I0457760

SOME ASSEMBLY REQUIRED

SOME ASSEMBLY REQUIRED

Rise of the Amazons Book 2

Amberly Smith

This is a work of fiction. Names, characters, places, public or private institutions, corporations, towns, and incidents are the product of the author's imagination or are used fictitiously. Any resemblance to actual events, locales, or persons, living or dead, is coincidental.

No part of this book may be reproduced or transmitted in any form or by any electronic or mechanical means including information storage and retrieval systems without permission in writing from the author, except by a reviewer who may quote brief passages in a review. This book may not be resold or uploaded for distribution to others.

Kuznya Freelance
Boise, Idaho

Visit author website at www.amberlysmith.com

Copyright © 2015 Amberly Smith, All rights reserved.

ISBN-13: 978-0692535745 (Kuznya Freelance)
ISBN-10: 0692535748

DEDICATION

To all the amazing men in my life but especially to Jim Burdick. Dad, you set the bar impossibly high. I miss you.

ACKNOWLEDGEMENTS

I want to thank James from Humble Nations for the beautiful cover. Val Roberts, Andrea Howard, and Stephanie Berget for their encouragement and critical eyes. I owe you.

Chapter 1

Dianne Fender's thoughts, and those of the hundreds of people in the church, flipped through her mind like a slide–show set on extra fast. She knew, even before she left the hospital, that her grandmother was dead. The new goal—keep Liesel Grant alive.

Grandma Maggie should have been buried in an Indian ceremony, not this grand-scale chapel and graveside service. Dianne was pretty sure that thought was hers. With little effort she could take a mental survey on A) how many people felt the 'service was lovely' or B) those who wished there'd been candles instead of the brightly lit overhead electric chandeliers. Option C) that Maggie had never died in the first place. Dianne choose that one.

At least the pallbearers would be Amazons.

The solid wood pews were worn. The funeral flowers were buried three arrangements deep, ten across, and had no scent. Dianne adjusted the long sleeves of her dress, pulling with a nervous twitch to cover her burns. Part of her mind knew the burns were no longer there but she tugged at her sleeves anyway.

A young girl sang the words to Britney Spear's Toxic. *Damn it.* How dare they allow such a song to be part of this sacred ceremony? But Britney was in somebody's head. Or rather, some young girl had the song stuck in her head. When Dianne laughed, the thoughts flooding her mind switched to thoughts of Dianne. Which was freaky-ass creepy. The drugs must be wearing off.

Escaping now would be good. At least to the rafters, her camera in her hands. The rafters weren't anywhere near far enough to avoid the torrent of thoughts, nor would the camera shield her. But to have her equipment, to be dangling from a high dangerous point, that was familiar. Hell, necessary.

The only reason she'd ventured forth was Maggie.

Grandma Maggie had taken her to her first pow-wows. Before her abilities kicked in. Rich memories of colors, the sharp swish of shiny beads and the chanting rhythm. Her first photos had been of dancers, bonfires, her white grandmother, and the tribe that had adopted her a hundred years before. Pictures of people. Before being that close caused pain; before she became a hermit.

Liesel, the young Amazon leader, gave the eulogy. Tears streaked Liesel's face as her kind voice eloquently paid tribute to a lost friend, a mentor. Liesel had worked tirelessly to connect all Amazons and Mightys—women and men of extraordinary strength. She had guided them to the answers they so desperately wanted, Dianne and Grandma Maggie included. Dianne owed Liesel more than just her devotion and respect.

Liesel had explained why she was different and that she wasn't alone. Her Amazon mother and her father, the stiff empty man sitting next to her, the son of Maggie Mountain Fender, both carried the Amazon gene. Two Amazon genes were unmixy. Made a Blue Hair. In Dianne's case a FUBAR human. And the drugs that helped block all the thoughts, that made the pain tolerable, breathable, were fading.

Dianne fumbled in her purse for a glass vial. Barney, her agent, had taken her to Wise Woman Daisy, a Navajo Indian who sold herbal medicines. She'd needed something for the pain and none of the drugs at the hospital had worked to block out the mental noise of those around her. The doctors had thought her quick recovery from the fire was a blessing from God for her great self–sacrifice. *Please. As if.* There was nothing shiny enough in her karma bank to pay for something like that.

"Maggie lived a life to be proud of. She died peacefully in her sleep and now is with her soul–mate. In her own words—" Liesel said. What Grandma had said Dianne didn't hear.

The carousel in her head paused a short second longer on a man. The man knew that Maggie had been killed. Just like Dianne knew that Maggie's death wasn't a quiet passing in the peace of sleep. The slide was gone, and with the cold vial clasped in her hand, seconds away from peace, she closed her eyes to focus. *All* the thoughts, not just those of the mourners, but the thousands of people in a three mile radius, flooded her. Hot painful air caught in her throat. Her mind staggered under the weight. His oily presence was torn out of her grasp. She could no longer find him in the sea of noise.

The groan pulled from her tight chest sounded feral. She couldn't do it, not even for Maggie.

She tipped the vial into her mouth, painting her tongue with the tart fluid, and felt her father place his arms around her. His grief and fear of loneliness made her black out for a second but then she felt him. Not his mind or his thoughts or anyone's thoughts, him. Just the physical feel of her father. Solid, warm.

It was the first time that she had physical contact with another person in...a very long time. Unless you counted the painful touch of each doctor or nurse; of Barney, helping her walk out of the hospital.

"Liesel is stalling," her father whispered. "You've been out for almost ten minutes. Are you okay?"

She straightened and nodded at Liesel. Sending a mental thank you. Probably a bit loudly, if Liesel's jerk and then smile was any indication.

Dianne yanked at her sleeves again as she stood with the congregation. Her whole body shook as if she had Parkinson's and her mind could only focus on the immediate.

Stand. Wait. Watch. Watch as six women, dressed in long black dresses, spread around the coffin. Who was in that coffin? Oh, Grandma Maggie. Right.

And the women weren't wearing black, she just couldn't take the time or effort to figure it out. She was watching.

The ladies lifted the solid mahogany casket easily—Amazons, her mind explained—and walked out of the church, carrying it on their shoulders to the waiting hearse.

Was it too bloody much to ask that her powers make sense? That they be useful? For almost fifteen years Dianne had lived on her own, traveled, photographed and finally, *finally* found peace. Found acceptance. Then she had a vision. What the fuck? If she was meant to make a difference, to help, was it too much to ask for a guide? Her very own Watson or Gandalf? Instead a vague sense of doom and she was sleeping on a couch in a city, bringing her mental baggage to Liesel, who deserved her own peace.

Yet Liesel was the only one who believed Maggie had been killed. So, until she knew what happened to Maggie, she would stay close to Liesel. She'd have another chance to make this right. She just needed to suppress her powers enough to cope.

Having psychic abilities was like reading a novel with all points of view present. Today, because of some street-acquired Mary Jane, Dianne only heard the points of view of the five women present.

"I don't need a point guard," Liesel said and thought, *My life is so screwed up.*

They might not believe Dianne's vision had predicted Maggie's death but they were determined to protect Liesel. She'd already been kidnapped, shot at, and her home broken into. Plus, there was a very powerful family of Mightys—the Mathews—that had made it quite clear they disapproved of HOAX, the rising Amazon community. All of which didn't include inside threats.

"All queens have, at the very least, a set of body guards," Tammy Griffon said. Tammy personified the suburban housewife, conservative dress and manners in neutral colors.

"I am not the Queen." Liesel buzzed around the room, sorting through mail, wiping off the kitchen counter. She was doing her best to be polite to these women but was growing weary of their bossy insistence. She even smiled, thinking how ironic it was to be designated queen. She didn't have enough influence to get them to stop pestering her about a guard detail. Again.

All four women were shorter than Dianne's obnoxious 6'1" height and, worse, Dianne was suffering major hair envy for Liesel's red curls—a thousand black exclamation marks covered Dianne's head. She placed her hand over her recently bald scalp, as if that would hide her short hair.

Liesel tried again. "I can't be called Queen, that's just ridiculous. This isn't a country. I'm a political figurehead for an organization. A web-based organization."

Dianne's drug oblivion from the funeral had lasted the night and she awoke on Liesel's couch ashamed of her retreat. That man in the congregation had known something about Maggie and she couldn't suck it up long enough to learn his secrets, whether or not he was the killer. If Maggie had been killed at all. Like a selfish child, she'd hidden behind the drug, used it instead of fighting.

Dianne stayed on the couch as Liesel's baby sister Harriett started loading the dishes. It would be nice to stay busy by helping, but she couldn't risk being that close to everyone.

"So Madame President, you still need to consider—" Harry, the only non-Amazon in the room, didn't broadcast her thoughts like the others. If Dianne concentrated on the blonde she could read emotion and surface thoughts. But the whole point of the marijuana was to not think. Harry blocked her mental scan. How? Dianne was busy not thinking about it and envying the long, straight blond hair.

Liesel interrupted her younger sister, "I don't like President." She was putting leftovers from a late breakfast into the fridge and looking out into the back yard where Tammy's girls chased each other.

"What about Monarch?" Tammy said.

"The butterfly?" Liesel asked. She rolled her eyes and pictured herself lying in a huge bed, thick blankets and a warm male body surrounding her. Jim Griffon, the boyfriend and Tammy's brother-in-law. Dianne felt a deep ache of desire in Liesel's stomach that made her own skin flush with heat.

Dianne shook her head to get out of Liesel's thoughts. Out of Liesel's and into Anna's, Liesel's assistant. Anna Marie Fort-Porter's brain was like a super computer. Dianne wasn't sure what a super computer was but had learned not to ask Anna questions. Dianne would get encyclopedia-level details.

Monarchs, Danaus Plexippus, Greek for 'sleepy transformation'. Related to the Greek myth, the daughters of King Danaus of Libya. The information rolled through Anna's mind, who ignored it.

Each adult butterfly lives four to five weeks. In autumn a special generation are born that survive seven or eight months. In human terms, 525 years old.

"Then isn't that fitting? Since we live a long time. Or can," Dianne said to Anna. Unlike Anna's thoughts, Dianne spoke out loud.

The two sisters and Tammy looked at Dianne. Anna groaned and slumped further down in her chair in the corner. Liesel thought, *I don't know how to help her. I need to get a hold of Sergei. Maybe he can help.* At the same time Dianne heard Tammy's *Freak.* Dianne brushed their thoughts away. Whatever. Nothing new there.

"Who's Sergei?" Dianne asked.

"Even though you can read people's minds," Anna said, "doesn't mean you should say what's in their heads. It's in there for a reason." *We're all hiding something.* Dianne knew Anna's cynicism, unlike that of other eighteen year olds, stemmed from battle-weary experience.

"Let's get something clear." Liesel smiled. "Tammy, you live in San Francisco with Frank and the girls. You can't be my bodyguard. Harry, you're my sisters and I love you but you need to work and can't be here twenty–four seven. Anna is in her first year of college. Nuff said."

They were due in Las Vegas for the first national convention of HOAX, Home Of the Amazon eXchange. There Liesel would be voted in as leader—title to be determined—and a board of directors appointed. Surviving in Vegas would make Dianne's visit to Boise look like a fun field trip to a sunny park.

And me? Dianne asked Liesel.

Liesel smiled at her. "We need to figure out a way you can survive in a city." She rubbed her fingertips against her temple.

Preferably without weed, Anna thought.

"I heard that." Dianne glared at Anna.

Anna just smiled and said in her head, *Welcome to my mind, Jean Grey.*

"Who?"

Anna laughed again and got up to get a glass a water from the fridge. Her mind filled with old comic book pictures of a red headed superhero who could move things with her mind.

"I'm not telekinetic," Dianne clarified.

"What?" Tammy asked, irritated.

"She can't move things with her mind," Harry explained.

Stop. Stop. Liesel pushed at her temple, feeling pain throb there.

Dianne didn't think about it, she just scooped Liesel up like a young child and carried Liesel to her bedroom. The weight of her queen in her arms, the scope of light bleeding into shadows, were still muted by the drugs she had taken during the service and the marijuana. So it felt like carrying a pillow in a dim room.

"What the hell are you doing?" Harry demanded.

"She's in pain." Careful not to touch Liesel skin to skin, Dianne angled sideways to avoid bumping the narrow hallway walls. The house was both home and office to Liesel's web design company and headquarters for HOAX. What if the threat wasn't a potential killer but an illness? Breast cancer ran in the Grant family. Dianne checked Liesel's mind for her last physical.

"I've just got a headache. Dianne, put me down," Liesel said. She wasn't frightened of Dianne, but still she was fully capable of walking to her room on her own.

"No," Dianne said. Liesel had had a full exam and blood work done after she was kidnapped. Everything looked fine.

"D, you need to chill," Anna said.

Tammy had her dander up and Dianne sent a mental command to stay the hell back, do not touch. Sometimes they listened.

The women followed them down the hall into Liesel's room. It was messy, and Liesel cringed in embarrassment.

Then as she realized Dianne was carrying her she jerked still in her arms. *Dianne!*

Understanding her friend's concern, Dianne said, "I'm being careful not to touch skin." She stumbled at the bedroom's threshold as it switched from hardwood to carpet. Startled, Liesel grabbed Dianne's neck.

In that brief instant of touch, nightmarish images took over. Dianne stood in a glass cube where Griffon bled from deep gouges. Her sister Harry sobbed and a small child, muscular like a circus carnies' sideshow, cowered in the darkness.

Someone tortured Griffon. Sliced deep. Blood pumped in rhythmic streams down his body. Harry, the gray of decay, dripped pungent water and didn't breathe. Dianne tried to offer Harry comfort, save Griffon and lead the child into the light. Her muscles tore away from her bones, pulled in three different directions.

Dianne dropped Liesel onto the bed. She experienced a brief moment of black sharpness before all the other thoughts flooded back in. And not just the house. Dianne swayed on her feet and fell like a cut tree. Liesel made it out of the way just in time. She lay stomach down, face turned to the side on Liesel's bed.

Before Dianne succumbed to unconsciousness, she saw Liesel reach out to brush the hair out of Dianne's face. Oh god she wanted that, a motherly touch, soothing, strong. Liesel stopped, remembered not to touch.

I'm so sorry.

It happens.

How was she supposed to help protect and support Liesel if she couldn't be within miles of a city without her life being totally fucked up?

Doctor Sergei Sky ran his hand over the top of his head, feeling the short blue bristle of his hair. He was wet. Runny–wet. If you stand in the shower or in the rain then you are dripping–wet but water from inside—sweat—runs off skin. Runs at different speeds in rivulets; runny–wet. He grabbed a grungy towel he kept for the purpose and wiped down his muscular arms and scrubbed his head. His t–shirt and the towel were tossed in the hamper and he took the single step required to go from home gym to office.

Enjoying a rush of endorphins and adrenaline, unwinding a bit before his vacation, revved him up. He flipped a page in his battered notebook and read page three for the eight hundredth time.

"Nice abs," crackled across the walkie–talkie.

Sergei started and laughed looking outside to the apartment building across the way. He placed a finger in the notebook to keep his place. Yeah, as if he would forget what it said. Somehow the answer would present itself. It had to.

He picked up his walkie–talkie and pressed the send button. "Well, Veranda, that's why I leave the drapes open. To enhance the view." He made his voice slick and flirtatious. He turned his body toward the window and undulated his hips once to really show off the goods. He laughed at how ridiculous he probably looked.

"If you got a gym membership you'd have a reason to get out of the building. Maybe meet someone."

"Veranda! Are you breaking up with me?"

His neighbor had a motherly tone to go with her sassy, wise-woman persona. "Darlin', I'm too much woman for you."

Sergei laughed and tossed the notebook into his carry-on. Every word Liesel Grant had translated from ancient texts, the gene research, even the sporadic bits of the Amazon codex—before it was stolen, was in that notebook. Everything he'd ever found on Blue Hairs.

"I'm going to miss you next week," Veranda said. He pulled his water bottle out of the fridge and chugged it while she spoke.

"You could come to Las Vegas with me." He wiped his mouth. "We'll take in the Blue Man Group and get married in one of the cheesy chapels." Sergei walked to the window and waved to Veranda.

The seventy-year-old woman was wearing her favorite bubble-gum pink sweater. It engulfed her frail body and made Sergei think of those coconut stacked sweets—pink, brown and white.

"Can't afford it." It was a difficult subject, money. Veranda lived on bread bought at wholesale and the 'discounted groceries' Sergei took in twice a week. Shortly after moving in, Sergei saw the old woman, who he smiled at in passing, fall on a loose rug. It was late and hard for him to see but Sergei knew she didn't get back up.

He alerted the police. She'd broken her hip. The walkie–talkies were his idea. Him eating his only non–microwaved meals at her apartment, was Veranda's idea. She was a nice enough lady that he occasionally felt bad for taking advantage of her generous nature. The groceries were an attempt to make up for his general lack of a heart. Okay, as a doctor he knew he had a heart, but not much of a soul. Those great-tasting meals and the home-like feel of their visits was worth the price of compliments and the time Sergei spent.

"You'll bring back pictures?" Veranda said.

"And shot glasses and pink M&M's from M&M world." He could

see her laugh even from this distance because her whole body shook. "Your nephew Tony's coming on Monday and his wife Sarah on Wednesday—" The walkie-talkie squawked and stuttered as she interrupted. Her version of sticking her fingers in her ears and going 'La-la-la.'

He released his button.

"Get cleaned up and come over. I'm making spaghetti."

He rearranged his mental schedule and kept his sigh to himself. She'd be alone until Monday and it wasn't like he had anything to cook here. His chest twinged with guilt over his reluctance. She was a good person. She deserved a faithful and grateful friend. Instead Sergei dragged his feet.

"I need to check my email. Half hour?" Sergei said.

"Ten four, Blue Hair."

Sergei set his walkie-talkie down on the small coffee table that also doubled as a kitchen table. The place was small but just a block from the D.C. hospital where he had done his residency. If he had had student loans to pay back like most new doctors, there was no way he could afford it.

The flat consisted of three rooms: bath, bed and catch all. The minuscule bathroom had needed a shower head extension, which he installed the first day. The old one didn't reach above his shoulder. At least on the top floor the ceilings were all high. Just as long as he remembered to duck in the doorways.

He turned on his radio and set the volume to the piece of tape marked 'approval line.' Above the tape and the neighbors started pounding to turn it down. He nodded his head a couple times and gave a snap to The Ramones' Blitzkrieg Bop. Above the radio hung a framed photograph of a Life Flight medical helicopter landing at sunset. A blanket, his only successful sewing project from Home Economics class, lay on his bed. Every remaining shelf, surface, and floor space held his medical books.

He left the radio on as he checked his email. Credit card offer. Couldn't they just stick to snail mail? Monthly subscription to an online doctor's magazine. He'd read that on the plane. Save on your car insurance. What? No, penile implants? The last was an email from Liesel Grant with the subject line 'I need your help.' His body tensed, the press of his heartbeat against his chest so much stronger than when he'd been exercising.

Serg,

Maggie's granddaughter Dianne is a Blue Hair with extreme psychic abilities. She's suffering in Boise but refuses to leave. I know you don't start your new job until after Vegas but could you recommend something?

Liesel

Crap. He knew exactly what was wrong and didn't need the hassle. He had finished his residence. Three years of being the bottom of the totem pole. Little sleep, almost no social life and every spare moment filling his notebook. Not only was this his first adult vacation but he hadn't had more than two days off in nearly four years.

He would start his new job for NEWCo Labs in a couple of weeks. The company had helped him obtain his research grant to study the effects of different medications on Schizophrenic patients. A disease the world believed his father suffered from. He wanted to help Blue Hairs before it was too late. Help those who suffered like his brother had, like his father did. Like Dianne was suffering.

The email waited his reply.

Liesel had sent the email an hour ago. He still needed to pack, eat with Veranda, clean out his fridge, and sleep before his flight in ten hours. Shit. He'd just ignore it. Pretend he didn't get it until he arrived in Vegas. He looked at his carry-on and his notebook still on top.

He couldn't ignore the email. Dianne must be in a lot of pain. Plus, maybe working with Dianne would help him, a look at the problem from a different perspective. Because, ready or not, his sister reached motherhood in less than three months. One more child who would suffer.

Besides, Liesel owing him a favor was a good place to be.

He clicked on the reply tab. *I have some ideas. Call me on my cell.* He added the number. Knowing Liesel's inbox alerted her, he waited to click send until he headed out the door for Veranda's.

He'd just locked up when his cell went off. He dug a hand into his tight low black jeans and pulled out his phone.

"Are you going to make me Vice President?" He said in way of a greeting, putting off what he could do today.

"No! You're way too busy as it is. And your work is too important," Liesel said. Her voice sounded rough, tired. Double shit. He loved his queen and would do anything for her because she cared, heart and soul intact. To outsiders, electing an officer to an international nonprofit group might seem odd. They wanted to recognize all the good she was doing with the medical and historic research into their abilities. She had stopped a kidnapping ring involving Amazon children. Hell, she had given them a place to find each other.

"I was just joshing. Are you crying?"

Liesel's hitched breath came across the two–thousand miles from Boise to D.C. scalpel sharp. "No, I've got a headache."

"Lie down." He jogged down the stairs.

Liesel growled.

"All right, stand on your head then."

"Sergei!"

No more teasing and no more avoiding. He couldn't cure Dianne and he couldn't cure his father. He would deal with it. Just because his spine was tight enough that he worried it would rip out the back of his shirt, just because his hands were tingling and his mouth was numb, didn't mean he could let this go. Time to help as much as he could. "Is she there?"

"Yes," Liesel said through clamped teeth.

"Let me talk to her." If Dianne was susceptible to treatments, he could give her some relief.

He nodded to a neighbor as he stepped out of his building.

Autumn in D.C. was a totally different menu item. Winter was steak and red potatoes, solid. Spring, the malted taste and texture of geopolitical hate. Summer, the scraping glass shards of waste. But fall was the smoked and roasted remains of political careers, detached control and agenda-driven. Whatever the hell that meant. Cold and filthy. The weather echoed the people's attitude.

While he waited for Dianne to answer the phone, he pressed Veranda's buzzer. He hollered into the speaker, "It's me pet!" People walked behind him on the sidewalk, a busy shuffle of bodies.

"Who?" said a small voice into the phone.

"Dianne? This is Doctor Sergei Sky," very professional tone, perfected after hours of use.

"How old are you?" Dianne said.

"Why do you ask?" The buzzer sounded and the door clicked and he entered Veranda's lobby.

"Because Anna Marie wonders if you're hot but are probably really old—?" she coughed a few times. "Why would that bother him? It bothers you?" Clearly she was talking to someone on her side of the continent.

"Dianne," he smoothed his voice. Rhythmic. Mellow. His father, in the early days, had responded to hypnosis. It helped him focus. Sergei had never tried it over the phone before. But what the hell. "I want you to focus on my voice. Just sit down somewhere comfortable for a minute."

"They're all thinking about me." Her voice rippled like lake water; sloshed on drugs, or alcohol, or adrenaline, or even exhaustion. It was a rich voice, deep in tone and warm.

"What are you using? What kind of range do you have?" Sergei said.

"One question at a time." Her words were careful, precise. He started up the stairs, had no problems speaking despite the several floors.

"What are you on?"

"I got some Mary Jane," she said.

"Marijuana? Isn't that illegal in Idaho?" Pot often numbed the psychic's mental pain but it was a short fix. Like a college student on caffeine, the crash could be harsh. And they quickly needed more in greater amounts to find the numb they sought.

"And?" Dianne said. That made him smile.

He'd finished the five-floor climb to Veranda's door and let himself in. He shook his head and indicated the phone so Veranda would know he was sorry he was talking on it.

He would still get his vacation, the chance and time to figure how to help his sister Portia. Just this favor first, but nothing else; he was responsible for more important things.

Dianne didn't want to work with some stranger. What if he didn't really want to help her? Was only doing this for Liesel? But she needed a solution and Liesel thought he could help. She would listen to him recite the alphabet, if it helped her stay and help Liesel.

Dianne listened to the quiet voice over the phone.

"Think of a safe place." He didn't really sound like a doctor—at least not scary or with a tone of reprimand. She tried to think of a place she was safe. Will Smith had it great in that movie, with the overgrown New York City. That was where she would be safe. Alone. *Come on, try.* The Sawtooth Mountains had turned out not to be safe but it was the last place she'd been alone. Dangling off the cliff into the ravine. Before she saw the vision of Grandma Maggie and Liesel. Before Maggie died, that had felt safe.

"You're there and it is empty of all others. Just the two of us," Sergei said. "And you can't hear my thoughts. Trust that."

She couldn't, he was more than three miles away. "Okay."

He took her on a verbal journey, his voice at first measured and soft, his cadence slow. She remembered sliding her hands into her long hair and pulling it through a scrunchie that she kept on her wrist, then a second time halfway, forming a messy knot at the back of her head. The sun sucked dew off the wild flowers. Idaho mountains were beautiful in a parched third-world, undeveloped way. Once inside the tree line, the evergreens—those devious bastards—hid the lack of water. She tugged on her climbing gloves, said a prayer to the goddess Athena and pitched backward over the edge. The rappelling ATC caught and gave her a nasty jerk but held. She laughed and looked around her as she descended into the canyon.

He pulled her a foot further down that rope into the ravine, held her tighter than her climbing gear.

"It does not matter what I am saying. It matters not what those other people are thinking." The switched sentence structure, in the middle of his description of how they were alone, felt off. Jangled. Pounded. Yet, she dropped another foot into the ravine. From there she no longer heard the thoughts of those outside the immediate house. Her heart thumped and the skin on her arms tightened, raising the fine hairs to attention along her body.

"It's working," she whispered. Scared that it would break, this connection, if she spoke, but scared that he would stop if she didn't.

"Serendipity. That is our word. You and mine."

She almost corrected him, yours and mine. But realized that she couldn't hear Liesel. Couldn't even see Liesel. From the bottom of the ravine she could only hear the voice on the other side of the phone. She pressed it tighter to her ear. Her shoulders hunched forward, she pulled her legs up. When had she sat on the floor? Magic, this was magic.

"Ser—en—dip—ity."

"It's our word," she said.

"That's right. Serendipity. To us it means this place, this tranquility. When I say it again to you, you will sleep. You will sleep when I say it again."

"Promise?"

He laughed. It was a great laugh, awkwardly natural. He continued talking and she listened. Happy to just absorb the peace of the ravine bottom. She could feel the rope in her hands, felt the pack on her back, smelled the earth in front of her.

After some time he said, "I want you to get amber. It can be found at health stores or Wicca shops."

"What's amber?"

"Fossilized tree sap. Add it to some hand lotion. Are you listening?"

The deep quiet worked better than any drug she had used. It may have been hours or just minutes. The fall sun still shone through the windows when she peeked below the weight of her eyelids. But even awake she only heard her own thoughts. Amazing. "I don't know." It was so blissfully quiet.

"Let me tell this to Liesel. Let me talk to her," Sergei said.

"Liesel? I'm not sure...." How long had it been? She was climbing back up the rope. Surfacing slowly, yet still in her happy place. She opened her eyes and Liesel's thoughts slipped into her mind before she saw her across the room. Resting on sisterly orders to get rid of her headache, Liesel was propped up in bed, dressed in her pajamas. She stopped reading a book on ancient Greek culture—which she thought was drivel—and tucked her long wavy red hair behind her ear.

"She thinks I look better. Not so scary." Dianne knew that below that soft body, the strong woman could break people in half. As an Amazon Liesel could do almost anything. She choose to heroically help people.

"Do not surface too much. Stay close to me," Sergei said.

"What are you doing?" Dianne said. She wanted him near, wanted to have a hold on him as strong as his on her. He was her dealer of peace and she was hooked.

"Me? I'm kissing Veranda goodbye and heading back to my apartment to pack for Vegas."

"Veranda?"

"Nope, you don't get to hear my thoughts," Sergei said.

"You're out of my range."

"Wouldn't matter. Besides my hair being blue, I block all psychic abilities."

Was that true? It sounded true. "Oh." She didn't know what else to say. Her whole world had a coating of fog stretched like tinfoil around her.

"Liesel," he reminded her.

She gave Liesel the phone back. She extended her shaking arm, her fingers clenched white and numb, tethered to her life line, her rope down into the ravine.

She, Liesel, was to get amber and bergamot and mix it into a hand lotion. It would diminish Dianne's psychic range. Or so Sergei told Liesel. Liesel didn't believe for a moment that some potion would help but, with a mental sigh, would try it. Dianne had noticed that Liesel didn't believe in much of anything. Concrete, solid evidence was still up for debate.

If the hand lotion worked she could travel to Vegas with Liesel. Medicine Woman Daisy would approve the organic method.

Liesel gave Dianne back the phone.

"When I fall asleep, leave me here," Dianne said, indicating the floor. "It won't matter. And no, I won't sleep on the couch. And no, I won't sleep on the bed. I'm still trying to recover from the mental image of you and Griffon in that bed. The floor is good." She was still talking as she lifted the phone to her ear. "Why would that embarrass you?"

"Serendipity."

Chapter 2

He was nervous about this trip and Jim Griffon didn't do nervous well. From across the Las Vegas airport's luggage area, Griffon heard the dulcet tones of his younger brother Frank.

"Damn it, Jimmy. I go all the way to Boise, Idaho, and you're not there to show me the sights? Then I have to chase you to Vegas?" His little brother said Idaho like it was Timbuktu. They had been raised in San Francisco, and compared to their home town, Boise was a twentieth-century version of Mayberry. But not as far as Timbuktu. He could have come to visit sooner.

Frank, his wife Tammy, and their two daughters had just arrived. Griffon knew they were coming, it just wasn't the reason he'd fought rush-hour traffic on a Friday night in the city that never sleeps to get to the airport. He hugged his sister-in-law and punched his brother in the shoulder, not all together good-naturedly. He settled to a knee to hug his nieces. He kept hold of Amy's hand as he stood back up. Her strong grip soothed an ache in his chest, reassured him and put things in perspective. She was quieter, yet carried an air of patient confidence that hadn't been there last year.

"I had a case here in Vegas. Finished last night," Griffon said. "Why were you in Boise?" Griffon was a private investigator. His brainy brother designed gadgets. They weren't exactly co-workers.

Griffon scanned the luggage area around them out of habit. The digital ching and whirl of slot machines that no longer needed to whirl smothered the noise of travelers looking for their luggage and each other. The heavy air-conditioned air held the desert heat outside as the automatic doors opened and closed. He made note of security cameras and the different exit points.

"I was hired to investigate a couple of bank robberies. I think you would have been much more capable. I'm in the business of preventing them." Frank designed bank technology and security systems. "Either way, we didn't catch the bad guys, but the banks are more likely to prevent such thefts in the future."

"He's being modest," Tammy said. "The bank managers have all raved about him. The robberies involved safety deposit boxes. Frank got a huge order for his voice recognition ones." She watched for their luggage on the closest conveyor belt while she handed out cheese and cracker snacks to her girls.

"Thanks hon. Let's get the kids together," Frank said, a step behind his efficient wife. "Did you meet us at the airport to give us a ride to the hotel?" He drew out the pause, a smug grin on his face. "Or is Liesel's plane coming in soon?"

"Liesel's plane is coming," Griffon said.

His brother's family had been on an earlier flight than Liesel. "Good luck," Frank said with plenty of sarcasm. Tammy jabbed him in the stomach and had already grabbed two suitcases before he recovered. "He's my brother. I have to give him crap."

Griffon helped them get their luggage loaded on a cart and watched them head for a taxi. He turned to watch the escalator again. There she was, and he suddenly wished he'd brought flowers. Wait a minute, scratch that. It made it sound like he had a reason to feel guilty.

He watched her walk towards him, he smiled, and raised his arms to embrace her. The heated scent that was unique to her shivered up his skin and filled his nose. She stepped close and hugged him in greeting. Her red curls drifted past her shoulders. She was in tennis shoes and, yep, a pair of his button-fly jeans.

He swallowed and smiled his appreciation of the lush body in his arms. They were both almost six feet tall and she—when she wasn't pissed at him—molded perfectly to his body. But right now her shoulders were stiff. "I've missed you," Liesel whispered, before pulling away. It wasn't a confession of feelings, more an accusation of mistreatment.

The baggage claim area was a huge square room with several luggage carousels. Tired, crammed passengers from around the world stood among the slot machines. Fifteen-foot-tall billboards advertised Vegas shows and the available skin fests.

He kept his focus split, still tight across his gut from his latest case. He knew the apprehension he felt was just residual adrenaline, but something about the airport had his gut trying to communicate with his instincts. "I had a case."

"I know." She squeezed his hand and he stared in her eyes for a second longer, lingering in the warmth of sappy happiness. They didn't fight. Went better than he thought. But his gut twisted as if in warning. The tension mixed with lust probably wouldn't go away until he had a chance to be alone with Liesel.

When first asked to be the Amazon Queen, Liesel Grant had scoffed, then rebelled, then accepted her fate. Now? Well, now a fire burned in her heart fueled by the prideful rush that she was helping these people, that she could make a difference. Though pleasing everyone was impossible. She had racked up her own set of opposition, but, with a few called shots, she would knock them down the corner pockets. Meanwhile she ignored the haters.

Liesel had considered driving. Boise wasn't that far from Vegas, and with Dianne, avoiding the airports was using your noodle, but she booked her flight weeks ago and gotten a good deal. Plus, the time between funeral and conference was too tight.

With Sergei's lotion, Dianne felt it worth a try.

She watched her sister nod to Griffon from across the way. The nod felt like Liesel was being handed off from one keeper to another. Harry had gone off to search among the kiosks for pamphlets on different shows and tourist attractions. Each stand was themed to match its sponsor hotel; an Eiffel Tower for the Paris Hotel, a velvet-lined carriage for the medieval themed Excalibur.

Among the jumble stood Limo drivers holding white signs with black lettering, enabling them to meet their assigned customers.

Liesel rubbed the back of her hand against the back of Griffon's as they stood next to each other. She squeezed his shoulder, using the excuse of a large advertisement she wanted to point out, but she left it there. It felt so good to touch. She slid her hand down his arm, stroked the cut of muscle at his bicep, and watched his eyes darken. When she got to his elbow, his eyelids drooped. At his wrist, he sighed and leaned toward her. She took his hand and a barbed current went over her.

"Want to share a room?" Liesel asked.

"I was going to ask you, after I did some groveling," Griffon thumbed her knuckles. "To get back into your good graces."

Which made her cringe. The man was a patient saint.

He rubbed the tense muscles of her neck knowing it curled her toes. "Why so tense?" It was unfair how quickly he melted her. She smiled. Heat rushed through her body and she wanted him naked and above her. She closed her eyes and tried to focus on what he had asked.

"Dianne."

"The psychic?"

She appreciated his restraint with the sarcasm. "Of the two of us, you're the believer."

"True. Where is she?" Griffon had a powerful set of eyes and a rugged look that kept people at a distance. All around them people were scrunched together trying to reach for their luggage on the conveyor belts, but around Liesel and Griffon there was a two-foot clearance. Those who stepped inside the circle took one look at Griffon and put as many bodies between them as fast as they could. His sinister exterior was almost as hot as his gentle core.

Liesel stepped out from under his hand and turned toward him. Griffon scanned the area. Worse than Harry, always on guard.

"I sent her and Anna straight to the hotel so she could rest. Though I don't know if the hotel will be any quieter." He leaned toward her and inhaled deeply, his nose an inch from her neck. Liesel swallowed the wave of lust the subtle move made.

"How-How'd the case go?" He'd been unable to call for two weeks. She wasn't mad. Not really. Achy, yes. Homesick even. Not mad. She understood the deep cover the case had required but knowing he couldn't call didn't make her okay with not talking to him. Not his fault, but she'd worried.

Harry came over and pointed to a limo driver. He stood away from the main group of drivers. His sign read Liesel Grant and Party. Like all the drivers he wore a too-big monkey suit and generic features.

"Did you get us a ride?" Harry asked Liesel.

"I didn't. Griffon?"

Griffon shook his head and looked back to the driver. Why wasn't he standing with the others? Like huge river rocks, they stood their ground in the main flow of traffic from the arrival gates. "It could be a coincidence. Someone else named Liesel," Harry said.

"Or one of my clients could have hired it. I do work with that condo developer here in Vegas." She designed websites for a diverse clientele. Jeans weren't limo riding clothes but it wouldn't do to offend a paying customer.

"Maybe," Harry said.

"I'll go see." She let go of Griffon's hand and walked toward the guy. "You're looking for a Liesel Grant?"

"Yes. The Amazon."

"I'm Liesel Grant." The driver pulled the sign to the left and reached for something in his jacket.

As Liesel left his side, Griffon stepped forward so he could see the driver better. She had an easy gait and had already smiled and extended her hand.

A man shoved between the driver and Liesel. Griffon saw the brassy flash of sharp metal and his gut twisted. "Liesel," Griffon yelled as he raced forward.

The driver's knife cut across the stranger's upper arm. Blood welled and then gushed down his sleeve. The injured man staggered, knocking Liesel down beneath him, shielding her with his body.

The driver had already dropped the sign, shoved past the other drivers and run.

As Griffon reached Liesel's side, he crouched and touched her shoulder, made eye contact. God, this wasn't going away; this driving need to be with and protect her. He just got more and more vulnerable.

Lots of blood. *Not hers.* Not Liesel's, he reminded himself. The stranger had immediately rolled to his knees. Griffon ignored him.

"Harry?" She'd been by his side the whole time.

"I've got her." He knew Harry was capable, had a gritty determination to protect her sister.

In the next breath he was up and running. Griffon couldn't draw his weapon in the crowded airport. It would cause panic, and he couldn't get a clear shot anyway. He took off after the fake limo driver, leaping over luggage and weaving through travelers. The runner dropped the knife, which was kicked and shuffled beneath a conveyor belt. People yelled at the man to watch out, screaming obscenities in different languages as he barreled through them. Griffon didn't call out for people to stop him. He didn't want the man to know how close he was or for other people to get hurt.

Didn't they realize what had just happened? Griffon's heart still felt the piercing contraction of fear.

Liesel's attacker didn't run for the exit but farther into the airport, heading toward the departure gates. Griffon saw him just ahead and he finally called out as the man reached the escalator, "Stop." People screamed and fell out of his way.

He wanted to inflict pain, carve the man's flesh for what he had tried to do. The driver swam upstream on the escalator, grabbing people and carry-ons and throwing them out of his way. One dog in a designer mesh carrier landed between the feet of the pedestrians and with a kick, slid further from its owner.

The security guards at the top, alerted by all the screams, ran forward to grab Liesel's attacker. Nimble, he dodged them and climbed the plexi–glass railing reaching for the huge advertisement for the *Thunder from Down Under*. He tried to swing across to the other side, intent on avoiding the security guards and Griffon, trying to escape.

With a wrenching snap the cord broke and the man fell fifteen feet, landing with this sick grace. He had no time to flail or scramble. There was a desert-themed floor mural, with stone statues, as if they crawled out of the marble floor. The man's bones snapped on impact and the sharp point of a lizard punctured his throat. After a spurt like a broken spigot, the man's blood pooled and seeped across the floor toward a stone turtle.

Griffon jumped and twisted, catching the escalator's side to slow his fall, then landed on his feet in an easy crouch. Finally, people alerted to danger, cowered against the walls or ran like the blossoming point of oil on water away from death. Griffon walked to the man's side and stooped down to check for a pulse. Dead.

Adrenaline hooked to Griffon's blood and whistled through his body. He drew his wallet out, flipping it open to show his ID, and stood clear of the body as security rushed forward.

What did this mean? A hired hit? Too amateur. He couldn't ask now, but someone knew. Until Griffon knew why and who, they would treat this like a warning shot on a much bigger issue. Liesel was in danger. Her life could be cut before he could reach her. He hadn't been in time today. Would he next time?

Harriett Grant took a cotton t–shirt from her carry-on and used it to apply pressure to the stranger's arm. "It doesn't look too bad," she said. She checked his eyes for dilation and his pulse felt elevated.

"It feels bad. The shirt smells like you," he grinned, "Alluring."

The blood didn't bother her. Knowing it had almost been Liesel's did. She swallowed the rush of bile back. This was a told-you-so she could have lived without. It was hard standing in the wings, waiting for your heroic sister to rush forward again and again to help others. She'd seen Liesel pull people from burning homes, rescue people from drowning, over and over, doing the right thing but making herself a target. Harry was fiercely proud but also terrified. All cop families and military families must feel this split conflict of wanting to encourage but also wanting to caution.

A doctor in the crowd stepped forward and began giving instruction. *Apply pressure while I check his stats.* Thanks so much for the guidance. Harry shook her head and bit her tongue. It wouldn't do any good to tell the helpful bystander that she knew what she was doing.

"Is Liesel okay?" The man pushed off his good elbow to look around Harry. The tile beneath her knees was cold, and she felt a buzzing tingle across her shoulders.

She didn't ask, just thumped him in the head to get him to lie back. "How do you know her name?"

The man looked at her for a moment, face empty, and then smiled. "Is my jig up?"

The terminal's noise level altered in waves as travelers gasped, yelled or hushed each other. Some were frozen in shock, others turned their heads, determined to stay separate of the reality around them. Some were still running around in panic. A group had formed down by the escalators, cellphones out, recording as security and paramedics streamed through the travelers. Harry scanned the crowd, looking for her sister or some sign that Liesel and Griffon were okay. It was too far down for her to see what was going on.

"She went to check Griffon. How do you—"

"What? No—" he coughed and struggled for breath as the doctor pushed on his throat to get a reading there, "hey thanks for saving the day?" He smiled again and for the first time Harry's heart had slowed enough to realize how good looking this man was. That smile—a mixture of come-hither and I'm-totally-innocent—made her heart creak like a rusty pipe. He had a hard square chin, beautiful lips and soft brown eyes.

A paramedic arrived and took over. "Thanks," he said to the paramedic. "I just want some butterfly bandages and fruit juice and maybe a ride to my hotel." They pulled the t–shirt away and were surprised at how small the knife wound was. The amount of blood suggested a much more severe wound. Or rather how shallow it was now.

Figured. Harry leaned close and whispered in the handsome man's ear, "Welcome to Vegas, Mighty."

Chapter 3

Dianne rocked back and forth. She sat on a bench in the lobby of the hotel and tried her best not to puke. She tugged her long sleeves down, trying to keep as much warmth as possible against her overly chilled skin. She'd tried to go to her 'happy place' on her own but it hadn't worked. She didn't like going straight to the hotel while Liesel and Harry got the luggage but she looked like a strung out heroin junkie—three different people had thought so as they passed too close. Airports were full of security and Harry was just as determined to keep her sister safe as Dianne. No matter how firmly she told herself that, doubt had her swaying in her seat. Go back and be in the way or stay here and wait?

"So basically a group of freaks?" a man waiting to check-in spoke with a lady behind him. That particular f word always drew Dianne's attention.

At the front desk Anna was talking to the hotel clerk. "This reservation was made over two months ago. My boss is head of this convention and if we don't get a room—" Anna continued to berate the lady behind the counter. The clerk had looked haughty until Anna had started to get loud.

The lady in line told the man in front of her, "People who are super strong."

Dianne pulled the lotion out of her pocket. The stuff stank but it took the voices in her head and deleted all but a few. She squirted it into her palm. It was the pale green of guacamole mix gone bad and smelled like hemp. She rubbed it to in hands and the back of her neck. She would probably get a fungus.

As the heat there absorbed the mixture her psychic senses focused, the couple behind Anna in line shifted to the top of her conscious. She realized they weren't a couple. The lady was medium height and dressed like an accountant on vacation. The man was five feet nothing and had the blunt build of a dwarf.

"Yes, I understand that you have both the National Convention of Little People and Fitness Freaks booked this week. But you hold—"Anna again. Thanks Miss Exposition.

Short guy again, "Babe, proportionately I'm very strong. Want to see my largest muscle?"

He was cute. The accountant thought so and since Dianne couldn't actually see much of him behind the other people waiting in line, she'd take the girl's thought for it. But he was one of those little people and the accountant felt both embarrassment at thinking that way and awkward for thinking him cute anyway.

"I'm trying not to be rude," she told him.

He thought she had a nice voice and sexy curvy hips. Dianne didn't read any true animosity or dislike off the man, despite his use of the word freak. He was genuinely curious. "And doing a fine job of it. Look I just want to hear more about this freak group. I'm a member of the Little People."

Feeling the need to be rude now, "Obviously."

He laughed. He flirted for all he was worth and had an *I'm-going-to-go-for-it* attitude. Dianne whispered encouragement in his head. Not words so much as a warm flow of emotional support. "But that's just the way I look. Let me take you to dinner."

"You're just not my type." The liar—his dimples made heat rush through her stomach—smiled and used her sweetest tone.

He went to back down. *I'll see you around then, no problem*, he was about to say. Dianne whispered *chicken* in his head. She'd not 'whispered' in a person's head before meeting them previously and felt a bit guilty for it. Encouraging feelings were different.

"How about if I can lift you, you pay. If I can't I'll pay."

"You? Lift me?" No boyfriend had ever been able to lift her. As an Amazon, the accountant's muscles were more tightly woven. Which made them stronger but also considerably heavier than they looked.

"Agreed?"

"No, I'm just saying—"

"Agreed?" He smiled again and her heart stirred. Those dimples. What a nice feeling. Dianne hadn't felt that way on her own before. The giddy, joyous doubt of attraction.

The accountant thought, *This way I've given him a chance and can let him down easy.* "Sure. I'm heavier than I look...." Her voice faded and Dianne heard her gasp. "Oh, my." The accountant's head emptied.

But Todd—his name was Todd—imagined carrying her to his bed. "You are absolutely gorgeous when you're flustered."

"You're a Mighty?"

"Am I? Thought maybe I was just a freak."

"Your word, not mine. And dinner? Would be great." The female accountant sighed, a gush from her heart rather than her lungs. Even their thoughts had muted and Dianne realized she no longer shook or swayed.

"Dianne."

"What?"

"Dianne?"

"What?" She shifted her mind and focused on Anna. This lotion stuff worked but it made her stomach as slippery as a frozen turkey. It didn't help that she was hungry. Anna was too.

"I thought Liesel would be here by now. Can you, you know." She waved at Dianne's head.

"What?"

"Stop saying what."

But Dianne wasn't talking to Anna. The airport was less than two miles from the Las Vegas strip so she had no problems finding Liesel in the mental noise. Dianne felt the weight of Griffon's anger and Harry's worry hit her mind like a falling brick wall. God, Liesel was worried about her boyfriend and her sister instead of her own safety.

Liesel had almost been killed and Dianne had been living, again, vicariously through strangers. She couldn't muster a whole lot of guilt since it proved Liesel needed protection and because Liesel was okay. Having a jittery junkie standing next to her wouldn't have prevented that killer from going for Liesel. She tried to look beyond the three viewpoints but there was too much mental chaos. Layers of worry, mixed with annoyance that the incident had caused a flight delay.

"Liesel was almost stabbed at the airport." She had to try, seek out answers in more than just Liesel's mind, so she pushed. Stupid move. The mental images and voices flooded through her body and she lurched forward to head to the bathroom. But it was too late. Dianne turned and vomited into a potted plant. She shook with razor sharp shivers, each rack of electricity sharpening her mind, erasing the fuzzy effects of the lotion. "She's okay but dealing with the police. She says not to worry about her and make sure I get you fed." Dianne pressed a hand against a pillar and puffed out a breath.

Anna wanted to yell or smack Dianne for the abrupt, unhelpful, rude way she shared information. Instead she tried to take Dianne's arm. "Let's get you cleaned up." Dianne jerked out of reach then presented her sleeved elbow instead of her hand. "Sorry."

"I forget too. Did you see that midget and the short Amazon? They're making eyes—"

"Dianne."

What?

Anna just shook her head and guided her to the hotel elevators.

Griffon positioned his body to best protect Liesel. His hands shook and he knew from the look Harry gave him that he was pale as paper. He really wished the guy hadn't fallen, and not just so they could figure out what the hell happened, but so he would have something to kick the shit out of.

"I haven't seen you on the website," Liesel said to the stranger. Griffon had walked with her, his hand resting on her lower back. Now they stood next to the injured guy. Griffon continued to scan the area, making note of possible security footage, and the best people to question.

The Mighty adjusted the bandage on his arm. "Website? I'm sorry, miss, I'm not sure—"

"Bullshit. You know who Liesel is. We know what you are." Griffon had finished with airport security. He'd shown his identification and they'd acted like it was an FBI badge, toeing the line and deferring to his orders. That was sure to change when the city police showed up. A lot of their response stemmed from his feral reaction on top of his everyday mugger-in-a-dark-alley look. People gave them plenty of space.

Harry handed the guy his wallet which she'd obviously pickpocketed. "I just peeked long enough to get your name, Tydus Vaughn McKinley."

Griffon's opinion of Harry shot up a full ten notches. The wallet was leather and the guy stuck it in his back pocket. Right handed. Taller than Griffon by a few inches.

Tydus shook his head. "That was rather unethical, don't you think? I'm the good guy here." He was all easygoing smiles. If it had been Griffon being questioned he would have presented his business card, stayed stern and professional. Yet, Griffon was of the uncommon opinion that smiles were false fronts to truth. Hell, sometimes when he smiled at Liesel, he was really just thinking about getting her alone. What was this guy's play?

"I am grateful for your help, Mr. McKinley," Liesel said. "But at the same time, a bit surprised by—"

"The timing is suspicious as fuck," Griffon said. He'd pulled out his smartphone and entered Tydus's name, then showed it to Harry to make sure he'd gotten the spelling right.

Harry watched as Tydus laughed and rubbed his hand across his face, wincing when the muscle in his bicep pulled. He was very distinguished looking. And Harry wasn't sure what about him made her think of that word. Distinguished.

Working in construction she was surrounded by men all day long, in all states of fit and unfit and a spectrum of ages. Yet, with a very few exceptions, they looked like construction workers. Tan year round, hands rough. But Tydus was suave. Handsome and smooth and clean, and he smelled better than a cold beer at the end of a scorcher working welding. And the tangy, crisp sent came from aftershave or maybe even cologne rather than sweaty armpits.

The area had been sectioned off and the medics had propped him up in a chair against the wall. He'd refused further medical assistance and the medics had hurried to help travelers with injuries or concerns from the escalator.

"I'm here in Vegas on business." Tydus lifted his hand to halt Harry's protest. "Which, happily enough, puts me here for the convention as well. I only found HOAX a month ago. I've sent my application in but haven't heard back yet. I thought I'd crash a banquet or two if business allowed time."

He had a charming smile and he knew it. He moved into it slowly and lowered his tone as he finished speaking. He made eye contact with Liesel then moved on to Harry, upping the wattage when it got to her. She needed a fan. That look made her hot. And truly it was nice to be seen, despite her powerful and beautiful sister standing right next to her.

"Liesel?" Griffon said.

"It's possible," she said to him then explained to Tydus. "We had a recent...death in the family and with conference, things are behind at the office." By death in the family, Liesel meant Maggie Fender. The old lady hadn't been a relation but part of Liesel's online family. Harry hadn't ever met her. In fact, she'd never been on HOAX. Liesel talked it up and Harry had done what she could to support her sister's efforts, but she didn't really belong on there.

"I heard about Maggie. I'm so sorry," Tydus said. He said it without any difficulty, used to speaking and being heard. No problems dealing with emotion politely.

"You got any more questions?" Harry asked Griffon.

Griffon did a bit of his death stare. Which okay, was scary as hell, even when it wasn't directed at you. He was a bad ass MoFo. "For now," Griffon said. "The Vegas detectives will contact us at the hotel."

"Good. Turns out a limo driver was hit over the head and his uniform and keys were taken. Very Hollywood," Harry said. While Griffon and Liesel had worked with security, she'd found the guy, looking lost and worried. "He offered to give us a ride to the hotel. Reward for saving his car. The police are done questioning him for now so.... Would you like a ride Tydus?" The ride would give Griffon time to grill the driver and sort out any clues, if there was any.

"That would be great."

"If the guy had a limo, why didn't he wait to attack Liesel until we were out of the hotel?" Griffon already or still in private investigator mode. Harry liked the way his mind worked. Their older sister Karma might have reservations about Griffon dating Liesel but Harry knew he would take care of her. Plus, hell, her sister was happy so what else could matter?

"I don't think he knew which limo was the right one. The driver was in the bathroom when he was attacked. You can go into full question mode while we ride. I'm for getting Liesel closeted away." As much as Liesel would allow, Harry thought.

Griffon's protective streak was Harry's favorite thing about him. Her friends on the Boise police force had vouched for him early on but once she had a chance to actually meet the guy that was the thing she liked best.

Her sister said, "Ha, ha. I'm fine." But the patient voice Liesel used to let all and sundry know she would help them was gone. Dangerous territory that. "Hungry—"

"Of course." Griffon smirked.

"—but fine." Liesel picked up Tydus's luggage and her own carry on and Harry got Liesel's bag and her own. Leaving Griffon's hands free to pull weapon or kill, which was probably the only reason he didn't protest.

"No, I can get—" Tydus said.

Harry adjusted her grip on the bag.

"No. You can't," Liesel said. "You might heal fast Mr. McKinley, but I'm not taking chances with that arm. Besides, it's the absolute smallest I can do to repay you."

"Please, call me Tydus." There was the smile again.

Griffon growled and grabbed Liesel's free hand. "Let's go."

"Don't you dare smoke that in here," Anna warned. She was babysitting and she didn't care that the peeping–tom–of–her–mind heard her thoughts on watching over Dianne. "You'll set off the fire alarms. This is a non-smoking suite." The two bedroom suite was usually used for the high rollers. Anna had threatened and quoted customer service requirements at the overgrown bellhop until the clerk shoved the keycards at Anna to get her to leave. Now Liesel could have her own room with Griffon and it was clear on the other side of the sitting area so Anna wouldn't die of embarrassment hearing them.

"Don't really think she's a yeller," Dianne said. She sat on the couch, twirling a joint between her fingers. Dianne had acted like she was about to explode on the elevator.

"Shut up Jean Grey." Anna threw a pillow at Dianne. Then laughed at her own antics. Felt like she was often throwing pillows. Guess that was better than punches, since those landed her in trouble. This week was going to be awesome. It didn't matter that she wasn't twenty-one so couldn't gamble. She was skipping over a week of classes at Boise State to come. She could use her fake id to get into some of the dance clubs, meet up with a bunch of the other members of HOAX that were her own age. Now, instead of lounging by the pool she was going to make damn sure Liesel was safe. Liesel had taken a chance on her, believed in her. She would put her life on the line for her boss and friend.

"Someone's coming to the door. I don't think you'll get to keep this suite."

"Crap." Anna hurried to put the chain in place.

"No wait. Wrong room. The hotel guy is kicking someone out of the room below us." Dianne's eyes looked like she'd already smoked the pot, vacant, eyelids droopy.

A tear slid down her cheek. "Why am I even here? Can I do anything to help her if I'm like this?" She gestured with her hands, her eyes moist with rainbow prisms. Anna had pretty much thought the same thing so she didn't raise any arguments.

"She's in danger and I'm this," Dianne stood and ripped the phone out of the wall, "worthless—no worse, I'm," she threw the phone at the door, "a problem."

Anna simply stepped out of the way and let Dianne storm around the room. "One more thing on her list of things to do. People to help. How," she took the drawer out of the end table and tossed it, bible and all, against the door, "is that protecting her? How?"

Anna felt like she was back in the juvenile detention center. When they brought a newb into the girls ward they went through stages. Tough reserve eventually exploded into rebellious anger. Some took longer to reach the guarded acceptance stage. It hadn't turned personal or physical yet, so Anna wasn't worried.

Perhaps Dianne's journey was the opposite path. Freaking because she had been freed from her mental prison. Her mind scanned through different articles and books on institutionalization. She probably needed specialized help from an expert and no matter how much reading Anna did, it wouldn't replace practical experience.

"I don't know how you're supposed to help her," she told Dianne. "Or even what the threat is." Anna was tempted to do the hugging thing. But couldn't. If physical touch really forced Dianne to relive the other person's worst memories, Anna wanted to stay clueless about which memory would be her worst. She let the thought absorb her mind so Dianne would know she wished to help, wished to comfort. She didn't know the photographer all that well but losing your grandma, then fighting pain and addiction. That shit was rough.

Dianne started to openly weep and then jumped a full foot off the ground when there was a knock at the door. "No one is there."

"Of course someone's there. They knocked," Anna said. She shook her head, Dianne being surprised just confirmed how much her ability was malfunctioning.

"I don't hear anyone there."

"Says the crazy woman whose powers are totally out of whack?" Anna headed for the door and swept her foot across the entry way to remove the debris as she checked the peep hole. "Yeah?"

"I'm looking for Dianne? Liesel's friend." The concaved image of the peep hole showed a man with spiked blue hair, hands stuck deep into his pockets. But it may have just been the hall lights.

"Yeah?"

A bit impatient, "I'm Dr. Sergei Sky."

"He says he's Dr. Sky," Anna turned to tell Dianne.

Dianne blew her nose in her sleeve. "Is he a hottie?"

"Try not to be an idiot for a minute will you?" Anna said. She opened the door and nodded approvingly at the man before her. "Nice t–shirt. Reproduction?"

"Nope. It's an original. Got it on EBay." It was an X–men shirt, the team in their original bright yellow outfits. "Sergei Sky."

"Anna Marie." They shook hands. Strong hands, solid cut build, guy was a hottie, and having recently finished his residency, probably not too old. But Anna didn't feel any particular sparks with the guy.

"Like in Rogue?" No surprise that he would catch the reference as a Marvel fan.

"Ya, like in Rogue. Nice hair."

"It's real."

"Sure it is. Come on in." Trying for sincere but it sounded sarcastic to Anna.

"Hey!" He stormed across the room and snatched the joint out of Dianne's hand, careful at the last second not to touch her fingers. "This stuff isn't helping you. It just makes the sober moments worse." He headed for the mini bar built into the wall and shoved the joint down the sink as he turned on the water.

Anna groaned. She would have liked some of that, though she hadn't smoked any in several months. She needed to keep clean until her probation expired, she reminded herself.

"Don't worry I have more. Who the hell are you?" Dianne said.

"We spoke on the phone." He dried his hands on a tea towel and did a turn, eyes scanning, eyebrows up at the posh digs.

"Are you like super stupid or something?" Dianne asked.

"What did you just say?" Sergei said.

OMG. What was she thinking? "Dianne, this guy's going to help you," *Dork*. The guy had already helped, they wouldn't have been able to fly without the cream. "Thank you would be a good place to start."

"His head is empty. Correction, he is so void like that I can't even find his head," Dianne said. She pointed with stern disapproval.

Anna shook her head and tried to calm the other Amazon down. Keeping her hands open and at her side. She had talked her share of chicks down from the panic ledge. This one might be a bit older and taller but Anna had no doubts she could take Dianne down without much fuss. "Maybe there is too much clutter—"

"No." She pulled the lotion out of her pocket. "This stuff works. I can pretty much only hear this floor and the one above and below us. You do not want to know what the guy next door is watching on TV." As she spoke she stepped toward Anna, in protective mode.

Be nice Dianne.

"I told you on the phone. You can't hear my thoughts. I'm immune to psychic readings. Comes with the blue hair." He hadn't left his spot by the sink, but Anna didn't buy his laid-back attitude for a minute. He was in prepared-observer mode, same as Dianne was. Prepared-to-pounce telegraphed in his tight shoulders and focused eyes.

"Yeah," Dianne said with crisp sarcasm.

"Yeah." He nodded and pushed away from the counter and Dianne stiffened with an inward breath. "Since you're in a functioning state let's start out with you cleaning up your mess. I assume it was your temper tantrum." He nodded to the pile of broken plastic and split wood veneer that lay next to the door. Perhaps the room wasn't so posh underneath.

"Don't tell me what to do," Dianne's voice rose.

"Why not?" and his just got quieter. Crap, this was going south faster than Anna could process.

"Okay, I can see you've got her well in hand. I'm going to turn her over to you and go check out my bed." Both ignored Anna's sarcasm. But she felt a sudden charge to the room, the rumble before mutiny or a ward riot.

"I can't read you," Dianne's voice peaking the edge of shrill.

"We covered this." He took a step toward her, hands open and down at his sides.

"Anna. We're not safe, Anna."

Holy shit. Terrified, Dianne started to herd Anna, pressing close but not touching, waving her hands. *RUN*, Dianne commanded. And Anna almost turned. Almost listened.

"Serendipity." It was an odd choice of words but as he finished speaking, Dianne fainted. Sergei caught her.

Holy fucking mojo. "Shit. What did you do?" Anna didn't know if she should fight to get Dianne back. But as he lifted Dianne, Anna saw deep pain etched in his eyes as he clutched her close. He might strut like everything was cool and he had no worries but the man had seen horror. Would it be from his time working in an ER?

"Hypnosis," he said. His face cleared and he pulled the charming smile back into place.

One word and Anna's head was scrolling facts; she ignored the majority. The seers and female prophets at Delphi utilized self–hypnosis. Frederick Anton Mesmer used magnets to affect humans and cure disease. Thus the word Mesmerize. Anna sighed and led Sergei into her and Dianne's room.

Sadly not her weirdest roommate. At least this one knew how to keep her hands to herself.

Sergei lifted Dianne, surprised that he could. He wasn't a physical person—give him a white lab coat or something to read, that was his element. And it wasn't astonishment over his ability to. *Hello, Blue Hair here.* Plus, working in the ER, especially once the nurses knew how much he could lift, he heaved bodies around plenty. He was surprised that he had the chance to touch.

He worked out with weights because the adrenaline release helped him sleep. Exhaustion kept the nightmares away. If Sergei slept too much or if he rested enough to remember his dreams he spent the day impersonating a zombie, physically there but mentally struggling. He couldn't prevent the dreams but he could control how they affected him, and control was everything.

"I think it's pretty cool," Anna said.

"What?" He smiled at her, direct eye contact so she believed he was listening.

He had come to meet Dianne, pay his dues and wish her luck. Maybe even convince her that she shouldn't be in Vegas. If he was going to work on his vacation it would be on his notebook, figuring out a way to help his sister Portia. Yes, he'd considered using her for an additional perspective on this issue. However, he realized that she was so dysfunctional that he would spend the whole week working and get little if nothing accomplished.

"That a punk like you can also be a doctor." She said punk and doctor with the same amount of awe to her voice.

He smirked at the wise-man-on-the-hill act and thought about adding a bit of his Russian Great Grandfather's words on life. Instead he kept it to, "The shell is our protection from the world. Our minds are our tool for survival."

Dianne's black hair was very short and her clothes—jeans and a t-shirt—too big and baggy on her. She had a collection of different colored hair bands on each wrist and a few more on her fingers at different knuckles. He'd only had a brief chance to see her hazel eyes, but they had a glint of defiance that appealed to him. From behind in a crowd she'd look like a boy. Long lean legs and hips hidden in loose clothing. Until she turned and looked with those delicate eyebrows and thick lashes. Until she walked with the alluring sway of her hips. Until you saw the catch of material along a pert curve of her breast or hip. A covered peek-a-boo.

He groaned and reminded himself that he hadn't seen her walk. Still, she was a damn sexy temptation.

He carried her slowly to the bed Anna indicated so he could enjoy the touch and feel of Dianne. When she was awake she wouldn't allow him to touch her. It was hard not to touch. Infinitely more desirable because you shouldn't. A rule his rebel heart couldn't break.

"So the cream is working?" Sergei asked Anna.

"It seems to. She made it here and didn't break out the Mary Jane until we got to the room." Anna slouched in the doorway, thumbs in her front pockets, fingers out.

He tilted his eyebrows, communicating interest, a learned ability to be more friendly, approachable. He could be a right cold bastard so people skills were important. "Did something set her off? Did something happen that—"

Anna sighed heavily. "Liesel was attacked at the airport." She put a hand up to hold off his questions. "I don't know more than that.

We were checking in at the lobby and suddenly Dianne says that and then...well, she started shaking."

"Her psychic powers can be extremely painful." No longer able to hold onto her, at least not for a good reason, Sergei laid her on the bed, let his hands smooth over her. "Her body is not made to process more than her own thoughts and yet it tries to do thousands." His brother would pass out or vomit in response to the pain.

"I hadn't thought of it like that."

Yeah, people didn't. Sergei took off Dianne's shoes but Anna stayed back. He pulled the covers down and then picked Dianne back up and put her down in the open bedding.

Checking her pulse, feeling her forehead. His hand slid over her scalp, her hair almost as short as his own hair. "Interesting hair choice."

Anna shrugged but Sergei wasn't really talking to her. He touched because if felt surprisingly right, because whether or not he wanted to now, he wouldn't be able to touch later.

His mother had often stood in his brother's room while he slept and touched his hand or hair or cheek. Sick fuck that he was, if he didn't have an audience he'd might lean down and kiss her. She had a full kissable mouth. It was Sergei's turn to sigh. He rolled his shoulders to release some of the tension.

"Have Liesel call me once she's settled and if Dianne comes to before that give me a call." He wrote his room number and cellphone on a pad of paper from the hotel's nightstand. As Anna looked at the information, Sergei ran his hand over Dianne's head again, feeling the short spikes vibrate against his palm, melt between his fingers, stir his blood. Yep, sick.

And worse he wasn't just going to walk away. And not because she asked if he was hot which made him laugh. And not for some noble reaction to the desperation he had seen in her eyes. He would help because it worked to his advantage. It gave him a chance to be close. He liked her fire and he'd probably get burned but, with one brief look, he thought it would be worth it.

"Do you know anything about magnets?" Sergei asked Anna.

"More than most." Anna's shoulders pulled back in a type of backward shrug. Anna, a few inches shorter than Sergei, had dark blond hair, and both a pierced eyebrow and lip.

Might as well lay the ground work for his next attempt. "Magnetic fields can affect blood flow and mental focus. I've got some magnets I want to use on Dianne once the cream wears off."

"It won't last?" Anna placed the note on the side table and led the way back to the sitting area.

"It's more that she'll build an immunity to it." That sounded believable and if Anna and others believed it, thought it, so would Dianne. He'd never had much trouble getting people to believe him. He picked up a few pieces of the broken drawer and Anna finally moved in to help him.

"Thanks for your help Anna. I appreciate it." She blushed. "I've heard about a comic museum. Fan run. Maybe we could go check it out before we return to our prospective haunts." He knew instinctively she would respond not only to his use of big words but the comics.

"Cool," she said. Another person won over by Sergei's incredible charm. He rolled his eyes as he left the hotel room.

Chapter 4

Liesel had brought an army with her to Las Vegas, she just hadn't realized it. After the airport threat her people flooded the hotel lobby like an orchestrated attack. But Griffon needed her secure. Liesel could feel him vibrating at the seams, about to come apart. She needed to reassure him in a very physical way that she had survived.

He guided her through the throng of people, allowing her to hesitate long enough for an 'I'm fine,' and a couple 'I'm glad you're here.' She even hugged Jesus Corby hello while Griffon shook hands with Jesus's father, Emilio. They kept it brief and she moved closer to the elevators.

Most understood, but not Valasca Perch. The woman had a strong voice on HOAX, including a following of her own, and seeing her across the lobby, Liesel knew this wouldn't be a quick in and out. Valasca stepped forward and Griffon stepped between them. He could read a challenge and a hostile person in the dark.

Crap. Liesel placed a restraining hand on Griffon's arm. "Valasca? Ms. Perch?" Liesel said.

"Leslie, at last we meet. Or will once this—" Valasca lifted her delicate nose as if she smelt something nasty and looked right at Griffon. Brave or a risk taker? Probably just ignorant that her life was in danger if she pushed Griffon too far.

"Liesel, like diesel with an L. We had a bit of an incident at the airport," Liesel said. "I'm so glad you could make it this week. It'll give us the chance to discuss your ideas for the group."

"I do feel that I could be of help to you. Steer you in the right direction," Valasca's words sounded diplomatic, and though not outright hostile, it set Griffon's growl off and Liesel stroked his arm.

"Great. But right now my room is in that direction." She pointed. "I'm sorry to be rude—" Sure she was. Okay, so even she needed the empty bliss of Griffon's body to remind herself she was alive. He stroked her neck. She closed her eyes and focused on her words "—

but I...have had a hard day." She opened her eyes. "I'll see you at our breakfast meeting?"

"Yes you will. The meeting is for us. It is not open to the public," speaking to Griffon. Yep, risk taker.

Griffon's complete focus centered on Valasca. "See you in the morning," he said. Man, Liesel loved him. Four star General of her personal army.

Buffet Riot. Liesel should have expected it. Put over three hundred Amazons and Mightys in line with the regional supervisors of Fitness Freaks and then tell them they are out of bacon. Yeah, buffet riot.

After getting to her suite the night before, the police had been by to ask more questions. A leader of the Japanese group—the Shishi—had needed help at the front desk. And oh, the small matter of ten Amazons camping out in her living room area. She had had no sleep, no sex and no food for way too long. The only reason she hadn't started the riot was someone had beaten her to it.

A mouthy little Mighty named Todd had demanded to see the chef. The Fitness Freaks thought he was cutting and made a derogatory comment about special privileges for special need people. Maybe that would have blown over. Todd, he assured her later, was use to close minded, tight-ass idiots. But then someone had stumbled and shoved and chaos ensued.

It was like a bank run when the stock market crashed and to make it worse the frightened hotel staff had tried to fix the problem by closing the buffet until they could get it sorted out. Then there really was a run on the bank.

Rule number one, you do not tell a starving Amazons they must eat elsewhere. They had torn down the security gate and Todd had jumped onto the counter, "Pay cash people, and get this line moving. Exact change or we will consider it a tip." An Amazon named Amanda helped move the line along.

Liesel had agreed to pay for the gate, but only after they promised not to close the buffet. She relinquished her cell phone number so she could be on call if anything else happened. As the manager left, taking half of the building's security with him, she turned to find Griffon leaning against the wall, arms crossed, waiting for her.

Griffon had gotten his own room and she'd hoped to make her way there after sorting everything out. "Missed you last night," he said.

"Missed you too."

Dianne had shadowed her all morning but stuck to the walls, bare hands tucked beneath her arms to protect herself. Why she would venture this far out of her room, Liesel didn't know. Of course the amount of mental noise probably didn't increase outside of the room.

"Did you get everyone's room figured out?" Griffon took Liesel's hand.

"Some rooms became available this morning and I cleared everyone out. They'll be sharing but it also means they can split the price. So no complaints." At least there shouldn't be any for the next twenty minutes. She planned to hold Griffon's hand across the table while they each put away a stack of pancakes. Love then food. No worries.

After the airport, the police and hotel security, she had answered too many questions. This point forward things would go as planned with a bit of organizing.

"Griffon, we need to have a talk," Dianne said as she stepped toward them.

"Talk?" Griffon said. His faced cleared of confusion as Dianne whispered in both of their heads. *Dianne, psychic freak.* What a way of introducing yourself.

The washed out color and drawn look to Dianne's face didn't diminish the freak look. Shit. She probably heard Liesel think that. Hopefully she realized Liesel was just concerned, wanted to help her.

"I know you'd do anything to protect Liesel. She's in danger. I feel it." Dianne sighed, squared her shoulders. "No, I don't know specifics."

Dianne pulled at the bands around her wrists. "I'm not going to watch her today. Not even a mental link. Dr. Sky wants to do fieldwork. You'll watch, I know, but I want you to know I know. Okay?" It made it sound like Liesel was some important dignitary. She kept the derisive snort to herself.

"Sure," Griffon nodded.

"Great." Dianne stared at him a moment. "Ashley was one sick twisted bitch. I'm just saying." She shivered. "Plus, don't touch me. I don't want to feel what I've just seen."

Griffon nodded.

Shit. Griffon's former partner on the police force had tortured him. No doubt, on top of whatever Dianne had just 'seen' in his head, Dianne had seen some of Liesel's anxiety of Griffon's safety when she'd touched her back in Boise. Plenty of her nightmares involved his abuse.

Thankfully he believed in Dianne's psychic abilities and wouldn't think Liesel had betrayed his trust. Liesel squeezed Griffon's hand and Dianne turned to leave. Before Liesel could politely thank her—Dianne did mean well—she sent a mental, *No problem.*

Chapter 5

"You want me to do what?" Dianne held the camera in her hands, like a musician picking someone else's instrument up. She knew how to use it but it felt awkward. Too big, too small, too heavy and she needed to twirl the knobs, get the feel for it.

Sergei had come by that morning as Liesel showered and, with a monotone lecture about magnetic blood flow, had told her where to place the magnets. He said that she was to meet him here on the foot bridge with her equipment. The bossy attitude sucked but Anna and Liesel thought he could help and wanted her to work with him.

Dianne didn't startle. She knew people were there, always. She'd seen it with other people, surprised when someone came around a corner or tapped them on the shoulder. She knew that feeling second hand. Hell, most of what she had experienced was second hand. So not mentally seeing Sergei scared the crap out of her, like a constant surprise.

Liesel and Sergei had known each other for several years, she trusted him. Griffon had run a full background check on the guy and the worst he'd turned up was an odd lack of debt. Yet, hearing these things from their minds didn't ease her apprehension over not hearing anything from his.

Once Griffon was in place to guard Liesel, Dianne headed outside to meet the doctor. The bridge arched over a side street from the main strip. Covered in scuff marks and the flat, black spots of old gum, the bridge had no flare or design, unlike the hotels it connected. Practical, it kept the traffic flow uninterrupted by pedestrians.

"Go with it," Sergei said. It didn't sound like he cared if she did or didn't.

"It's lame."

"The magnets will help." She could feel, even after a couple of hours, the two spots of cool metal. One pressed against her left breast and the other at her lower spine, held in place by the waist band of her jeans.

He obviously didn't understand how her psychic abilities worked. "But if I focus it'll open the flood gates and I won't be able to close them," she said.

"That's why we are going with the huge angle." He nodded to the camera.

"It's called a wide lens." Barney had bought the camera for her knowing she would need it to heal, to function. Her regular equipment had melted in the fire.

He wasn't behaving like he had with Anna, or how she saw in Liesel's head. Liesel's memories where of Sergei's wicked sense of humor and overly formal manners. The first word that came to Liesel's mind was charming. Today on the bridge he was stiff, distant.

Sergei lifted an eyebrow and she wondered why. "What's with the eyebrow?"

"Guess."

Dianne laughed and lifted the camera and took his picture. The lighting was all wrong, not to mention what the wide lens would do with his close features, but it felt good to take a shot. Sergei's short blue hair reflected the sun. He wore a white button down with no sleeves. Little threads hung where the sleeves had been ripped out. His defined muscles glowed golden and a black hoop earring pierced his inner ear rather than the outer lobe. A blue shadow of growth sat just below his full lips like a pointed exclamation.

He didn't look like a medical doctor. A drool-worthy club DJ maybe or a punk teen. Then, as she took another picture, she saw the pyramids behind him. Nothing really heroic about them, which meant they didn't fit her general theme but it might be fun to take a picture just to have a picture. She use to do that. She wanted to scope out the right angle, fiddle with different lens but Sergei had stashed the rest of her gear in his backpack and she didn't think she could get into it without touching him.

The lotion had worked, was working, and so were the magnets. Thoughts floated by like the people walking on the foot bridge. But ten feet, maybe twenty was all she heard. It was manageable. She could ignore most of it. She'd give the camera idea a try. "Okay. Tell me again."

"I want you to look through the lens and pick that area to hear. The people in your lens." His voice was neither welcoming nor off putting. "That's why we are using the big lens—wide lens," he corrected himself. He leaned back against the metal railing in his tight black jeans and sunglasses.

"Could you at least take those off so I know if you are looking at me or not?"

"No."

Dianne sighed and lifted her camera to the pyramid. There were construction workers. Hard hats, dusty overalls, repairing a column, adding to the pyramid hotel. Working before the heat of the day climbed. If she had her telephoto lens she could see the tools they used or if they were right handed. But even zoomed in with this lens, she saw them as a group.

"Not the picture, the area. Focus on the people." His voice changed to that soothing hypnotic lull.

This was ridiculous. She'd hear thoughts but what would prove that it was their thoughts if she didn't know these people?

He continued talking in that voice, slid closer, kept his tone low. The serendipity thing chilled her blood; she should make him take its power away, but right now his voice drew her in. She knew the precise position of each of his arms, where his legs were. How much room he took up. How good he smelled. How rebellious he looked. She heard the depth and frequency of his breathing. She couldn't focus when he filled so much of her awareness. Even the people who passed them thought about him and tried not to stare. They wondered what they were doing on the bridge, about his hair.

"Just focus on the view in the lens. The people are the only ones you can hear," Sergei said.

"Stop. Wait." Dianne placed a single fingertip to his chest—one of the buttons for the extra layer of protection—and pushed. She took a step to the side for good measure. "You're making me all hot and it's hard to focus."

The corner of his lip shot up for some reason and an eyebrow lifted above the sunglasses. She flashed the camera at him again and turned back to the construction workers.

"What are they thinking Dianne?"

"See that scaffolding?"

After a moment. "Barely."

Her long sleeves provided armor but she hoped by Athena she got inside before she died from the heat. With her hands in her pockets at least she was fully covered.

"There's three of them up there." She needed to know when they would leave so she could photograph the site while it was empty. She didn't photograph people. And thinking that, needing that information, her focus hit its mark.

One turned to the guy next to him and answered the question, not realizing it was Dianne asking. "Done by eleven."

The other guy had heard too and figured his coworker was confirming with him. "*Si*, yeah dude, I've got lunch plans and then I'm headed to job number two."

A minute later, Dianne told Sergei, "They're talking about how expensive it is to live in Las Vegas."

"You can hear them talk?" Sergei stepped toward her. He slid the bag off his shoulder and placed it at his feet. Dianne wanted to shush him, make him hold still.

"More the thoughts as they say them. Speech is thought first."

"What about the third guy? And are you getting other feedback?" Sergei said.

Avalanche. As if she'd lifted a pile of laundry to look at the towels in the middle and now the tower of fluffy white fell on her head. White static, a hundred at once, rough and blurry. She nearly dropped her camera and had to brace herself on the railing.

He put a hand just next to her shoulder. Close. But didn't touch. She saw him move, so deliberate, and wondered how he knew not to touch.

"I'm done," Dianne said, agitated, buzzing with weariness.

"Take a break and—"

"No."

She could look through a camera and hear specific people's thoughts. What good would that do her? Lame.

"Who have you helped that's like me?" She looked at him. The rough edges of the white static rubbed her nerves raw. "You're so aware. And the lotion and stuff. You've done this before."

He shook his head.

Saying no to what? "I don't have to remind you not to touch."

Sergei sighed. "I'm not likely to forget. Ever," he whispered. She leaned closer to hear. "My father and..."

And who? At least it seemed as if he would say another person but instead—

"And he never held us. No hugs." He blew out a rough breath and worked his jaw side to side. "He and mom live in New Mexico. Total hermits."

No touching? Then where did Sergei come from? As a child, she always meet her father at the door when he came home. He would scoop her up and press her close. Until things got rough as home, until she couldn't be picked up anymore. No idea which came first. For once Dianne kept the thought to herself. She kneaded her forehead and temples, still feeling the smoother of thoughts, even if they were blunted.

"We'll go back inside and get something to eat. No more field work today." Sergei scrubbed the back of his neck, cupped his skull. His flexed arms, emphasized his defined muscle tone. Looking made her mouth dry, and she swallowed. No way would the task master let up with such a small distraction, just after a couple probing questions.

She swayed, locked her knees to stay upright. "No field work? What then?"

A little girl bolted up the steps at the end of the foot bridge, giggling and running from her fat nanny—the child's opinion—and plowed into Dianne as Dianne stepped away from the rail. Dianne reached to steady the child who squeezed her hand in gratitude.

During the brief touch, Dianne feared the dark. The creep of monsters just beyond the cast of hallway light. Not bad enough to black out but she dropped to sit on the concrete bridge and started to dig in his bag for a green vial, her last one. The next person she touched would surely make her gibber for a week. And she had a mile of hotel hallway and casino before she reached any kind of safety. She pulled it out and felt some of the worry melt off her shoulders.

Sergei reacted as if she'd spit on him. All laid back ease gone to reveal a hostile energy. "Go ahead and take your fucking life." He yanked the vial from her hand, narrowly missing touching her. "Do it fast instead of this slow decay." He threw the vial over the heads of tourists and the traffic to the top of the hotel's lobby section, at least the distance of a football field.

"I hope that broke," Dianne said, clenching and releasing her empty hands. That strong of a dose could kill a normal human. Hell, should she get someone up there to wash it off?

He shook his head and started to head back the way they came. She shouldered his bag and ducked in quick behind him. He wasn't all that bigger than her but with his edgy look and punk hair people avoided direct contact of him and she could swim through the sea of people behind his divide.

His silence unnerved her. Still consumed by that brief touch, Dianne said, "She was afraid of the dark. The little girl."

He didn't pause. It wasn't like he sped along the path, more a casual swaggering stroll. "The one that touched you? Why?"

She thought about misunderstanding him on purpose but decided not to. "She's had a ... safe life. The dark fear was one night when the nightlight went out. Probably a power outage and she cried and no one heard. The baby monitor was a plug in."

"You can tell all that from a second of touch?" He turned his head to look at her. When she only shrugged he stepped toward the front curb of the hotel. He leaned in the meager shade against the cool stone of the building. She stepped to his side, keeping him between herself and the people coming in and out.

He scrubbed a hand at his face then slid down the wall to sit on the ground. Dianne sat next to him. He turned his head toward her and she could see her reflection in his sunglasses, the palm trees and traffic behind her.

"Didn't you wear that yesterday?"

Dianne always knew the reason behind every question asked her so his words rattled her. Not an intriguing cozy mystery but as if she was being threatened. "Why the fashion question? Isn't that rude?" Hostile much? Why would he care what she wore? How did she figure out what he really meant? She looked for the answer in the minds around her.

Not that it helped. "I'm supposed to know what you mean by your tone? What the hell?"

"Dianne, did you wear that yesterday?" Sergei asked again, his tone didn't change.

"Yes. So?"

His shoulders lifted, dropped. "Why?"

She couldn't say that she had lost all her clothes in the fire. It sounded whiney. "I don't own very many." She'd had a few things in storage that Barney had gotten for her, the rest she'd picked up at a thrift shop on the reservation.

"Hard to shop?"

"Yeah. I usually just order stuff online or buy at truck stops." Which often meant men's jeans and t-shirts. For the girlier stuff she could take a tape measure and order the size she needed. Plaids when it got cold, though she tended to stay south when the temperature dropped. Or at least had. This winter she'd be in Boise, in Grandma Maggie's house watching over Liesel and hopefully would have better control of her abilities. She suddenly remembered the press of her grandmother's cheek and the feel of the blanket she kept on her bed in the RV. Had kept. She sighed to dispel the grief.

"If the magnets are really working you could go shopping. Like in a real boutique." His voice was sweet, charming, like a stranger offering a little girl candy. The voice he had used when he spoke to Anna at the hotel room door.

The voice wasn't off or odd or in any way suspicious. Unless you accounted for his not using it until now. Until he wanted something. "What kind of doctor are you?"

He gave her the long of it, including his school degrees. Before she could ask him if that meant he was rich, he asked her, "What kind of reclusive photographer are you, spending time in Las Vegas?" At least the sugary charm was gone.

"I do landscapes, abstract theme shots—"

"Why are you here, Dianne?"

"Why didn't you just ask it that way the first time?" What the hell did he want from her?

He waited her out. She sighed and shielded her eyes to look across the street at the increasing traffic. Most were billboards on wheels, taxis with advertisements and literal billboards on wheels. There was a waiter in the coffee shop just behind her who was trying to do simple math in his head. He'd been tipped thirty percent. The heat was pressing the moisture out of her like a sponge, trickles running down between her breasts and across her forehead.

"Dianne?"

"A few weeks ago I was taking some shots in central Idaho when I had a vision." She stopped to look at him and saw herself reflected back in his glasses. She fiddled with the scrunchies at her wrists and slid her fingers through her still-too-short hair.

She reached up and took the sunglasses off him. He couldn't stop her without touching her hand and that's probably why he conceded. His eyes were brown. Just brown. Not particularly thick lashed or dramatically shaped. Just eyes. Perhaps intelligent eyes. But against his pale blue scruffy cheeks and thick, bright, blue hair they were...They were wow. She took the lens off her camera and took a real picture of him. "Beautiful."

"We were talking about why Vegas."

"I had a vision that my grandma and Liesel were in danger. Now Grandma Maggie is dead." She blinked several times to stave off any tears. "I want to protect Liesel."

"Which you can't do if you're—"

"In the way? A problem? I know." She stowed her camera away in his bag. "Why didn't you compliment me back?"

"What?" He turned and looked at her then down at his glasses.

"Why the glasses? To make you look cool?"

He laughed. "The glasses are to warn people off," he took them back from her open hand with two fingers. "And I didn't compliment you?"

"When I said you were beautiful. You've been charming everyone but me."

"Hmm." He tilted his head to the side in a type of nonchalant shrug minus the shoulders. "Maybe I'm hoping that you like me as me."

"That could work." Her jeans were starting to feel muggy.

He checked his watch. "Dr. Kandi's presentation is starting soon. She's giving a lecture about genealogy and the Amazon gene research she's doing."

She couldn't imagine sitting in her day-old clothes listening to a prestigious doctor give a fancy lecture. "I'm going back to my room." She braced a hand on the wall and focused a moment on Liesel to check her whereabouts. When she opened her eyes to look, Sergei was gone.

Stairs or Elevators? Dianne was much more likely to touch someone on the elevator so she took the stairs which started as a series of escalators through the casino, clubs, and restaurants. It was like a field of land mines. No, not exactly, more like explosive Frogger. You had to time your movements, foresee possible obstacles, weave and float around the unexpected. Because one touch, one jostle from the crowd, would bump her into another, then helping hands would reach out to assist her, burn her.

She tugged her sleeves down and stuck her hands in her pockets, glad the AC was on high, even if it was a shock after the heat.

She tried to stick to walls, which provided a side that didn't require watching, but security thought the behavior odd enough to send someone to shadow her. George from security thought she had a nice ass but quit following her when she left the wall and stuck to the higher traffic areas.

Tired from the field work, she navigated the hallways alone. Dianne sent Liesel a reassurance that she was safe and asked Griffon if she was needed. He was kind enough not to laugh at her question; it wasn't like she could do anything. He gave her the all clear.

She headed up the escalators as she listened to Anna, acting as moderator, introduce Dr. Sima Kandi with an impassioned speech about Amazon and Mighty genes and the research Kandi and Sergei had done.

Dr. Kandi did not acknowledge Sergei's presence and Dianne could sense a deep knowledge of Sergei in her mind, someone he had worked with, someone who could give her insight. Maybe if she focused on Kandi she'd learn something about the blue Doctor. Yet, it felt stupid to push past the barriers the lotion and magnets provided, a filter she would have given her best camera for. Except now it kind of felt like that was exactly what she had done.

Distracted, she stumbled into a man reading a paper. She jerked back out of touch zone and apologized. Then she yanked the paper out of his hand. He thought she was upset that they nearly collided but she was shocked by his thoughts on an article.

An article about her.

The man yelled at her to watch where she was going and how bloody rude she was. She dropped the paper and pulled out her cell phone. It only had one number in it, seeing how it was new and given to her by her agent Barney.

The newspaper had one of her photos of the Florida Animal Rescue. Florida had been way too hot. Of course it had been early August. She pressed his contact number icon and tapped it again to dial Barney. "You scheduled an art show?"

"How are you? Feeling better?" Barney was from the Midwest, spoke as if he was from San Diego, and looked like a sports agent. She smiled thinking of him. He had saved her.

He didn't wait for her answer. They didn't normally do the hi,-how-are-you's. "Yeah, the hotel sold-out within two hours of posting on your website the actual appearance of Defender. Most people think you're still a guy."

"Still a guy, like I had a sex change?" Her voice echoed oddly in the stair well as she started up from the third floor.

"You know what I mean."

"You sold tickets to an art show?" Did they do that?

"D, it's for charity. You know, minus the gallery fee. Babe, if you found a way to handle traveling in an airplane and can be in Vegas, then you can have a show. No more excuses." Barney had been her agent from the beginning. Sold her first piece, got her artwork on the cover of the New Yorker and Life. He knew about her psychic problem and created the Defender name to sell her art work under.

"Not excuses." Hello, she hurt. She added a put-upon sigh for affect.

"Yes darling, they're real but still holding you back from worldwide stardom."

Her art kept him well paid and with her trailer and stuff gone in the fire she'd need the cash flow. Plus, he made her hermit-like existence possible so she would repay the favor. "When?"

"Two days. I'm coming to Vegas myself in an hour. I'll set everything up." Damn straight. Of course he would love every minute of it. She had called his cell number so he could be anywhere. But the lack of traffic noise or carpentry made her think he was probably in his office.

"Two days. You can't set a show that quickly." But even as she complained she thought of setting up shots during the gallery show. Of seeing other people see her work. The hemp-smelling lotion and magnets would make it possible. No matter how much an enigma Sergei was, even though his body had her buzzing, even though his moods swung without any discernable push, she was grateful for that. Barney was happy. She'd get to go to a real art show. Hell, except for someone trying to kill Liesel, life was going pretty good. *Fuck.*

"I can if I don't sleep. Plus, I already had everything packed up for the LA showing. I just loaded it on a truck."

"You're insane." She reached the seventh floor and pushed the metal door open.

"I believe in my artists." He loved her. They were friends. "Still having dreams?"

"Only when I'm awake." Dianne didn't have to explain. He got it.

"You could do a series on forest fires in California. Expand on your rescue series. It might be therapeutic," he murmured.

"Maybe."

"I'll call you when I reach Vegas," Barney said.

Dianne headed down the hall to her room. It would be nice to rub some cream in, take some pain pills and take a nap. The thought made her yawn until her jaw popped and her eyes watered.

"I'm inviting your father. Do you want me to call your mom?"

She pulled her keycard out of her back pocket and slid it into the door. "No." Barney read her silence well.

"Maggie would be so proud. Your first show. Speaking of which, Sgt. Sparks would like to meet you. Heard, somehow, that you were in Boise." I.e. from Barney. The other photographer was an artist Dianne had discovered and talked Barney into representing. "I could set you up on a blind date when you get back."

"Absolutely not Barney!" She knew enough from the Sgt.'s work to know he had seen hell. Lived and breathed the worst kinds of tragedies. That was how she knew his work would do so well hanging with hers. They both could look at rot and decay and see hope.

She made Barney promise no matchmaking and added a command, "Bring the Sergeant to Vegas."

For Sergei the bridge had just been an excuse to see Dianne. Sure, if she could learn to manipulate her focus, strengthen her abilities, it would probably help her cope in the long run. It just wasn't that altruistic for him. The morning sunlight contoured around her body, sparked in her green eyes. She was good looking and then she mouthed off or said something outrageous and his body just perked up and wanted more.

They had separate lives and she couldn't stand to be touched while *his* body would go into anaphylactic shock without regular bouts of sex. All key indicators that there was zero chance of a future. So in a total dipshit move, he left her to find her way back through the hotel and headed for Dr. Kandi's lecture.

Sergei had worked, when he could, with Dr. Sima Kandi, a geneticist and genealogist. He'd gathered genealogy charts, analyzed data, worked the lab every spare moment he had. It added to his notebook on Blue Hairs plus improved his work credentials.

In front of the Las Vegas group, she spoke with confidence and ease. "It's not that we can't ignore the instinctive drive to protect or that all Amazons are born with it—in fact a third aren't—it's more that if these urges are ignored, it affects our hormone levels and our mental health."

He knew all of this. Coming to this workshop when he could be playing Black Jack or Pinochle was masochistic. A pair of swim trunks and a bottle of sunscreen and he could work the ladies at the pool, get laid by dinner time. Though in this particular hotel they might all be married with kids. Not his type.

He wondered if Dianne ever went swimming. Probably some ice cold creeks or rivers. He'd followed her website and art right after purchasing his Defender original. Liesel had clued him into the fact that the photographer was an Amazon. He didn't realize until this morning that the Blue Hair and photographer were the same person. Seeing her struggle had raised painful memories, and made his desire to help his sister's unborn child catch fire, fry his nerves.

He tried to turn his attention back to the presentation. He'd make nice with Liesel, rub elbows with other conference attendees, and keep his sex drive gagged and tied down.

Liesel pointed Tydus out to Sergei. Tydus stood to let an older lady sit in his seat. When he noticed them he smiled and nodded in Liesel's direction, who waved back. Tydus was handsome, in a polished sort of way, and the other attendees were giving him a heroic welcome for coming to Liesel's aid at the airport.

Kandi had already covered why Amazons had high metabolisms and longevity. She continued to explain Amazons' and Mightys' instinctive drive to protect. "Whether the transfer of this aspect of the DNA is connected or latched to the rest of the Amazon gene spectrum is still unknown.

"I'll be publishing my results. This study was one of the most comprehensive comparisons between family heritage and DNA analysis." And this was why Sergei had stopped working with Sima. As the only non-Amazon in her family, she was determined to gain some fame for herself, especially at the exposure of her Amazon sisters.

"Our DNA may continue to develop as I believe it has in the past. But to truly know what we are capable of, more research needs to be done. A broad spectrum of tests to showcase our abilities."

Our abilities? She wasn't an Amazon and shouldn't suggest otherwise. Sergei kept his eye roll to himself. He leaned back in his seat and let his mind wander to where Dianne had taken his picture. He felt cranky and awkward around her, like his first day working at the hospital and uncertain how to impress his mentors.

All those long limbs covered except as she reached, bent, stepped and little peeps of smooth pale skin would draw his eyes. Oh, if he could touch, push the cloth out of the way. She'd be overly sensitive, might come from just the erotic play of his fingers over her nipples.

Sima stepped back from the PowerPoint presentation and the audience clapped politely.

"Questions from the floor?" Anna asked.

"How does the DNA in a Mighty differ from the Amazon gene?" Emilio Corby asked. Sergei knew him and his son were both Mightys, Jesus was one of the kids Liesel had saved.

Sima stepped back to the mike, "We first believed that the Amazon gene was passed like mitochondria, through the mother only. But now we know that the Amazon gene is dormant in male carriers. The Mighty gene is directly linked to the y—or male chromosome." She showed the corresponding slide.

Sima wasn't interested in solving the problems. Amazon children went through periods of painful growth. They were prone to injury at an early age because they could lift more than their bodies were ready for. They often developed Unbreakable complexes, they were sure they could not be hurt. Sima obsessed over the power and finding a way of breeding it into all humans. Sergei just wanted to protect his family, help Blue Hairs cope.

Portia's due date was only four months away. Her husband John carried the Amazon gene dormantly and Portia was a Blue Hair. Ax, ay plus Ax, Ax. A fifty percent chance that their child would be a Blue Hair. Sergei would do anything to prevent that child falling down the same path as his brother.

Tydus asked the next question, "Dr. Kandi, first I wanted to say on behalf of the community that you've done a wonderful job. Thank you. My question. Can you give us an explanation why the double gene mutation varies so widely?"

Sima preened at the attention. "I believe the double gene, or Blue Hair mutation, is similar to eye color mutation. With eye color, a family with a long tradition of brown eyes on both sides can still have a blue eyed child.

"Studies show that eye color, a composite of pigmentation, is not only affected by the type of pigment—the gene—but the production of that pigment by the body. Two Amazon genes or an Amazon gene and a Mighty gene prevent the body from producing the proper type and amount of certain proteins and amino acids."

Sima laughed, a flirtatious sound, "Which is way over simplifying. Perhaps Blue Hairs adapt to their environments, as they develop rather than slowly over several generations. An evolutionary reflex." She shook her head and smiled at Tydus. "Honestly, so much more work needs to be done to truly understand Blue Hair mutations." If what Sima said was true, Dianne's evolutionary reflex had been to read people's mind to protect herself or survive. Sergei wondered what the stimulus had been and for his brother, active upon birth, was it just because their father had already developed those abilities?

Chapter 6

"What do you do?" Harry adjusted the straps of her climbing harness and passed the chalk to Tydus. His arm was healed except for a series of puckered red flesh along the curve of his bicep. The marks went in and out of hiding underneath his sleeve as he reached for the next hand hold.

She clarified her question. "You've talked about all these places you've been but not why you were there." The rock wall was in the basement of the hotel and extended into the third floor rec. area, offering both climbing and rappelling.

And yeah, maybe she shouldn't have worded it that way. She'd only known him two days. It wasn't like they were dating. Though what the hell it was she didn't feel comfortable speculating. He kept turning that smile on her but neither had tried to pursue past the point of friendly. She'd seen him in the lobby after breakfast and asked him to come climb with her.

"I'm a business consultant. Companies hire me to analyze what they are doing wrong and how best to fix it." He made it level with her and leaned back in his harness to rest. He offered her a bottle of water.

She took a swig then passed it back. "Sorry, but it sounds boring."

Tydus laughed. "It can be. But the traveling is a plus. And I'm pricey." He chalked his hands, sniffed at the powder. "They add talcum powder. Nice."

As a blonde she found that people dismissed her words if she talked about important things. It didn't occur to them that she, a construction worker, would have a valid opinion or useful thoughts on other subjects. Sometimes it bugged her, but she'd learned early that a quick way to scare off men was to make a fuss about it. She didn't act stupid, just kept the conversations light. Women were different. They wanted to use her as a handy man, liked when she showed off her knowledge of scotch or the financial market.

"So, what are you doing after the rock wall? I've dominated so much of your time."

"Manicure appointment. Then I'm meeting with clients this afternoon," he said, secure enough in himself to talk beauty care without giving excuses. He was wearing a snug t-shirt and a pair of khakis shorts, both high-end labels and neither looked particularly worn. She had bought a few new items for the trip as well. Nice excuse to buy clothes you didn't plan to sweat through on a job site.

"I'm actually going to the salon myself. Rogue booked us a pedicure while Liesel has her haircut. She didn't have time back in Boise."

"Rogue? Is that the blue hair?"

"No, sorry. Rogue is Anna Marie. I call her Rogue because it pisses her off."

He laughed. That great laugh that made her heart race and crash. Pitter, patter, boom. "No, wait then. Who is Dianne?"

She is a total basket case and ugly and not the girl for you. Harry sighed and tried to not be jealous and a petty shrew. The photographer was mad talented and had beautiful features and skin. "Dianne Fender. Maggie's granddaughter. She's tagging along."

"A great loss for the organization."

Shrug. It wasn't like Harry was part of that. "She was a very nice lady."

To deter any further questions about other women she chalked her palms. "Race you to the top? I win you buy me dinner."

"If I win I buy you dinner. Go." In a quagmire for an instant, she took off after him. He wasn't holding back and used every muscle to propel himself up the wall. But Harry had the advantage of weighing less and not being afraid to fall.

At the last second she planted her feet on a steady footing and leaped upward. The muscles of her legs protested and her hands caught on the edge just before his. A hand reached over the edge and snagged her arm. With a single pull she shot straight up and Liesel steadied her.

"Harry."

Pissed sisters are no fun.

"I win." Tydus's arm pressed over the climbing wall edge.

"I got to the top first," Harry ignored her sister.

"Exactly. I win." He kissed her check. "See ya later." He deserted her to deal with the worried sister on her own. But since her toes were curling and her check radiated heat, she didn't care. Bring the angry sisters of the world on. Release the hounds of dates gone bad. She could take it all.

One day of conference down and, except for the buffet riot, things had gone smoothly. Liesel adjusted her skirt and smoothed her hand down her shirt. Her heart lodged in a frozen lake each time she thought of Harry nearly falling off that wall or the fight they had after. Keeping her family safe would always be a top priority.

At least Sergei had helped Dianne. The pearly green color of Dianne's face had disappeared. If either one of them complained about working with each other she would knock heads. She was much too busy with meetings and workshops to make sure they were getting along.

After the day's meetings she only had the welcome dinner and she could retreat to Griffon's arms. Tomorrow she had been asked to go down to the police station and answer more questions about the attack at the airport. Yes, she recognized how sloppy an attempt it had been and agreed that someone could still try to get to her, but it didn't feel personal or real. All of that at the airport, it was probably a misunderstanding or a hot headed reaction to some slight. Hell, how much damage could a knife really do to her?

"So you have to go glad-hand for a while? A little smoozing?" Anna asked.

Liesel glared at the teasing. "Anna, it's not glad-handing, it's—"

"Ah, you will not handle me? I'm disappointed." The woman's voice sounded like cultured wind chimes.

"Ping." Liesel turned to embrace the lady. "I'm so glad you could come. No more problems with your room I hope?"

"Well, being what it is, we figured it out. Tell me who this little Amazon is and then lead the way to dinner. I'm famished." Ping spoke English like people often do after being taught at Oxford. Precise. Clean. With confidence.

"Kee Ping this is Anna Fort–Porter. Anna is my assistant and Ping is the leader of the Japanese Amazons, the Shishi or lion warriors." Turning to her long distance friend, "How did I do?"

"Your pronunciation was passable. Anna, you may call me Ping." Regal, elegant but welcoming because of the warmth and sincerity. Ping had the rich skin and slanted eyes of her Japanese heritage and a crooked nose from a bar fight. Her full lips and sharp cheek bones added to her beauty even in her sixties. For over a year, she had mentored Liesel through emails and phone calls, tirelessly answering her off the wall questions and offering advice with patience.

Ping and Anna shook hands and Liesel asked Anna to take Ping into the dining room. "I need to wait for Jennifer Hadley."

Anna, answering Ping's inquisitive look, "A recent transplant from New Zealand who is acting as the Aussie representative."

Liesel continued, "Valasca Perch and Maldecia Farina are also joining us."

Ping nodded, "The European representatives. Don't be too long."

Valasca and Jennifer arrived just as the banquet doors closed behind Anna. Valasca was talking with a fierce determination, "We can't allow science to distract from the divine that makes us Amazons. God has seen fit to grant us special talents and to use science to—"

"Not Dr. Kandi's intent." Jennifer's strong kiwi accent, a sweeter rounder tone than Australian. "Science doesn't eliminate God."

Valasca ignored Liesel but Jennifer nodded briefly before continuing her argument.

Though their words were civil, each woman vibrated and Liesel expected the next words to spit venom or make their faces blush with frustration.

Maldecia swept between the two. "My sisters, debates before dinner? No." She raised her arms like a bird and gathered her chicks under her wings. She ushered them forward, a natural respect instantly in play. Maggie would have done the same thing, diffused the argument and gathered them up. Liesel had discovered Maggie dead herself and until Dianne arrived hadn't once thought it was anything but from natural causes. Maggie had lived over a hundred years, so old age was way more likely than foul play.

If the airport attack was somehow connected...She gripped the door handle and felt the metal sink below her hand, contour to her fingers. The hole left by Maggie's guidance would never be filled.

Dianne asked from her room if Liesel was okay.

Griffon is keeping an eye on me and so is Anna.

Dianne said, *I miss Maggie too.*

Anna approved of the table arrangements. Her mom's strict attention to manners—one more mental file in Anna's head—had taught Anna the proper placement of foreign dignitaries and the salad fork. One of the conference rooms had been set with two tables forming a large square. Professionally set with linen cloths, it held more silverware per person than they could possibly need and enough food that no one would leave the table still hungry. Liesel had doubled the courses and told the waiters to keep it coming.

"There is a wedding tonight," Liesel said.

"In Vegas there is always a wedding," someone said.

Statistics and procedures from the official Clark County website on obtaining marriage licenses ran through Anna's mind for a moment. The first course, salads and bread, was served on generic but good quality stoneware.

"Tiffany Sven is marrying a man she met through HOAX." Determined to keep the subject light and happy, Liesel said, "His sisters are all Amazons. She wants me to give her away. They actually asked me to marry them but I don't have the authority."

After the heated words Valasca and Jennifer had traded over Dr. Kandi, and the general tension in the room, Anna didn't blame Liesel for wanting to avoid controversy. Who didn't love a wedding? Anna scrutinized each diner's movements. Who waited until everyone was served? Who used the correct fork? But she was also looking for subtle signs of anger. She knew that Griffon had this case well in hand. The guy had been a great cop and had really made a name for himself in private practice. Yet, people tended to overlook Anna because she was young, because she had more piercings than clothes on. She worked hard at maintaining that image. It allowed her to dwell in places others couldn't, hear and see different things. Liesel had taken her in, offered her a job and shown her why she healed so quickly, could lift so much. HOAX answered so many questions, filled in all those gaping doubts. So she would use her natural invisibility to snoop.

"You might consider it. Supposedly if you go online you can certify as a preacher," Harry said.

"Depends on the state," Anna wished Harry had sat next to her. She usually kept up with Anna's deeper and occasionally morbid conversations.

"I don't need more to do," Liesel carefully ate with her left hand. Probably holding Griffon's hand under the table.

"You are the closest thing to a religious leader we have," someone said. Anna couldn't see who the speaker was from this side of the table. Flowers and other diners were in the way.

"Not true," Kee Ping said. "Many of us are Muslim or Catholic or Protestant. As Liesel's initial study of the codex revealed, our ancestors did their best to integrate themselves into their new cultures."

Only Amazons could read the codex. The ink scrambled and shifted for non-Amazons or Mightys. Some believed a spell had been cast on it. Anna believed it was the type and color of ink. Similar to how only certain people could hear high frequency sounds, perhaps the codex creator had found a way to do the same with people's eyes.

Someone had stolen the leather pages from Liesel's home office before she could finish translating it.

Anna rubbed a hand around her neck. The bruises from the thief were long gone but just the thought of them made her hurt.

"But we were created by the Greek Gods," possibly the original speaker, Anna didn't know. The codex told the story of the Greek goddess Athena activating the blood of Zeus in Amazons and freeing them from a repressive culture, teaching them to fight and forming a powerful matriarchal society.

Matriarch. That could work. Anna focused on her food. Kept an eye on Liesel.

Liesel's rescuer Tydus sat at the other end of the table next to Harry. Not Anna's type, too strait-laced, but he had sensed danger and acted to save Liesel, which was cool. Anna felt uneasy around him, a shivering itch across her shoulders. Like she had poor posture, or used the wrong fork or just embarrassed herself.

She watched his body language change as they spoke of the codex, listening carefully, unaware that his body tightened. Anna remembered he was new to all this Amazon stuff. For her, adjusting to the truth had been a wild self-destructive ride. Hopefully he took to it better than she had.

Liesel directed her answer to the Greek Gods comment to the whole table in storyteller mode.

"Were we? There are all kinds of creation stories. And I believe that each one holds, like most myths, many truths. In an attempt to understand why they were different such stories were written—"

The dinner guests all spoke at once. Some encouraging words, other outraged protests.

Griffon straightened in his chair and moved their clasped hands to the top of the table. A declaration of his own. Anna felt the power of his eyes, like Cyclops minus the glasses. The X-man with laser vision, not the mythological monster. He looked the room over and people quit talking. Anna did her best not to laugh.

"Yes," Liesel said. "I'm not saying that there wasn't perhaps a divine hand—"

"I believe in justice," Griffon said, interrupting her and pitching his cop voice above the noise.

Liesel turned to look at him. "Well, of—"

"And freedom," Griffon continued. "Freedom to think what we want, believe what we want."

Liesel smiled at him. "I hope to give people knowledge and support, not change who they already are."

Tension seemed to ooze across the room even though the conference had barely begun. With someone out to get Liesel and everyone else on edge, Anna didn't know how they'd make it through the week without a few fist fights breaking out at the very least. Imagining what Dianne would do, Anna sneezed as loud as she could. Sounded real, even if she did say so herself. "Goodness sakes that was loud. Can you imagine what that would sound like if this place was empty? Echo off the walls."

People shook their heads and returned to eating and visiting amongst themselves. Maybe Dianne wasn't always oblivious; Anna would have to study her timing.

Maldecia had sat next to Anna. She smelled of smoke and Anna could see the nicotine tint to her hands. As a recent non-smoker the stale smell made her fingers twitch and her lungs quiver with longing. Would she ever not crave?

"What part of Europe are you from Mrs. Farina?" Anna asked, mostly to distract herself.

"My father was French. My mother Italian. And I live in Greece with my Spanish husband. He's in politics," she said the words with familiarity like a friendly epitaph that she broke out for parties. An opening to conversations designed to put the listener at ease and bring them in to Maldecia's confidence. Very slick.

Anna's usual crowd leaned more toward, "S'up?" and nods.

"Sounds a bit like the convoluted mess I call family." Anna sat posture perfect, medium smile. The right level of polite interest. She liked Maldecia or she wouldn't have bothered with the effort. "What does your husband think of your name?" Anna changed her smile to let the gray-haired lady know she was teasing. In Spanish Maldecia meant to curse or damn someone.

Maldecia laughed. "My husband calls me Mal unless he's very mad."

Farina? Her husband was the famous political advocate and known advisor to Greece's President of the Republic? Holly cow. He had serious political clout with the UN. Anna's head ran stats and articles, even brief glimpses of his name in articles about others, anything she'd ever read or heard that could possibly relate to him. She doubted Maldecia would want to talk about any of that though.

"The chat boards on HOAX said something about your love of

handbags?"

Off Maldecia went and the differences between Gucci and Coach would forever be stuck in Anna's mind.

Two hours later, after a stuffy boring party heavy on the rabbit food, Griffon pulled Liesel into his room and shut the door. As conferences went, this one was longer and more social than any of the security-themed ones he had attended. Liesel had been running around like a mediating guru, knowing just what to say to gather her people, directing workshops, answering a gazillion questions, often the same ones, with patience. Holy shit, the woman was great at this stuff.

He had Max, his assistant back in Boise, looking through the background of all the registered attendees. He called the airport security and local police multiple times to get updates on their progress. It had been hours since the attack but he still felt the edge of danger. As if it lurked in the shadows.

This night was important. He needed to anchor himself to Liesel and finally express the love he felt for her. The time they'd been dating was the happiest months of his life and he'd almost lost all of it at the airport. He couldn't put this off another day.

Liesel's hair was still red. Griffon asked her how often she colored it and she said she didn't. Her stylist, however...

He laughed at her smile, at the playful way she twisted her body about in his arms, at the pure joy of just being together. He smiled at Liesel, and not because of the hair joke. He could admit that, though only to himself. He had matured, learned, and fallen hard for an Amazon that could bench press him easily.

She trusted him knowing the temper and strength of his body and he trusted her. He proved it by starting to strip. Liesel groaned. He laughed at her sudden and strong reaction.

"Oh, baby." She stood motionless watching as his scar-riddled chest inched into view. Her nipples tightened, he could see them tent her shirt. She breathed in short pants of air. He thought about teasing her. They always brought a lot of humor to bed. Which was wonderful but also a crutch, a way to hide from the tougher emotions.

"Come here Liesel."

She must have noted his serious tone because her smile dropped away and she approached him pulling her own shirt over her head as she went. He brushed his thumb down her stomach to her belly button above the waist of her skirt. His thumb rough, her skin smooth and soft.

He looked her in the eye. Determined to do this right. "You're so beautiful."

She quirked an eyebrow at him, "And you're so serious."

"Is that okay?" Laying himself open, so painfully vulnerable, he looked in her eyes and waited through the silence. Just as he was about to smile, cocky grin, pull her close and kiss the mood away, she finally spoke.

Her voice quivered, "Oh, James, I missed you."

I missed you too, but he didn't say the words. He showed her. Saying with his hands, *I can't get enough of you.* Lingering long and deep at her mouth, *we have all night. God you make me burn*, with his moans and shivers. Griffon kissed down her belly and pulled her panties out of the way. The last article of clothing joined everything else on the floor.

They made it to his bed and he slid a finger inside her. "You're so wet." Her hips lifted off the mattress and she touched his hair, keeping him close. He used his teeth to ply Liesel's skin along her hip bone, not quite a bite but not a kiss, leaving it wet and breathing on it as he moved down slowly to her apex.

He breathed in her musk, nosed the soft hair nestled over her clit. His finger slid in and out, in and out, then he added a second finger and his tongue and she lifted her hips again and moaned his name. "James." So glorious, so beautiful, and she came, the little and big muscles in her thighs and pelvic clenching, shaking. "James."

He kissed up her body and nudged her knee out of the way so he could brace himself above and between her. Griffon kissed her chin and lips and nose. "Let me just get a condom."

"No. Don't leave." She clutched at his shoulders and dug her nails into his skin and he throw his head back as he burned with a wave of desire that shook him. "I'm clean, you're clean."

"Shh. Leis, next time," he said.

She ground up again, pressed her hips against his hard length and he bit his lip. "I'm on birth control."

He kissed her silent. "When I'm not pleading with my dick, when we can think, we'll decide together."

Liesel groaned and shoved at his shoulder to reach for the condoms herself, tearing one open with her teeth. He tried so hard not to laugh, not to smile as her hands shook but then he was totally incoherent as she rolled it on and he jutted his hips forward into her grasp.

"Hold still," she whispered.

"I can't," he groaned. So close. So good.

She pulled him down and in and he was thrusting. The burn would be banked, manageable, only to flare again as he pulled back, felt the wall of her wet heat cling and pulse around him. *JamesJamesJames.*

He could feel her build a second time and he wanted that, Liesel coming, wild and free in her release. Wanted that more than his own orgasm, but his body wasn't cooperating.

Please, just hold it together a bit longer. She shifted her hips and shouted with joy. The little minx. He came hard with shuttering waves, a clench and release of power. Her power up his back and back down into her. A circle. A completion.

He laughed into Liesel's hair at his lovesick thoughts. "I love you."

"Oh, we have to wait to talk about contraceptives until were sober but you can spout love when you're in afterglow?" She poked Griffon in the shoulder. "I don't think so buddy."

It hurt and he had to rub at it. She pushed his finger away, kissed the bruise already starting. "Sorry."

"That's okay. It broke the afterglow and now when I tell you I love you—I love you Liesel Grant—you'll know—"

She interrupted him with a deep kiss and rolled him over with little effort, pinning him to the bed.

In a Tarzan voice he said, "You cave woman. Claim—"

She kissed him again. A quick smack to shut him up. "I love you, James Griffon."

Chapter 7

Sergei leaned against the bar's counter in the hotel's lounge. The place had been reserved for the afternoon. The sound system played quiet Jazz. The only kind of Jazz Sergei's ears could tolerate. People mingled, sipping beverages, eating canapés and tapas. Jim Griffon, Liesel's boyfriend, had just come over and now occupied space near Sergei, keeping the room in front of him.

Liesel and Dianne were attending a meeting in their hotel room with just the conference coordinators. For Dianne short interactions were manageable with the lotion and magnets. Sergei had known she would be susceptible when she responded to the hypnotism over the phone but he was taking copious notes on the success of the lotion and magnets. A child might have a completely different response, he might need to find another Blue Hair at the conference to test his theories on.

Griffon leaned back against a pillar. "So you what? Donated sperm?" Sergei couldn't remember how this conversation started. Somewhere along the lines of 'I'm Griffon, what's this party for?'

Why Griffon had come, Sergei didn't know. Perhaps after Liesel's attack at the airport he was checking everyone over. Whatever the reason, no one would risk offending Liesel or draw unwanted attention by asking him to leave.

"Little Katelyn there?" Sergei pointed to a fiery little spark plug of a girl, climbing the stage's curtain pull-rope using her upper body strength only. "Making her, or her as a successful fertilized egg, paid for college plus a monthly check home to the folks."

He indicated a little boy making Choo–Choo noises and pushing little wooden trains along the carpet, "Thomas, the train, paid for medical school and a little extra for savings." Actually it had also covered his sister's wedding, one sister's college tuition and when the bonus came—for a boy—that had gone into savings.

"That's a lot of money." Griffon wasn't drinking. Sergei figured it was either to keep his hands free or to stay alert.

Sergei shrugged and shook his glass to swirl the ice in his vodka. "The Amazon families couldn't have children of their own and wanted to guarantee the continuation of...special skills? With me, all kids are Amazons. Guaranteed. Or in Thomas's case a Mighty." With a non-Amazon egg there was no double gene. No chance to create a Blue Hair.

"So the party's a social for donors and families they've helped." Seeing it from an outsider's perspective made it sound elitist and extravagant. Sergei had never negotiated prices or put himself up for sale but both times he was asked, he'd accepted. "Plus, a chance to scope out the next donor. Make family connections."

"That's just weird," Griffon said. His voice was gruff but held no real malice, and it *was* weird.

Griffon looked him up and down for a minute. "So, you are both a Mighty and an Amazon. What's your mutation?"

"Blue hair."

"Yeah, Liesel says you call them that—"

"I have blue hair," Sergei tried again.

Griffon just stared.

"This isn't a dye job. It's really this color. Everywhere." Most people responded with 'No. Really? Are you sure?' Which made Sergei think, Are you sure your parents didn't drop you on your head? Why else would you ask such a stupid question?

"That has to suck," Griffon said.

No shit, Sherlock. "It wasn't so bad in high school. It's cool to have neon blue hair and a nose ring when you're being rebellious." Sergei played with the hoop in his inner ear. The nose ring hole had sealed up during college. "But as a professional...."

Griffon grimaced, too menacing to be a smile. "What do the ladies think?"

Sergei smiled. "They don't believe it's natural, at least at first." They laughed together and Sergei sipped his vodka again. This Griffon wasn't all that bad. Liesel had mentioned him from time to time, just in passing. He should have clued in she had the hots for the private detective.

"Even on your arms?" Griffon seemed glad that Sergei didn't take offense to his many questions. They were being sociable and why the fuck not.

Sergei trusted Liesel and loved her like a cousin. He wasn't checking Griffon out, or protecting Liesel. This consisted more of a greeting, a welcome-to-the-clan.

Sergei raised his arm and leaned forward to show Griffon his pale blue, almost white, arm hair. "People think it's the lighting making it look blue. Or that I spend way too much time in a hair salon."

"So others get, telekinesis or whatever, and you get blue hair?"

"Yeah."

"It's got to suck."

"You said that," Sergei said. But he smiled to let Griffon know he was okay with that. Maybe he could talk Griffon in to going to the casino together. Play the roulette table, or hell, with Griffon's menace factor, he probably rocked the poker tables.

"At work do you...." Griffon made a buzzing noise and moved his hand over his scalp.

"Have to. People don't want to hear clinical explanations from a guy who looks like he carries cotton candy on his head." And yes it had been compared to just that.

"We'll at least you're a good sport about it," Tydus said as he approached them. He wore a suit, complete with tailored, creased slacks. Something neither Griffon nor Sergei would feel comfortable in. Sergei had on his black jeans, the nice ones without safety pins. Griffon was in cargo pants and a t-shirt even tighter than Sergei's jeans.

Griffon stepped away from the wall, feet shoulder length apart. His chest lifted as he breathed in. All intimidation. It looked like Griffon didn't buy Tydus's smooth operator act, either. However, Griffon definitely didn't feel the need to intimidate Sergei, and Sergei wasn't sure how to feel about that. Like what? Sergei could totally be a bad ass when he wanted to.

"So you're just a Mighty?" Sergei asked.

"Just a Mighty?" Tydus said. "That's all it usually takes to impress the ladies." He laughed. "Damn, that sounded cocky. I really was going for confident."

Working in the ER, Sergei had seen all types of people. Strung-out druggies looking for a score. Stressed mothers short on time and patience. Do-gooders fighting their own level of jaded. Tydus didn't fit in any the categories, just off center from being right. Of course neither did Sergei, so he tried to stay open minded or at least act open minded.

Tydus continued, "I might be wrong, but I get the impression neither of you like me—"

"You're not wrong," Griffon said.

Griffon did intimidating better than a review board made up of the world's top five heart surgeons. The shorter man had no problems stating very clearly, all nonverbally, that he could and would kick their asses. Short? Fuck, the man was six feet tall and fit, but Mightys averaged six-six. The P.I. had dark curly hair, sharp features and hands made to squash lesser beings.

Tydus nodded at Griffon's words, yet stuck around. He had some balls in that suit of his.

Griffon continued their conversation. "Marriage and baby mart?" Indicating the room in front of him.

"Even before Liesel's website there were places you could go, to arrange marrying an Amazon. Or to have an Amazon or Mighty child," Sergei said.

"How did they find each other?"

"They have their ways," Tydus said. "Especially the Mightys. My great uncle talked about belonging to a secret organization. I always thought he meant the Elks or the Masons. Turns out he was a Mighty."

Sergei's great grandfather had been the same way. Long stories about mother Russia and meeting in secret with his brothers. He'd chosen the wrong woman to marry and had to flee to first England and then America.

Tydus drank his martini, two olives. He told a few stories about being a kid and asked get-to-know-you questions. Griffon stayed closed lipped, no surprise there, but Sergei couldn't bring himself to be charming either. He didn't know why.

Maybe to keep on Griffon's good side?

"Dr. Sky, I heard you just finished your residency?" Tydus said.

"Sergei's fine," offering his first name, a polite knee jerk response. Sergei realized what bugged him about Tydus. The guy reminded Sergei of Sergei. Tydus stood with his back to the room, giving them his full attention. He said polite things, balanced the conversation about himself with topics that would interest Sergei and Griffon. The man knew how to work it.

Hopefully his own charm was a bit smoother, or when it was awkward it was endearing rather than trying too hard. Eventually Tydus drifted away and Sergei saw his sister across the room. She had just started her third trimester. As she approached there were no trills of glee or gushing greeting, but she hugged Sergei, her large stomach pressed against his waist. He'd expected the girly overt reaction so the subdued made him analyze each of her movements, search her face and body for additional clues.

"Yours?" Griffon said.

"Gross, no way." Sergei snorted a laugh. "This is my sister Portia." Sergei introduced them and she hugged him again, cried a bit. "Hormones," they said in unison.

"How are the 'rents?" Their parents lived closer to her than any of the rest of them.

She just nodded.

"John?" asking about her husband.

"Great."

What the fuck? Taciturn much? Griffon gently teased Portia and asked polite questions about the baby and Sergei as a kid. The brute turning all gentle for his sister earned him big brownie points in Sergei's book. But his sister stayed stiff, tense.

Okay, so what was really up? "You're glowing," Sergei whispered to her.

"So are you a Blue Hair?" Griffon asked.

Portia looked at him a moment, weighing her answer. As the oldest girl she'd always felt a responsibility to help their parents, to be both companion and aid to their mother. Sergei figured he was the financial support to her physical support.

"She can fly," Sergei said, before she could fess up and maybe to make her laugh.

"Bullshit," Griffon said.

"Joshing. Portia's an interpreter. She can understand almost any language the first time she hears it." His other sisters, Bailey and Zeeman were just Amazons. The youngest had a year of college left.

"Though it took me a whole month to learn Mandarin." Portia rubbed at her belly. Her eyes watered even more. "Serg, it's a girl."

Shit. Fifty percent chance to be a Blue Hair had just turned into guaranteed, for sure, time to panic. "No worries." He gathered her back in his arms, rubbed her back. "It'll be okay." He'd fix it. He'd find a cure or a way to treat the symptoms. Had he ever failed them?

Embarrassed Griffon said, "I'll leave—"

She finally giggled, wiped at her eyes, waved her hand for him to stop. "No. I see John. Serg, dinner tomorrow?"

"I have an art show to go to. Come as my guest." Dianne would love to read about Sergei from Portia's head. He might dip into his savings and purchase another of her photos. It could be a lot of fun, getting Portia and John to come, it would give him someone to talk to while he awkwardly jonesed for the artist.

"Art? Boring. Maybe. If not I'll catch you for breakfast one time before you leave." She gave a little wave to Griffon and headed across to John. John nodded to Sergei. He looked worried too.

Liesel finished reading the proposed bylaws out loud. She waited for the sign language and other interpreters to finish and reminded herself to thank Harry. Her baby sister had suggested they pass out written copies to the translators beforehand. So far the reaction was a tense shock and silence.

Liesel expected to hear crickets next and thought she could be out running. No, wait. This was Vegas. Much too hot to run outside. Didn't the hotel have a running track on one of the floors? She could put on her headphones, crank up Lindsey Stirling, and run until sweat soaked her clothing, until all the worries dropped away.

A hand went up in the middle of the crowd. Liesel said, "We recognize Roe Snyder from Pensacola."

For some reason Liesel had the ability to tell who was an Amazon or a Mighty. No contact required. Sergei had once nicknamed her the Santa Claus of super powers. If asked she could tell you all about Roe's history on HOAX, or almost any of the twelve thousand members. Thankfully not all twelve thousand members were present.

If someone was truly targeting her, the changes she was making to the group seemed a likely motivation. Dianne wasn't convinced it was the bylaws since she had first felt Maggie and Liesel were in danger several weeks ago. If it was somehow tied into the kidnappings, or possibly to the Mathews, Liesel would have to pull in her government contact. Valdez had warned that the viper's nest she'd disturbed would be looking to settle things. She hoped it wasn't as bad as all that.

Anna handed the man a microphone and he stood and cleared his throat. "Did you really pull a car from a canal?"

Anna took the microphone back. "Yeah whatever. Anyone have a question about what she just read?" They did and voiced them freely and simultaneously.

"Did you really say current gender?"

"Yeah, what the hell was that all about?"

"Who would be on this initial board?"

Meanwhile Anna waved the mike around, "You have to speak in the mike or it won't record for the broadcast."

A month before Liesel had read a rough draft of the bylaws to Griffon, Anna, and Griffon's new Boy Friday, Freddy Rayne. She thought about the words and their reactions.

I, Liesel Grant, founder of HOAX and acting leader, in order to establish this organization, convey our intent, insure order, secure the welfare of our posterity, do ordain and establish this constitution for the Amazons of America.

Our intent is not to define the lives of our members. We will support through information, guidance and legal representation our people here forth defined as humans of superior strength. No distinction shall be made based on race, age, gender, sexual preference or physical abilities. It is not our purpose to segregate ourselves from our land and we shall at all times up hold the law of the United States of America.

The business matters and political issues shall be represented by our leader. The (Matriarch), a man or woman, shall be elected by popular vote by members in good standing for a term of three years. The matriarch with continued support may hold office as long as he/she is mentally and physically capable.

The Matriarch's Cabinet, or directing board, shall consist of four members, at least one man (current gender) and at least one woman (current gender) shall be part of the cabinet. No person can serve more than two terms on the Cabinet consecutively.

Member information is private and confidential. To become a member of Home of the Amazon eXchange, also known as HOAX, one must submit a detailed application and a back ground check will be completed. Being wanted for criminal activity, under the age of sixteen, falsifying information on the application or disregarding the rules of conduct set forth on HOAX shall disqualify a person from membership.

The matriarch shall do all necessary to protect our people.

The board shall do all necessary to keep the matriarch in line.

The members shall do all necessary to keep the cabinet in line.

The Matriarch is answerable to the President of the United States of America and to the law and ordinances of the government of the United States of America.

"What do you think?" Liesel had asked as heads came up from reading their copies of her rough draft.

No one had said anything. Liesel had continued, "I'll give it to Sara to translate it into legalese and incorporate our nonprofit end for the website and conferences."

There had been some more lack of noise, also known as nerve-wracking silence.

Griffon had said, "Current gender?"

"If they have had a sex change operation or even just identify—"

Freddy then interrupted her, "That's what bugged you? Me? I was surprised by the—" looking back at his copy, "No distinction on physical ability."

"I know when someone is or isn't an Amazon, but the next Matriarch might not have that ability. What should we do? Fly around the country giving physical training tests? And what if an Amazon is injured and can no longer walk?"

Griffon had smiled and leaned toward her on the couch to kiss her forehead.

"True. But I still don't understand why we need one. A constitution," Freddy had said.

"I won't be put into power without one. Amazed by what they can do, Amazons seek out a higher purpose to their life. I don't want to be followed blindly and we don't need a bunch of amateur superheroes acting as vigilantes."

"Plus, you wanted to make sure your predecessors weren't followed blindly either," Griffon said.

"Isn't it predecessor or post—cessor—?" Freddy said.

"It's successor, from the old French word *succeder* meaning 'come next after,'" Anna had said.

"Did you read the dictionary?" Freddy teased her.

"Webster Collegiate Ninth Edition. When I was twelve."

"Anna, what do you think?" Liesel had lifted the copy in her hand and nodded to the one Anna had finished several minutes before anyone else.

Anna had turned her head then swung her legs off the armrest of her chair and sat up right. "I think you should ask Jordan—he is the poly-sci major. Then have Sara check the legality. Do we have to register with the state? That type of thing." She had then re—hooked her legs over the arm of the chair, her back to the opposite arm.

"That's the third time you've read that comic," Freddy had said when Anna picked up the Ultimate Spiderman she'd been reading.

"Fourth actually. I'm studying the artistic symbolism. Bagley is a genius. Or so my paper is going to prove."

"Hope the Art professor approves of comics," Griffon had said.

"He'll have hell to pay if he doesn't."

Now standing in front of this crowded conference room in Vegas,

Liesel thought about throwing up. She didn't really feel queasy—this leader stuff was getting easier—but if she swooned, fainted, was sick, a room full of maternal women and protective men would swoop to her aid.

She smiled then realized how bad that might look. She tapped her knuckle on the wooden podium, and her mike made it sound like a gavel. "1 hope we can answer everyone's questions. Let's start with Valasca Perch from Bainbridge, Alaska. Ms. Perch?" Better to meet her biggest foe head on.

"Point of order. Robert Rules state that we need to establish a quorum before deciding on or voting into practice major changes," Valasca stood when she spoke.

"Absolutely, and if as a board they decide to abide by Robert's Rules, not only will they be well organized but they'll establish a quorum for voting purposes. Meanwhile we want to welcome all comments and concerns." She took a large breath and pushed. "Do you have a concern?"

Anna had passed the mike to Valasca and stood in the aisle. "This should be for Amazons," Valasca said. "It might not be a popular belief but there are far too many male organizations that we can't let them control this one. Being an Amazon is about womanhood. Protecting our children."

She spoke clearly and with authority, her tone educated and sensible. If she had been hostile, they wouldn't listen, but the of-course tone seemed so agreeable. "Learning more of our heritage. I want my daughters to grow up proud of who they are. If accepted into practice, this constitution—"

There was an outcry of voices, those worried that they were somehow alienating themselves from the established government and those who had other grievances.

Liesel tapped her knuckle again. People quieted down. "I want to make sure everyone is heard with respect and clarity so if we could keep the interruptions down? Ms. Perch," calling her by her first name didn't seem right, "We all have men in our lives, fathers, brothers, sons. Men were a part of the Amazon past—"

"But they're not Amazons. You've said so in your research.

They're Mightys."

I didn't interrupt you, why are you interrupting me? Liesel nodded. "Yes, my initial translations of the codex—"

"This world needs strong women, and strong women are created by opportunities to excel and lead," Valasca spoke to the crowd rather than addressing Liesel directly. She had even turned her body and tried to make eye contact with as many people as possible, happily on center stage to their little drama.

"I thought we were born this way," another voice countered.

"What of the Blue Hairs? If you strike out the men? Only Female Blue—"

Valasca Perch jumped back in to regain control. She gestured with her hands. "I'm not saying they couldn't participate. But if we spread are focus too broadly, it will help no one and only serve to undermine our strength as a group. We need to focus on Amazons. The board should only be Amazons."

Liesel let her eyes wander the room as she listened patiently. The room's A/C wavered between frosty and frigid. A pyramid of glasses and pitchers of ice water sat on tables. The chairs were padded at the seat and back and were stackable, yet they pinched her lower back and her butt was going numb for sitting so long. She squirmed a bit to reestablish blood flow and focused back on Valasca.

Valasca, a plump brunette, wore red-rimmed glasses and a set of pearls. "Children are impressionable. What are we teaching them if we allow a group of men 'current gender' to lead women?" Valasca did air quotes, actual hands raised, two fingers on each hand flexing like claws. Liesel didn't think anyone did that anymore. She was very proud of herself when she was able to not laugh. Because, dang, that was ridiculous.

"How to survive in the real world," a woman in the front said. Several murmured in agreement.

Philip, from Ohio, stood up and cleared his throat. "My family— my family," he said a second time to gain their attention, Anna handed him the second mike "is Amazon, Mighty and Blue Hair. We are a family, we are equal and different. I want my children to know others like us, to understand the importance—"

"I'm not like you," a new voice yelled.

It deteriorated at that point. Liesel answered questions for another hour and then broke things up for lunch. "We'll vote on the bylaws tomorrow." Even as she finished speaking, like-minded individuals were finding each other across the room and grouping to rally behind a leader. Now she truly did feel queasy. Hopefully it was just hunger pains.

The part that was hard for Liesel to accept was that someone cared enough about all this to fight her, to kill her. She wanted two things in life, keep her loved ones safe and help people. Hell, she'd wash her hands of all this shit and find a different way to make a difference. If HOAX folded tomorrow, there would still be her research, still people in a thousand different situations that needed a helping hand.

Yet, the more she thought about it the more she realized how much it meant to others, especially the teens when they first joined, or for families with Double Amazon children. If they dismantled HOAX, she would choose the nuclear option, decimating it back to rubble, destroying every bit of code, because she couldn't stomach the idea of someone stepping into her place if they were going to jack these people's lives up. Fuck, she did care and that meant someone might actually care enough to get rid of her.

Anna sat in a centralized seat and listened to the splinter groups.

Valasca wanted to be a board member and flat out said she should be the Matriarch. Anna posted the title suggestion to the website and on twitter and it spread like fire. Anna used her smartphone to send a text to Freddy, asked him to monitor the responses to the video feed and the website looking for any extra hate or venomous responses.

After a while Valasca spoke with Maldecia and Ping. If she got their support it would only be a matter of time before they amended the constitution to fit her idea of what was proper. Maldecia and Ping kept their reactions to themselves.

"Mightys are capable of establishing their own groups," Valasca said.

Everyone generally ignored Anna. She looked young and added to the image of innocence by pretending to read off her smartphone. She could sit among the crowd and hear who said what without worry.

"It is a predominately online group. It is not a sporting event." Maldecia wore an elegant black suit and a silver Coach handbag that matched the color of her curly hair. "It is an attempt to provide community and information."

"What information? That medically we are the same as men?" Valasca raised her thick eyebrows and clicked her tongue in derision.

Dr. Kandi sat as everyone else stood. Her legs crossed and uncrossed every other minute. "If we can figure out what makes us the way were are—"

"What makes us this way?" Valasca crossed her arms and shifted on her feet, stuck out a hip. "How about god? There is nothing wrong with the way we are. We don't want to change it or fix it. We are healthy and strong,"

Dr. Kandi shot death arrows up her nose at the Valasca.

Anna tuned them out and listened to Philip with the mixed family. "And perfect? Better? No, we are people. All people are different in some way we just—"

"If it was a disadvantage like being short."

"Yeah, but it isn't," Philip told his listeners. His son who was a Blue Hair had been born blind. She knew because yesterday Anna had told Philip's wife Wendy how to get comics in Braille.

"Maybe not for you, but I can't get insurance because I weigh too much and my wife got kicked out of her college because they thought she was doing steroids." The Mighty or Blue Hair, Anna didn't know which, had black skin and a neck as wide as Anna's thigh. The guy was over seven feet tall.

Philip nodded, sympathetic. "Everyone has those types of problems."

A third listener, from Quebec if Anna remembered correctly, "We're not here to hear your problems."

"Well, we sure aren't here for you foreigners," the man with the neck replied. "This isn't a global—"

Philip calmed down the bickering, a natural mediator, and redirected the conversation back to the point he was trying to make.

Anna got up and left. She had a mental list on who she thought the new board would consist of. Valasca Perch, Philip, Dr. Kandi, Dr. Sergei Sky and Liesel. Both Kandi and Valasca would oppose Liesel but good opposition allowed learning. Toss Philip in to make sure no one killed each other and it could work.

Harry kept her eyes open for trouble, even though she wasn't on guard duty. And like it or not, when they got back to Boise she would finally train Liesel in self-defense. She'd been soap-boxing the subject for several months and Liesel came back from being kidnapped all determined to be taught. Then life got in the way. One more project, one more website to code. She relied too heavily on her strength, didn't know about disarming someone else, or what to do if someone aimed a gun at your head.

The MGM Grand's lion habitat had high grade plexi-glass walls which kept the visibility and provided better protection to the animals. Harry approved of the planning, the smart use of material, and the aesthetic integrity. The entrance from the exterior foot paths wound down the stairs into the casino and curved around the two story high viewable habitat.

Tydus had brought her here at a good time. The lion cubs ate from the trainers, frolicked with each other. She and Ty stayed on the stairs where it was easier to see over the crowd.

"So you were able to block Dianne reading you because you didn't want her to know that you dislike her?" Tydus picked their conversation back up.

The subject of other women had come up again but she was here, not them. That had to mean something. Harry shook her head, "No, because it felt so freaky."

"So you can tell? You know, when she's rooting around in there?"

"More when she comes knocking. I've managed to keep her out."

"Didn't know you could do that," Tydus said. "Once it thins out we can get closer," Tydus indicated the crowd in front of them. He made a few comments to point out the chubby cub rolling around in the grass and the pale fur of another. He put his hand on the rail behind her and said, "You're wearing that new perfume from Dolce and Gabbana."

"Do you like it?" She wanted to lean back against his strong arm, feel his heat.

She felt him shrug. "It's nice."

She turned her head to look at him. Eyebrow raised in question. He just shrugged again and returned his attention to the animals. "They're cute at this age."

"Didn't see you at the salon," Harry kept her tone neutral.

But Tydus heard her girly concern. "Client called. Sorry if you were waiting on edge for me to appear."

She elbowed him and he smirked. He raised his hand to wave at Liesel and Griffon. They walked hand in hand through the crowd, perhaps enjoying a minute away from the conference. Since the airport Liesel was always with someone. It would've driven Harry nuts.

Thankfully, Liesel allowed the precaution. And with Griffon here in Vegas, Harry knew her sister was safe. And okay, she could admit to herself that wanting it to be so didn't make the threat gone. Griffon and his office were checking every conference attender. Dianne, if she could ever get her abilities sorted out, could be a great asset. Harry was mostly focused to enjoying her vacation and keeping an eye out for possible threats.

Chapter 8

Dianne hadn't seen Sergei since the field trip to the footbridge. Twenty-four hours to shadow Liesel when no one else could, catch up on her sleep and do some online shopping for a new trailer. Except she couldn't get herself to press the buy button. Turns out there was an RV dealership right here in Las Vegas. Maybe she'd go take a look. Yet, it could be several months before she had the freedom to travel again.

At four that morning she'd photographed the scaffolding against the pyramids. The photos sucked. She didn't need to develop them to know that. Too dark, despite the street lights and flash she'd used. Too empty.

During all of that—the guard duty, sleep—since the moment she opened her eyes and found Sergei no longer standing in the heat with her, her mind had wandered back to those brown eyes. And even now, sitting across the table from him at a Vegas show, she was still thinking about him and those eyes.

"It has been brought to my attention that a fellow hypnotist is in the audience." The performer, Jack the Hypnotist, had expressed his derisive, humorous opinion about other hypnotist. "Damn that sounds snotty. Sergei? Get your butt up here. Everyone, Doctor Sergei Sky." Jack said Sergei's name with a break. Sir Gay. The audience already primed, laughed as if cued.

Sergei had summoned her for more 'fieldwork' by calling Liesel and asking if she would send Dianne to meet him here. As he unfolded himself from the booth she tried her best to remember that everything else, even the lame camera work, had been helpful.

People considered the red velvet-lounge style trendy-Vegas and the place was in decent enough shape to pull big performers. Sergei had gotten the tickets from the front desk. Dianne had asked him.

Sergei approached the stage and people clapped. They thought about his hair, some with severe disapproval.

"Yes," Hypnotist Jack said, "the hair is real." The performer took a fist full of hair and tugged; barely able to close his fingers on the length. Sergei shoved Jack away with his elbow. Sergei was wearing long black slacks and a soft looking polo. The monochrome of his clothes made his pair pop, especially surrounded by all the red tones. If she had her camera with her, found a way to sneak up to the balcony or maybe even just standing on the table....

"Maybe that should be your trick. Hypnotize the audience to believe your hair is real," Jack said, rubbing his gut.

"If they want proof...." Sergei unbuckled his belt, went to unbutton his slacks. Men and women cat called and whistled encouragement.

"Keep the pants on. This isn't that type of show," Jack said. Then in a drum rolling voice, "Can you, Sergei Sky, hypnotize this audience?" Jack knew his stuff and could gauge an audience from a single applause. Just ask him.

"I can with a little help from my friend Dianne Fender." Cue spotlight. Dianne's mental spotlight at least. Their table sat in the second row of round tables. Sergei pointed at her, the bastard. Her personal torturer, iron maiden and solace in one. Though no actual light shone on her, all thoughts swiveled in her direction.

One audience member knew she was the famous photographer Defender and leaned to her companion to pass the information along. Dianne closed her eyes to block out the staring and tried to focus on Sergei. She still couldn't find his thoughts. What was he doing? Why bring her here?

She rose with polite applause and joined the men on stage, who bickered back and forth to entertain the audience. The hypnotist thought Dianne had a nice ass, pity about the lack of tits. Dianne considered punching him.

"Dianne. With your help, I will convince the audience that my hair color is real," he picked up Jack's showmanship.

"Well that should be easy." She pulled his belt loose and, with a twirl worthy of a true Vegas Drag Queen, sent it to the closest male admirer. The guy caught it easily and his date imagined the belt on his lover. The belt and nothing else. Dianne blushed, had to quickly swallow to dampen the rush of sexual heat.

"With hypnotism," Jack reminded in a beleaguered and exaggerated tone.

Sergei turned to face her square and with the same tone as he had used on the phone, focusing only on her, began to talk, the audience was enthralled. "You can do it. You know my hair is real. You simply tell them."

She'd dressed up for the night in her best and only pair of slacks—only a slight tear along the bottom hem—and a long-sleeved thin sweater. It had something shiny in the material and looked nicer than her average jeans and t–shirt. But she felt shabby. No one thought about her clothes. She checked.

If only she could read Sergei's mind and see if he was doing this to help or to embarrass her.

"If I do it all at once they'll think it's over the P.A," Dianne said.

"How about in alphabetical order," Jack said. The audience laughed, slung back alcohol and begun to talk among themselves.

"First or last names?" Dianne said.

"Middle names," Sergei said. "Ladies and Gents, think what your middle name is."

They didn't need to concentrate. She read them easily, continued to stare at Sergei. He had really nice looking lips. And those brown eyes tipped with blue eyelashes.

Focus.

Three didn't have middle names. She told them first then asked them to stand. The shocked reactions from the three felt like being hit in the face with a wet pillow. But they stood. The people around them wondered what was going on, shifted in their seats, tried to reason about how a trick like this might be done.

Aberforth was next. Poor girl, who'd name their daughter Sally Aberforth Smith? Guess that would be Abbey and Fort Smith, her parents. Working silently, the audience's twittering dying down as each of them began to stand.

Then Carney, the new belt owner. Last was Zachery.

Dianne spoke out loud to the now-standing audience. "You were hard, Mr. Veshnijky. You have so many names." Mr. Veshnijky's wife began to cry.

Dianne's head had reached its saturation point repeating, '*It's a birth defect. It's really blue,*' to each person. '*Please stand.*' No thoughts entered her head. As if she'd stuffed the dam. Her mind wasn't empty but she had a firm grasp on the sand of memories that usually streamed through her head like a never ending hourglass.

Dianne started crying, unsure why. Happy maybe. Scared definitely.

"Tell them to tip their waitresses thirty percent." Jack's wait staff cheered at the suggestion and the audience, broken from the eerie silence, laughed and returned to their seats. They clapped in approval of Dianne's trick.

Her mind opened and the slide projection turned on. She stumbled forward, surprised by the sharp edged change. Sergei steadied her.

The mental noise flickered, added a clicking noise like a light switch. He let go. "I'm so sorry."

She'd almost blacked out from overload. "I think it was pushing it. We can try something smaller." Could it truly be as simple as having a focused purpose? Controlling the mental noise by using a specific goal to jam up all the neural pathways? She was back to thinking the man was magic.

Jack and the audience weren't about to be left out of their conversation. "Get off my stage, Sir Gay," Jack hollered with a smile.

"You've got to snap your fingers," Sergei taunted. Pale, his body shook as if cold. Had she done something wrong? Was he disappointed? She'd try again. She could get this right. She had to work harder. Be better. If her goal was to find Liesel's threat...yet even with just the list of conference attendees, the idea felt impossible. This room barely contained two hundred and fifty people, all of whom were open to general suggestions. Burrowing out a secret would me much harder.

"Get!" Snap, snap. Jack went to smack Dianne's butt and she turned and swung. Sergei caught her sleeved arm before she could land the punch to Jack's nose. Startled, Jack made a noise, half chortle, and half gasp, shaken not stirred. The audience was enthralled once again.

"I'll need to work on my technique," Jack said. "The last girl let me smack her...No wait, she smacked me. That's right."

"Come on." Sergei guided her off the stage, his hand holding her covered upper arm. Jack was already using his voice to lure the audience into the next stunt.

"Why did you...." It was like talking with headphones on, unsure if she'd pitched her voice loud enough to be heard. She lost track of her own thoughts, unable to see them buried among the clutter of the whole hotel.

"I think the magnets are wearing off," Sergei said.

That made sense. He'd said they wouldn't last forever. That she might need to replace them with new ones.

They'd made it out of the theater and stood on the edge of the casino floor. In Vegas everything leads through the casino. Want to swim? Through the casino and to the right. Want to eat in the buffet? Through the casino and to the left.

Dianne took the magnet off her left breast and handed it to Sergei. He was careful to just take the tip and not make contact. She flushed again to her toes. She knew where that magnet had just been, how warm her skin had made it. He tested it against a metal pole. It slid halfway down.

Dianne swayed in place, felt the blood rush from her face to her feet. "Someone is beating an old man." She said the words as that image solidified in her head. No filter, just pouring the overflow into verbal existence.

"Shit. Where?" Sergei said.

"I don't know." Her lip trembled and she sniffed. "It could be a memory. Or a TV show. I don't know." She cried, felt the tears run down her cheeks. It had been too good to be true. Dr. Sergei Sky her doctor riding in on his white horse to save her. The lotion had worked for a time. The magnets had worked for a time. But now it felt like all they had done was weaken her resistance.

Even with the goal of turning it off, simple, easy, yet she was useless. She didn't fight it. That way lay only more pain.

And as the intense burn engulfed her brain, charred her eyes and raked her nerve endings, she keened low in her throat.

She leaned against the closest wall. Then realized it was Sergei, not a wall. Solid and empty. "Are you dead? Only dead people are empty of thought."

"You just can't read my mind."

"Why can't I?" she said. She slid down his body. Maybe her mind couldn't get a message to her spinal cord to stand, or maybe she was exhausted. She wasn't sure. Just couldn't stand any longer. Disconnected from her body, the strings cut from the puppet. She stopped crying, felt only the fire across her nerves, her own thoughts strung among the others like white pearls on a black necklace. Odd little details about the way his hands looked, the color of the carpet, the pain.

"Shit. Don't do this now." He helped her sit on the floor then crouched before her. "Focus on me, listen to my voice." He tried to hypnotize her, yet the tone was wrong.

Don't look at his crotch, she told herself. "You're angry?" If he couldn't get the tone right, the safe word wouldn't work either.

"I don't know where to put my hands."

A lady walked by who'd once had an abortion that she now regretted. A little boy tried to sneak a cigarette from his father's pocket. An audience member contemplated bankruptcy over suicide.

She urged herself to just faint but nothing happened.

She groaned, "Touch me."

"But it could..."

She tried to focus on Sergei's face. Still pale, he looked like he was frozen. White skin, blue hair. Like they show cartoon characters that have fallen in a frozen river and pop back up in ice-cube form.

"Touch me. I'll blackout. Then you can carry me out of here." Through the casino and around the back.

He reached toward her face. Desperate for the black oblivion, she grabbed his hand and pressed his palm against her cheek. She took a breath at the same time, pulled his powerful, edgy scent in.

White. This oblivion was white. She opened her eyes and looked at Sergei. "Even babies have memories. Are you a robot..." she stopped. "Or a gift from GOD. SERGEI."

"Don't shout."

"I can't hear anything," she yelled. The headphones were off, yet she couldn't adjust the volume. Perhaps she was just too freaking excited.

"Everyone can hear you."

The fine hairs on her arm stood up, still trying to process what it all meant. "You've got blue hair."

"Point?" His tight voice sounded like he held his breath.

"Who cares if they can hear me? You should be used to people looking at you. Have you considered shaving your head?" His hand still pressed against her cheek. He had rough, heavy hands. Strong but clean. Nails clipped, cuticles trimmed, surgery scrubbed. Her own callused hand pressed him closer.

The burn had been banked and now only an ache throbbed sharp with her heart beat.

"I usually keep it shaved off. But I'm on vacation. Besides, this is Vegas," Sergei's thumb glided across her bottom lip.

As if to make his point, Dolly Parton walked by. Dianne decided it was an impersonator. At least the real Dolly wasn't over six feet tall, even in stilettos. She couldn't read the person's thoughts to know for sure.

She didn't hurt and she didn't hear. Dealers, gamblers, slot machines. Music played from the lounge. Lots of empty noise but no thoughts.

"I don't know what people are thinking," She whispered, afraid the magic would go poof if she pointed out the fact.

"No one?'

"Not even myself."

Sergei grinned, his full lip thinning as it stretched. He lifted his knuckles to rub his fingertips across her face. Like a bending caterpillar, knuckles up, fingers down. The softest touch and the longest touch she had ever endured.

Yet, she wasn't enduring his touch. She didn't relive his childhood hell. She didn't experience firsthand his worst memories. She touched and was touched. By a man. By another person. Deep in her gut something twisted, clenched. Like aloe on a sun burn, relief.

Her body warmed, relaxed, melted.

His eyes focused and darkened.

She felt hot and lucid. She wanted...more. More touch.

He pulled away from her to the point that only a single fingertip touched, pushed flat and flexed. He then straightened his finger, the point of contact getting smaller. Slowly. Slowly. To the barest tiny piece of flesh against her cheek.

"Please don't let go," Dianne said.

He lifted his finger. Hovering. Touching the downy hair on her cheek. "Can you hear anything now?"

"The security guard behind you is worried."

"What else?" Sergei ignored the guard. However, she was finally aware of the small group of people that stood around them. Just outside the theater, a mix of gamblers, the security guard and a bell hop who held a first aid kit and a walkie-talkie, stood in a semi-circle around them.

"Nothing."

One eighth of an inch. Nearly paper thin distance between her skin and his. "Now?" Sergei whispered.

"Half the casino, maybe. There is a man cheating at roulette. How far is the roulette table?" Dianne said.

The security guard left. Too easy. She kept the grin to herself.

"Any pain?"

"No."

He moved a half inch further away. "Liesel's worried about us." From the casino, Liesel's room was six floors up. She scanned Liesel's mind out of habit. There were two men trying to be menacing but Liesel had seen Griffon in full rage mode. These guys didn't intimidate her and Griffon and Anna Marie were there. Just the briefest surface look at the two men had Dianne inhaling liquid heat. She saw equal parts anger and fear.

"Pain?"

Touch me. Please. Now. "A little." He immediately put his hand back on her face. What a lovely new temptation. He took her hand and helped her stand up. "Let's get back to Liesel," Dianne said. "She has unwanted company she needs help with."

-#-

Sergei decided that Anna was right. Getting cryptic information from Dianne sucked. She gripped the escalator's railings as she concentrated on Liesel. She panted in little breaths through her nose. He saw her nostrils flare though her mouth gapped slightly.

The touch thing had wigged Sergei out. When he had accidentally touched her on stage, his own personal hells had descended and he couldn't breathe knowing she must see his brother hanging from the garage rafters. But she hadn't even noticed his skin meeting hers. Adrenaline and endorphins were still mixing in his gut and he was having a difficult time turning the memories off.

If she had seen that...experienced it.... He was desperate to fix it. The bug zapper swinging in the high wind outside the now open garage door. The orange hunting tape wrapped around Peyton's neck. The tool box on wheels just out of his reach.

To let anyone else see that pain? The idea made his stomach pitch forward and he gripped his palms until the nausea passed. He shook and tried to push the thought away.

He had thought the hypnotism would be a decent challenge for her. She could continue to learn focus and everything went astonishingly well. She took this nearly impossible task—take hundreds of minds and convey a message with conviction—walked that path with balance and precision. Then out in the hall with all her senses overloading and exhaustion engulfing her, the sexy brat got the security guard scurrying away by implying someone was cheating. She was such a kick.

They went past the restaurants on the second floor and headed for the elevators. "What are we walking into?" Sergei asked Dianne. She kept a hand on his sleeved bicep, her steps unsteady, her eyes half shut, her nose wrinkled as she continued to focus.

"Two guys came about five minutes ago."

Sergei pushed the elevator button.

"Shut up Anna, I'm trying to listen to Griffon," Dianne said, probably sorting through the different thoughts she had access to. So Griffon and Anna were with Liesel, which was good. Griffon was probably armed and wouldn't need to hold back in a fight.

Sergei looked at Dianne, stared at her lips. Suddenly the desire to kiss her flooded him. They could touch without exchanging horror. Better than that, his touch acted as the perfect pill for what ailed her. Turned off her abilities or at least shuffled them to the back of her mind. He wanted to kiss her and wondered if she had kissed anyone before. What would she taste like? Would the more intimate contact expose him to her psychic powers? When the brief skin to skin hadn't? Could he strip her bare, press her to the floor and pump into her?

"They're setting all of Griffon's sirens off. I can't focus on them yet. Maybe because I can't see them." Or maybe because they were still close together. He didn't say it out loud though because he didn't want her back to that dark pit begging for oblivion.

If these men had Griffon fired up it wouldn't be good. But then again, besides Liesel, Griffon didn't like anyone.

"Liesel is talking to them about a...Ronin they are looking for. What's a Ronin?"

Not someone Sergei ever wanted to meet. "Who are they?" Great Grandfather's stories included Ronins, raging animalistic men bent on destroying those they thought had wronged them.

"They're being cryptic." They both stepped into the elevator and he put his hand on the back of her neck as a jostle of kids piled in just before the doors closed, dripping wet from the pool and wrestling around.

"Sorry," one said as he bumped Dianne, then punched his friend in the arm and glared.

Dianne's big liquid green eyes, wide with surprise, looked at Sergei. Her mouth opened to a little oh as if pursing them for a kiss. "I can't hear the rest." She slowly smiled as if all these puzzle pieces were slotting into place and the world was glorious around her. She'd probably compare it to some photo technique.

"It's like I'm finally asleep." Hmm, he liked that even better.

"It'll keep." After working the crowd at the hypnotist show she had to be worn down. He didn't want her fighting through a stranger's touch when his touch would prevent it. Sergei squeezed her neck. The kids stepped aside to let them pass when they reached the six floor. Sergei liked the feel of her skin, having this dominant hold on her, guiding her easily to step where he urged. She straightened and arched up into the touch.

Her short hair wasn't quiet long enough to grip and pull. How long would it take to grow out? He pushed that thought away too.

She looked over to him, eyes still heavy as if emerging from sleep, her pupils dilated. Did she feel the spark of passion that coursed between them?

At Liesel's door she tilted her head as if listening to the voices inside. Sergei pulled her key card out of her back pocket, cupped her butt a second and felt Dianne shiver.

"Ready?" He raised his hand slightly so she knew he was letting go and to be ready. She nodded.

Sergei didn't knock: It was her room too.

"Oh. Hey." Aiming for surprise, so it wouldn't alert the strangers. Sergei closed the door behind them and was surprised when Dianne gasped and grabbed his hand, her whole body swaying like a boat mast. Liesel gasped too, staring at their hands.

Staring because Dianne touched Sergei. He felt like staring himself. Already an instinctive response to touch him. Holy shit. She shouldn't trust him. Not with something as important as her safety.

"Dianne isn't feeling well," Sergei told the silent room. He didn't bother looking at the two men, because he didn't want to alert them to the fact that he knew they shouldn't be there.

In a very sarcastic tone and with an extra sway, she slurred, "That'sss obbbvious." She tugged him into her room and shut the door, letting go of his hand.

"They're going to think you're drunk and—"

"A slap and tickle? Who says that?" she had her eyes closed and a pink flush with green highlights covered her cheeks. Definitely not good. He wanted to check her pulse and make sure she didn't go into shock. Had she been drinking enough water? When was the last time she ate?

She shook her head and pulled on his sleeve to bring their bodies close as she took a step toward the bed. Her brow tightened and her eyes closed to slits. She shook her head and took his hand back.

"Liesel is safe from them. Say it," she whispered.

Her fingers slide around his like they'd been holding hands for months instead of all of five times. They fit so nicely together. "Say what?"

"Say. It," she demanded.

Then as she whispered the word, he said, "Serendipity."

He pressed his shoulder against her hip and her unconscious body folded over his back. He laid her on her bed on top of the covers, shucked her shoes and pulled the blankets from the other side up and over her body. It was the second time he'd carried her to a bed and the most he'd gotten was that short grope in the hallway.

He shook his head. She had left him to figure out what to do. Decide if he should stay in here or go out and help.

Her brief claim that Liesel was safe didn't really help.

He took a deep breath and opened her door quietly, closing it with an exaggerated caution as if he were afraid to wake her. She'd wake when she was ready.

Liesel and Griffon stood near the couch. Anna stood by Liesel's room. And the two visitors stood across from them. No one seemed interested in using the sitting room to sit in. The men turned to look at Sergei.

They straightened and continued to stare.

Sergei's great grandfather back in Russia had been a Mighty from the Nevsky line. They had changed their name to Sky after immigrating to the United States. Great grandfather wrote about the recovery groups to terminate rogue Mightys, the Ronins Dianne had heard earlier. *ZhaTv Brigada* or Harvest Team. They'd sent a Harvest Team after his grandfather, the British spy, but great grandfather had stopped them. Did the American Mightys have something similar, even after all these years?

"Sergei, this is..." Liesel let her voice trail off. Giving the guys a chance to introduce themselves.

One continued to watch Sergei, but the other turned back to Liesel and said, "We work for the Mathews."

"Like that means something to us?" Griffon said.

Sergei shelved all the pieces of memory and tried to stay in the room.

The two men were built for movement. They wore different colors, khaki and blue, but the material was the same used to make camouflage, loose enough to move with the body but tight enough to the skin to prevent a hand hold. Similar to scrubs in a lot of ways. Same with the hair, business short rather than the military high-and-tight but they could wash and go, no fuss and no distinguishing style.

Liesel rubbed a knuckle along her thigh. "This is Dr. Sergei Sky. Perhaps he has met the person you are looking for."

The spokesperson turned to look at his partner who continued to look Sergei over. Sergei looked at Liesel or Griffon and tried to ignore the Mathews.

Finally the silent man shrugged and sat down in a chair, he slid his legs forward and slouched his back, head tilted to the side. Sergei checked Griffon. Griffon's body tightened the more the other relaxed so Sergei was going for the oh-shit reaction as well.

Everyone else sat down. Anna took up a leaned position against the wall and Sergei joined her giving her a brief nod and smile of hello.

Uptight soldier boy and apparent spokesman said, "We are looking for Arnold Ole."

"Do you have a picture?" Liesel asked.

"No."

"Why are you looking for him?" Griffon said.

Sergei expected him to say that it was classified or we cannot divulge that information. Instead Uptight changed the subject.

"Mr. Mathews requested that we inform you of our presence at the conference."

Liesel, "I can't see the Senator giving me a heads up about anything."

"Jordan Mathews," chatty clarified.

"Jiffy?" Anna asked.

Slouch and Uptight looked at each other, a brief glance, and Slouch straightened in his seat.

Jiffy was Jordan's online name, though Sergei hadn't realized

Jordan was one of *those* Mathews. Little Thomas's mother was a Mathew. Thomas's grandfather had been a cousin to the Mathews and had only daughters.

The Mathews ruled the entrenched secretive Mightys of America.

The Nevskys were, or at least had been, in charge of Russia.

Griffon's body language and attitude indicated trouble. Sergei didn't need Dianne's warning about Griffon's sirens going off. They might be silent but the man was on edge. His eyes full-on scary.

"Mr. Ole stole files from our offices and we were informed you had had a similar issue. We tracked him to Vegas," Uptight said. Slouch stayed silent.

"It's the same guy?" Griffon said.

"Perhaps."

They stood to leave. Just up. Conversation over. They'd done their duty by coming but weren't comfortable staying. Then the quiet one heaved a sigh, his chest lifting with the effort, and said, "This Ronin has gone over."

A Ronin, his grandfather had written, was a Mighty who had triggered a deep rage inside themselves they could not turn off. Slouch spoke with a heavy Latino accent though Sergei had assumed he was an American. "He's dangerous. Notify us if you find him."

"Or he finds you," Uptight said.

Supposedly rage consumed a Mighty and if not stopped he would, like the blue faced berserkers in Scotland, decimate everything in their path. Batshit crazy. Blue Hairs didn't have this problem. Dr. Kandi speculated that the more carefully bred families were prone to mental illness but the extended lines had healthier results.

Once they left, Griffon asked Liesel about this madness and she waved it off. "Fables. You have to remember I only heard about Mightys when I started translating the codex. But yes, if you speculate that super strong men in history are these Mightys it might account for the berserkers, Templars...vampires, come on. Let's contact the conspirators and see what they can put together." She growled and punched the couch cushion, which popped a zipper and a bit of cotton puffed out.

"If it's all hooey then why the tension?" Anna asked.

"It's just one more thing to deal with and I don't like the idea of these men 'hunting' someone." Liesel turned to look at Anna, still leaning against the wall. "You don't send a pair like that to take them in quietly."

"Eight," Sergei said.

Griffon looked at Sergei, using the full power of his intense eyes. "What?"

"My great grandfather, on my father's side, wrote about the Harvest Teams. That they worked in eights. That the number was somehow significant. Maybe the Mathews do things differently, call it something else, but let's not count on them being the only ones."

"Diaries?" Liesel sat up and her eyes widened. "Can I see them?"

Griffon laughed and sat next to her, taking her hand.

Sergei had read the diaries growing up. He hadn't realized what Mighty meant. The diaries were written in an unintended puzzle. Like a Christian writing about Christmas assuming that only other Christians would read it and not need the basics explained. He'd figured the word was a descriptive tag rather than a title.

"Well the Diaries aren't here. Portia has most of them in New Mexico. It was the first thing she read after mastering See Spot Run." She had taught her siblings to read Russian. Peyton had picked it up the fastest. Being bilingual made landing a residence at a major hospital easier. He'd even used the Russian a few times to translate for patients.

The Mathews had tracked missing papers to Vegas? If this person had also stolen the codex and was here then Dianne could find him, get the codex back and Sergei could help Portia's family. He would have a solution ready as his niece developed Blue Hair tendencies.

If it actually was the Ronin who had stolen the codex. If. Maybe.

He could keep his promise, look after his family.

"I'm going to wake Dianne up."

Chapter 9

"I am not a bloody search engine," Dianne seethed. Her teeth closed tight enough to reshape her jaw.

She sat with her legs crossed—she refused to call it 'Indian style,' Daisy, her medicine woman, didn't ever sit like this—on Liesel's hotel room floor.

Sergei told her what she'd missed and explained about the Harvest Teams. He used short impatient sentences. "Dianne, try again."

He wanted her to find the two guys from the Harvest Team. He didn't have names, or a location. Just here are thousands of minds, find these two. Then find the Ronin they were looking for. She snorted and crossed her arms, turned her head so she didn't stare at him. They were the only ones left in the room. The others had gone down to breakfast and promised to bring them something back. Dark smudges shadowed Sergei's eyelids. Had he slept at all?

Sergei pinched the bridge of his nose. There was a different energy about him today. The laid back indifference was gone.

"What's the deal Sergei? Why is this important?"

"Do you know about the codex?"

She didn't look at him but saw him move out of the corner of her vision. She nodded. "The McKinnon leather. It was stolen from Liesel."

"I believe it may contain information about Blue Hairs. Concrete stuff on how they started, ways they fought against the mutation. Practical stuff." He rubbed his chin and breathed a few more times. "My sister is having a baby girl in a few months. A Blue Hair. If they had a cure or solution, something."

"Could be normal. Might end up no big deal." She didn't want to search for these guys. She had looked just deep enough to know they weren't here to hurt Liesel, had in fact been sent by some prince named Jordan as a show of respect. The Latino thug didn't feel the same respect for Liesel as the Iowa thug but neither felt any hostility. Plus, if the threat she'd felt in her vision was this Ronin, then finding him would make it much easier to eliminate the big bad and move on with her life. She could be in California photographing the scarred earth left by the summer's fire season.

"Like your no big deal?"

"Yeah, mine isn't awesome, but you turned out fine. And there are others." Probably. She wasn't on the website enough to follow who was or wasn't a double Amazon. "Well, at least you can work around it."

"To a point, but for every Blue Hair born with blue hair, four are born with or develop a different mutation."

That was a lot. She remembered a few stories about people with an out of whack sense like heightened smell or touch.

Last night when they'd gotten to the room with the Harvest Team, Dianne had tried to read their minds. They'd killed people. They'd done so with relief. No guilt, no remorse. They feared becoming what they put down. Even now, skimming the surface of those memories made the hair on her arms spike up and sent a wave of cold through her head. A really bad brain freeze because it wasn't ice cream induced. Both the Ronin and finding the codex were great reasons on their own to find out more. Combine the two and she'd happily walk over burning glass to find answers, but wanting was different than doing. Wanting didn't make her capable.

Sergei took her hand and, as if all oxygen was gone, the icy fire went out. "Dianne why do you photograph heroic things?"

"Did someone tell you I was Defender?" Had she told him? She'd meant to invite him to the showing tonight. Especially after she realized what touching him did. After the hypnotist show and the Harvest Team she'd slept like the dead. Even now she felt drained.

"Liesel told me. Ages ago. I'm going to the show tonight. Thanks for the invite." Sarcastic but with a big flirty smile. "Why?" he prompted. "It's because you want to help people and can't. You use your work to encourage those who can." He tilted his head, teeth flashing, eyes hooded.

He was charming her and it freaked her out. She glared and

withdrew her hands. What happened to liking him for who he was? What had she done to change his mind about her? "Don't do that."

"I thought you wanted to be charmed," the sarcasm was oily this time. A rush of saliva flooded her mouth and her stomach sank. She recoiled.

"I'll try again." *Just stop.*

How could he be so sexy one minute and then, like an angle change on a knife reveals the sharp danger, he triggered her instinct to flee.

She filtered and focused, felt her body sway to a silent rhythm, a carnal, primitive beat. She gathered all the thoughts she could, placed them in her lap and imagined herself picking each up with her fingers like shards of a mirror. One side reflected what they saw, the other, shiny gray, showed what had been seen. She felt the bite of sharp edged memories but didn't look too close. Needed only to see—male, hunter, Harvest Team.

A long time later, her dry mouth stuck closed when she tried to speak. "Water, please."

Another piece, too young. Another, a mother. A cup was pressed in her hand and she drank the tap water, felt it dribble on her chin but ignored it as she worked her way through the pile. Kept her eyes closed.

"Wait. Go back," she said to herself.

She drank some more of the water. "I found them. But Sergei?"

He stayed silent until he realized she needed him to verify he was still there. "Yeah?"

"I can't get much. Surface stuff. They're almost out of my range and..." I'm scared to look too deep. I don't need to add to my nightmares. She swallowed. "They never raise their voices and are careful to regulate their breathing. Afraid to become what they hunt, Ronin, out of control." She saw a Ronin, tearing apart a room looking for anything to destroy. Oh, holly hell, who would do that to another person. "Once the rage kicks in they can't turn it off. Ronins eventually drop from exhaustion."

"What else?"

She flipped the shard over, pressed her thumb to the flat surface.

"Two guys, yes, but one is from Europe or South America. Yes, from Brazil. There is territorial pissing going on. Both sides were...wronged." Her mind felt the sharp stab of an edge and she swallowed and felt herself fall. That earlier memory of destruction had been the Ronin. She caught her elbow roughly on the carpet and the surface pain knocked her concentration out. She tasted blood but couldn't identify whether from her stomach or a bit tongue.

She lay back and opened her eyes to stare at the textured ceiling. Harry, Anna, Griffon and Liesel sat on the couch's edge watching her.

"Yeah, I'm okay." She wiped her forehead and felt sweat, pushed the damp hair back.

"Runny-wet," Sergei whispered and took her wrist, felt her pulse point. The remaining shards fell away when he touched her. It was like climbing out of a cold pool of water into a freshly dried, terry cloth bath sheet. Still bits of her felt the chill ache of constricting muscles but that press of warmth felt all the better for it.

"Something about obeying an order but knowing it would get back to the other group and seem weak," Dianne said.

"Jordan isn't in charge yet," Griffon pointed out. "Coming here was probably against SOP but when the king-to-be says jump....File a CYA."

Cover Your Ass, Griffon clarified.

Dianne swiped at her mouth, wishing she had more water. "The rest of the team is outside of town. Not close enough to read."

"What's the guy look like, the one they are following?" Harry asked. Boy Dianne must have really been out of it if Harry could come in, get updated, and her not notice.

Dianne shook her head. "No idea. Sorry."

"What do the Mightys call Blue Hairs?" Anna said.

"Tainted," Sergei and Dianne said in unison. Dianne realized she wasn't registering much. She felt floaty.

"You did well," Liesel said. She was taking notes in Griffon's smartphone. The offhand compliment felt nice.

"We can try again later," Sergei said.

Harry sighed and Dianne turned her attention to the murky

waters that were Harry's mind. "What's wrong?"

"When was the last time you ate?" Harry asked in response.

"Before the hypnotist. What time is it now?"

"Shit." Sergei rubbed a hand across his face and then reached down to help Dianne up. "You should have said something." Liesel winced and Anna pressed a hand to her stomach feeling her own pang of sympathy hunger.

Harry pulled a packet of peanuts from a pocket and handed them to her. "Eat these. I'll order room service. Anna, can you please get her more water, and a bottle of juice from the mini bar."

"I'll get them," Sergei said.

Yeah, lack of food would explain why she'd slept so hard and why, even now, she couldn't stop trembling.

She would refuel and work on catching this Ronin, stop this threat. Just like with the audience at the show last night, she had a goal and would use it to push everything else out of the way. She didn't know if this was the danger she had felt in her vision or not but she'd keep moving forward until she got it right.

Sergei wiped blood off her lips with a thumb. Nothing stung when he touched her mouth so the blood probably wasn't from a split lip. The rest—pain, weariness—was so familiar she set it aside. Felt at home. Dianne closed her eyes and let go of his hand. She sat on the couch, her knees shaking. "I need a shower. And a really good excuse not to go to an art show."

Dianne ate, showered, and coated her body in lotion. The extra attention was making her skin soft. She placed a magnet in her left bra cup, plenty of room there, and one at the small of her back. Then she went shopping with Sergei and Harry. He was adamant that she need the mental and physical break before searching for the codex or Ronin again. She had almost invited him into the shower with her. He could stare with his hot brown eyes while keeping a hand on her. Hell, he could wash her body and she would live in the moment, live in the comfort of his touch.

The shop they went to handled consignment and vintage items.

Stuffed tight with clothes, it required digging to find what you wanted. Big southern fans swept the hot air out of the high open windows and wide, planked wood and red brick made up the floor. When they had first come in Harry made a bunch of comments about proper restoration. Dianne liked the place. And oh, look. Black knee-high boots in her size.

"So, I've wanted to ask," Harry said, flipping through a sales rack. Harry's thoughts were unavailable to Dianne. Sergei's block was more an absence of thought, but Harry was a cloudy pool of still water that she'd been asked to stay out of. She sometimes caught emotional twinges as they leaped from the surface. The woman spoke her mind and protected Liesel so Dianne trusted her despite not being able to read her. Harry carefully tapped a scrunchie on Dianne's wrist. "What's with the hair ties?"

Dianne held still until the chance of skin to skin was gone and then moved her hands down to her side, snapping and rolling the bands around her wrists and then around some of her fingers. "I had long hair."

"Yeah? How long?"

"Long." The subject made her so.... Maybe what she felt was fear. She looked over her shoulder to the back of the shop where Sergei was looking through racks of leather and jean jackets.

Tired from her impersonation of Google, Dianne wanted to eat her weight in bacon, puke and go back to bed. Instead she got to buy jeans and shirts and bras that she actually tried on first. Way better than bacon.

Harry opened her mouth to say something and Dianne looked at the murky pool as it rippled then hardened. Harry closed her mouth and sighed. "When my mom went through chemo she lost all her hair."

"Yeah?" Dianne said.

"She'd always had short hair though. I bet the more...I bet it was hard." Harry gestured at her own long blonde hair.

"Yeah." Dianne could change the subject, pick an item off a shelf and discuss it, but she wanted a connection. Especially since she couldn't read Harry, if talking like friends provided further insight into the youngest Grant's mind, why not? "I don't know what to do with it." She laughed. People laughed when they felt insecure or were fishing for sympathy or empathy, didn't they? "I—"

"Could I help? I know you have that art show tonight," Harry offered.

"Barney is sending a dress."

Her voice must have sounded truly horrified because Harry laughed and went to touch Dianne and stopped. "Sergei?" She yelled across the store and didn't look up to see who stared at her. Sergei came and she whispered something in his ear.

An uncomfortable pain spread across Dianne's shoulders and sent a charge through her blood. She felt jealous that they could touch, that they could be close. The one person she had found that she could touch and he was leaning toward Harry. Not her. But maybe she could touch more people. What if this cream made a difference or if those who she couldn't read, she could touch?

Since Harry blocked her thoughts, her skin would block the memory transfer as well. Right?

She reached out and touched Harry and felt herself sink into a canal. The thickness of water gelled her nose close. She felt the weight of water with each forward and back motion. Dark liquid dragged her down, pulled at her limbs and hair.

Pressed her lungs flat.

Dianne gasped in air as she regained consciousness and felt Harry pat her hands with a brisk tap. So much for that experiment.

Sergei ran his hand over her hair which allowed Harry's touch. "You okay, Dare Devil?"

How did he know? Ignoring them, she stood up. "Been on the floor way too much today." A bit of sugared caffeine and she'd survive the afternoon of watching Harry and Sergei touch.

After nearly two hours of shopping, Sergei had bought more than Harry or Dianne. It was mostly for Veranda, the promised pink M&M's and a fuzzy pink pair of I-Love-Vegas dice, but also a few items for Portia and the baby. Now they sat at a table, Harry wisely trying to get the two super powered metabolisms fed.

As white as gauze, Dianne randomly trembled and took deep gasping breaths as she listened to Harry and Sergei talk. At least he thought she listened. He'd asked if she was okay and she just nodded. He considered touching her—giving her relief—but he didn't want her dependent on him. He had become her new drug of choice. She would either build a resistance or lose access to the supply when he went back to D.C.

The lotion smelled like hemp. Mental note to self, recommend something better smelling next time.

He brushed a hand over his head and sighed. Harry stared absently at the open area around them. The absent stare people get when they are standing in lines or elevators. Distant despite the physical proximity. No invitation to chat, not open to acknowledging those around them. Dianne wasn't talking and he figured getting to know Liesel's sister would only be to his advantage later.

"Sure is hot," he said.

"Sorry," Harry said. "You're trying to talk and I was off day dreaming." The look didn't disappear. Whatever she was thinking about was heavy stuff.

He laughed and shook his head, activated charming mode. "Besides go shopping, what are you doing today, Harry?"

They were both hand people, Sergei decided. Their hands were strong and used to work. Hers rough, his dry but smooth.

"I'm going to get a tattoo," she said.

"No way. Why?"

She shrugged. "I don't have one." She drank a sip of her soda.

"So, I don't have one either that—"

"You don't have a tattoo?" Bit too loud. She tried to tuck her reaction away.

"Neither do you."

"Yeah, but I look like I don't have a tattoo." She pulled her straw half-way out of her cup and tapped it down to break up the ice.

"Yet I look like I do?" He raised his eyebrows. He didn't know how to take her words. He kept the charmer in play and planned a couple of ways to work back from whichever hole they landed in.

She didn't let the power, the confident authority in his voice, intimidate her which he admired. "With the hair and the punk look."

"Okay, nice talking to you. Go back to your day dream." He turned toward Dianne. Her shivers had stopped but at Harry's raised voice she had stiffened. Was she worried that they'd fight? It wasn't like it was her responsibility if he and Harry got along.

Harry punched him in the arm. Not hard. But it got his attention. Dianne's too, who scooted back and stared hard at Harry's head. She pulled her feet toward the base of the chair, her thighs spring loaded, ready to bolt. He felt bad for how hard he'd pushed her to search for the Harvest Team and the Ronin. He'd need to ease back a bit or her body's immune system could be compromised.

Harry said, "Do you want me to lie and say you look like an angelic choir boy?"

"I was a choir boy." He rubbed his arm where she'd hit him. More as a reflex or to humor her. It hadn't hurt. He smiled at Dianne to let her know he was okay. He even laughed, a teasing chortle to even out the mood.

"Really? How did the blue hair go over?" Harry smiled and leaned back in her chair to open her body language. Whether a conscious reaction to Dianne's panic, Sergei didn't know but he appreciated it.

He thought back to connect her comment to the glib choir boy reply. "The priest thought he was saving my soul from a street gang."

Harry laughed. "I also think you're a brilliant doctor."

"I'm just trying to help Dianne—"

She spoke over him. "That article in *JAMA* on genealogy being a valid and important part of genetic coding, was very passionate. I agree that—"

He laughed, this time genuine, and Dianne leaned forward to smile at both of them, ate her last couple of fries. He hadn't even told Liesel he was publishing that article in the *Journal of the American Medical Association.*

Harry punched his arm again.

"Why'd you hit me?"

"It's a Grant thing, out of camaraderie," Dianne said. "Liesel goes around punching Griffon all the time. Though I think it makes him hot."

He felt heat infuse his checks and tried to remember the last time he'd blushed. "Okay, so point proven. Neither of us are what we appear to be."

Harry had to convince Dianne not to tell Liesel. If her sister knew her worst memory was drowning in that canal, she'd spiral into a raging guilt complex. When Liesel got it in her mind that Harry needed watching, she recruited family help and Harry would spend all her waking—and a few sleeping—hours verifying that, yes, she was okay.

They ate their lunch in relative silence, Dianne twitching and tugging on her short hair between ragged breaths. Wet breaths. Man, she'd just wanted to offer Dianne a helping hand. She was good looking with strong cheek bones and the short hair complimented her so well. But it was obvious that she was self-conscious about it. Harry wished she'd kept her distance.

"Okay, so point proven. Neither of us are what we appear to be."

Appear to be? Hell, that was worse than telling someone they looked better with glasses. What? They looked like shit before? What did she appear to be? Course, as the youngest Grant sister, plenty of assumptions were made. If the good doctor decided not to rely on those assumptions, well, another point in his favor.

"Dianne?" Harry didn't know how to even approach the subject. What? Just ask her to keep a secret from her queen and the woman she'd suffered to come to Vegas for, the woman she revered? She sighed and switched gears, "How'd you lose your hair?"

"It burned off in the fire. I have no idea what to do with it so I don't do anything. When it's wet it's curly and looks even shorter. I carry scrunchies out of habit—"

"Wait. Wait. Fire?" And not just a fire but an oh-by-the-way fire. She'd helped a friend do a remodel after a house fire. No one had been home, thank god, but the smell stuck with her.

Sergei took Dianne's hand. "What fire *Svyet*?"

She looked at both of them and shrugged her shoulders. "A forest fire. That's why I was late getting to Boise. I stopped to help a couple who were hiking and got caught in a forest fire. She was pregnant and I couldn't ignore..." She tried to laugh it off. It sounded to Harry like someone else had issues with coping mechanisms.

"I got them into this stream, burnt out gully behind us, and I look up to see an umbrella," Dianne and said as if telling a story, her voice hollow. Not empty of emotions but so full that they get trapped in your chest and your voice sounds void. "It's open, divided in sections, twisting in the rising heat. And I'm in a lot of pain but that's like, normal, my usual state, so whatever."

She stole a fry off Harry's plate with her left hand, Sergei still holding her right. She spoke faster with each word. "The umbrella had thoughts," the laugh, and oddly it didn't sound so broken. She might actually believe that being singed by a forest fire as you barely escaped being burned was no big deal. "I realized the umbrella was actually a parachute. A smokejumper landed in the fire to save us."

Harry had dated a Smokejumper once. Totally crazy, jumping into the middle of a forest fire.

Dianne sighed. "The unborn child had called to me. Almost wished I'd ignored it. Meant I wasn't there for Maggie."

"Diane, you did this brave thing and—" Sergei said.

"Brave," Dianne shook her head. "I didn't know about the fire. I thought they were lost. If for one minute I thought I'd be delayed, if I'd seen the fire? No way. I wouldn't have gone. I'm not trained for that type of thing. I take pictures. That's me."

Harry sputtered. Holy fuck. Didn't Dianne realize?

But it went beyond even what she could imagine. Sergei saw what Harry hadn't considered. "How long were you in the hospital?" He swallowed several times and his hand shook as he moved their joined hands to his lap.

"Two weeks," Dianne whispered.

"The Burn Center in Salt Lake?" he asked.

She hadn't escaped being burned. You were only sent to the burn hospital for third degree damage over the majority of your body. Her Amazon genes had kicked in and she looked fine now. On the outside.

"Yes."

"Shit. All those people, all those thoughts..."

Double Holy Fuck. Harry couldn't even conceptualize that level of pain.

Dianne blushed and changed the subject. "Harry, will you help me with my hair tonight? You said your mom had short hair. Do you think we can do something with mine?"

Harry nodded, felt very wooden and all her mental edges blunted by shock. "But—"

Leave it alone, Dianne said.

Harry didn't want to answer questions about almost drowning. She felt stupid about it. She'd dived into a pitch black canal to help Liesel rescue someone in a trapped car and instead almost killed them both by getting stuck down there. She'd freaked out and if Liesel hadn't saved her, she'd be dead.

So she understood Dianne's wish to pretend it didn't happen. But Dianne had to see that what she'd done was amazing. Made her more than worthy of Harry's respect and friendship. Shit, she'd been a bit of a brat at first. "Dianne, saving those people was the right thing to do. On purpose or not, you should be proud of that. I'm sure they're grateful."

Dianne just shrugged. "So my hair?"

Okay, one favor deserved another. "My drowning is what you saw when you touched me, wasn't it?"

Dianne wiped her hands with her napkin and slide back her chair to stand up. "Yeah."

"Don't tell Liesel." She wouldn't add please, made her sound vulnerable, and would mess up the important request.

"She's asked me not to tell you what I saw when she grabbed my neck," Dianne said, talking about Liesel. "So neither of you are getting each other's. You'll have to deal with it like sisters."

Harry could live with that. Sergei stood with her and placed cash on the table to cover the three of them. Dianne gathered up her bags, turning her body away to stave off any argument or further discussion.

Harry led the pair, still holding hands, out of the restaurant. For several minutes they just walked in silence, stepping around people

Dianne said to Sergei, "I've been thinking about the codex. Why would someone steal it?"

Harry answered, "We don't know. If Liesel did, they could track down the thief. We assume it's worth a great deal."

Sergei said, "I think the book was stolen because of the information it contained. Once Liesel came out saying that male Amazons are actually Mightys it was like she lifted the ban on this secret society and all these rumors surfaced. Even my Great Grandfather's diaries make sense now. Hopefully, once we recover it, Liesel will translate it and I'll find a way to help Portia."

They had shopped a couple of blocks off the strip but it was a simple walk back and the fall weather, though hot, wasn't so bad.

"Yes, you want it to help your sister. What does the thief want it for? Just the money?" Dianne asked.

"Whatever their reason, it's selfish. Liesel was sharing every translated word online," Sergei said. Liesel had told Harry that he was working on a cure or at least better treatments for some of the more extreme manifestations of Blue Hair. The man wore his heart on his sleeve but seemed oblivious to it.

"Maybe they didn't want that information out there. Who'd want to keep it secret if it would help people? That's horrible." Dianne said.

Harry nodded and then held the hotel's door open for them, "Like I said, worth a lot."

Chapter 10

Maldecia Farina was pitched up and over the railing of a footbridge by her killer. Built as second story thoroughfares between hotels, the footbridges of Vegas have high side rails. Only the billboards advertising all the great attractions stand higher than the rails.

Maldecia hit the pavement in a semi-crouched position between the rare gaps in traffic. The van's driver navigated back and forth, up and down the strip, as a mobile advertisement. He knew his day was truly screwed when he hit the old lady. Her glasses lay on his dash and her knickers were up around her neck. He rushed out to help her and the Las Vegas strip began to clear for the ambulance.

She was dead when the EMTs arrived. Electric paddles couldn't restart her heart. Vegas grime smeared her cheek and her blood stuttered into the sewer grate.

At the same time, a half a mile down the strip, the Bellagio opened its doors to the world renowned photographer D. Fender.

Dianne wanted to wear a man to her first gallery showing. Barney had suggested a deep cut purple gown. Suggested by hand delivering it to her room one hour before show time. And she'd obeyed but added a brand new pair of magnets and a layer of hand lotion as accessories. She didn't understand how any of it worked, but it did. Sort of. There were a lot of people in Vegas and quite a few thought about her. Her and her photos. The lotion muted the thoughts and the magnets limited her range to just her immediate surroundings.

Harry spiked Dianne's hair here, plastered it down there and added a purple barrette. It looked nice. The whole time Dianne's hand held Sergei's thigh, touching his skin through a slit in his jeans just above the knee. As Harry worked, Sergei read through a spiral notebook that looked like he'd run over it with a really heavy coffee machine, many of the pages stained or wrinkled.

Dianne plotted seven different ways to steal the notebook and read it.

The Fine Arts Gallery at the Bellagio had high-sheen wood floors, neutral walls, and black ceilings that were inter-crossed like a sound studio with lighting. The flat-painted walls looked sparse compared to the highly detailed interior of the hotel itself.

Dianne hadn't shown this much skin ever, willingly, except to the deserted landscapes she photographed. She felt exposed and vulnerable and she refused to wear the heels Barney delivered with the dress. She traded with Harry for a pair of flats.

"Gentleman and Ladies," Barney called for attention. He often felt the need to be different, say things to get attention. "Defender has shared beauty with the world. Showcasing the heroic efforts, the humanity of communities, and the harsh realities of war." He'd obtained a section of the art gallery in the Bellagio. The curator knew Barney from college and it had been available—the next exhibit not coming in for a couple of weeks. Luckily it was one of the best. Waiters dressed in black blended into the crowd with chocolate bars and wine glasses.

Avoiding pronouns, Barney gave a brief list of awards her work had received. Dianne wondered if her other shows had been like this—Barney, vague and protective of her privacy. Were there always this many people?

The press was in attendance. Even a New York Times news crew had shown up. The Times crew planned to reveal the hoax and then enjoy Vegas on the business account. The world knew only two things about Defender, the photographer was a hermit and didn't do gallery shows.

"Defender asked that before I open the show I introduce you to a new find. Defender received a post card and demanded I hunt down the photographer and represent him." The postcard from her grandmother had been of the Sawtooth Mountains and her whole reason for being in the mountains before the fire started.

Barney had displayed each photo to showcase it, sectioned them to complement each other or to tell a story. Most were shots of rescue buildings or equipment or historically significant sites. In series-shots the light changed, like the sun moving east to west, or setting. He had hung those in the same order she had taken them as she had captured different angles. Barney set them so you were drawn to look and linger.

It felt odd to see her work displayed this way, a thrilling rush of astonishment. Had she done all this? Some pictures stirred memories while others felt so vague she wasn't a hundred percent sure she could tell you where or of what location the picture had been taken.

"There is true talent there and we are happy to announce that Sergeant Christopher Sparks will have a full showing of his work in L.A. Sergeant? Please unveil your work."

Sergeant Sparks stepped toward a covered photo to remove the drape. He had worn his dress blues at Barney's insistence and looked handsome, several people thought so. The canvas hung from a wall all by itself, just to the side of the podium and the flat side of the semi-circle of people.

The audience gasped. The photo, blown up to the size of a small kitchen table, was of the aftermath of a suicide-bomber's attack on a marketplace in Iraq. But unlike the photos seen in newspapers, nothing was held back.

It was gruesome and intriguing and, with a brief glance, beautiful. The way it glimmered here, darkened there, kept your eye moving in a spiral toward the center, signifying an on-purpose composition. It was good, more so for its powerful message and the emotional reaction it generated.

Dianne felt several people who had firsthand knowledge of this cringe. They may not have seen this specific incident—one lady thought it was the Oklahoma City Bombing—but it made them respond.

The light floated over the surface, leaving the ground and base in shadow. Perhaps indicating a hidden truth. That we only see so much. Dianne clapped with the crowd.

Instead of letting Barney make even more of a fuss with an introduction, she approached the mike.

Recognizing someone in charge, the room fell silent. "My name is

Dianne Fender. D. Fender. Welcome to my show. I want to thank Barney for setting our wonderful evening up and Sgt. Sparks who agreed to come on short notice. I am honored that my work will be presented with such obvious talent." The speech wasn't too bad. Mostly because she'd pulled it word for word out of Barney's head.

Several people were surprised, others laughed and someone said, "It's a girl."

"Will you be at the L.A. showing?" The Times reporter asked, not buying this publicity stunt for one minute.

"No."

Barney groaned next to her and tried to make more appropriate suggestions of what to say in his head. Always the diplomat. Dianne ignored him.

"Why not?" The Times reporter asked. Sometimes she couldn't hear a person's name by reading the surface of their minds. They were so locked into their career, their achievements, that they saw themselves as doctors, lawyers, or Times reporters.

Dianne raised her eyebrow like Sergei would. "Are all reporters exempt from the rules of polite society or is it just you?"

"Just me."

"Can I join the exempt club?"

The reporter laughed.

She answered a few more questions and had the audience convinced that she was Defender by the time she broke them up, only a few mental nudges needed. The technical questions would come next, and since she had taught herself and didn't speak the lingo, she wrapped things up. "No more questions. Please enjoy your evening and thanks for coming."

Sergeant Sparks stepped forward and took her hand before Barney could intercept. The man was just grateful. She'd given his life a new purpose.

While all that was great, the hell of his time in Iraq as well as losing his young wife in a car accident, were now her hell. She reached for Sergei, put every mental effort into reaching his mind—it had to be there somewhere—and kept a smile on her face.

She released his hand quickly and turned back to the mike.

Clammy moisture clung to her skin. Nausea rolled through her. She could smell the dying blood of her wife, her lover's face jagged and torn from the windshield glass. Her wife. Her love.

Relieved that she hadn't passed out, she said, "Sergeant Sparks served during Operation Phantom Fury in Iraq. I want you all to know, I am genuinely honored to be in his presence. It is men like him, who sacrifice their lives, their peaceful dreams at night for our freedom that inspire me. Now I can share his great talent for catching beauty at its pinnacle. Twenty percent of all sales tonight will go to the Veterans of Foreign Wars. Thank you, Sergeant." She shook his hand again, her other hand tightly clenched at her side to prepare herself.

Sergei stepped out of the crowd to help her and touched her exposed lower back just as she touched the Sergeant. She smiled. Radiated. And the Sgt. thought he should have his camera. "You can take my picture later."

She read my mind.

"Yes I did," she answered. "I'll be buying your photo tonight. How much?"

He laughed, overwhelmed, but said nothing. Christopher Sparks had receding brown hair and deep brown eyes and his compact build was all muscle and capable will.

"Thirty thousand," she said. He stopped laughing.

"I'll talk to your agent. Hey, Barney."

People mingled and paused before her work to consider each piece. And she had no clue what they thought of it. Wasn't that great? "Barney, I want the photo but make sure I pay a fair amount for it."

"Thirty after my commission and the donation," Barney didn't even flicker. Always flexible as a rubber band but still able to keep things together. "What will you do with it? It's too good to put into storage with the rest of your stuff. It won't fit in your little trailer."

No trailer after the fire. "I'm going to donate it to the Walter Reed Hospital or perhaps give it as a present to the White House."

The Sergeant paled and started to shake. She could read his thoughts loop, unable to process beyond the shock. She focused on the touch at her back, just Sergei's fingertips. Barely there. Maybe that was why she could still read Sergeant Sparks.

"Sergeant, let me introduce you to someone." Sergei stepped around her, keeping his hand on her exposed back. "No, not you." His eyebrows went up. But she didn't want anyone to take Sergei's attention. She reached into a crowd of ladies talking about the Sgt.'s work and pulled a lady out.

The lady and her companions stopped speaking and stared with mouths gaping.

"This is Alice. She is a teacher from Ketchum, Idaho. She's here for a friend's wedding."

Alice, a mid-thirty blonde that Chris thought looked like Doris Day, said, "How did you know that?"

Dianne took for granted that Sergei would continue touching her and prevent the painful side effects of touching Alice.

"And she thinks you're sexy," Dianne told the Sergeant. "I'm psychic," Dianne said to Alice, then added, "You think he's cute? Wait till you see the tattoo."

The Sergeant blushed but offered to show Alice the rest of the photos and get her some wine.

Dianne turned to Sergei. "Thank you. For...for helping me. Who's Doris Day?"

She went through meeting the press. Her, in a one-of-a-kind elegant dress and Sergei, in his leather pants and piercing and blue hair. Rather than saying hello, she'd poke her head into a crowd and say, "This is my friend Dr. Sergei Sky." or "Barney says I'm to mingle." or "I hated that photo the first four times I took it. This time I think it worked though." It helped that she kept one hand tucked in Sergei's bare elbow and a glass in her other hand.

Not introducing herself or offering her hand, perfectly happy to just interrupt and smile. When they were offended she'd talk about how nerve wracking her first show was and all was forgiven.

Before she could dive into yet another group, Sergei pulled her around to face him, sidestepping for privacy in the crowd. "I am in awe, Dianne."

"Thank you?" She had avoided—rudely interrupted—the gushing

praise of some of the crowd. But somehow his simple words left her speechless.

"There is a picture between those two," Sergei said.

She turned to look where he pointed. He stepped close. His breath fanned her bare neck. There were only two pictures. "What?"

"I mean one taken between those. Light wise. It's the same place." He kept his voice low and she leaned close to hear him. Their shoulders brushed and she forgot for a second that they were talking. His mouth slid slowly into a sexy smile. He smelled good, probably shaving cream or deodorant, because he didn't seem the type to use cologne. It was nice.

She vaguely remembered that she had gotten three usable shots from that Life Flight helicopter. The metal blades cast great shadows on the green grass. "Oh, yeah. Barney sold that one." She'd taken them laying on her side just as a rescue patient would perhaps see the looming salvation.

"He sold it to a lady who then sold it on eBay at probably twice the price." He brushed his hand down her back, left it at the base of her spine.

"I don't care—" about the money.

"I bought it. I have that one."

Which meant he'd got it before they met, maybe even before he knew she was a Blue Hair. "Oh." She blinked back the sudden tears, shifted her jaw back and forth and smiled, a full expression of the giddy happiness overflowing from inside her. Dianne reached up and pulled on his earring, cupped his jaw before putting her hands safely away. Not knowing how to respond but needing something. Feeling needy.

People asked why she chose different subjects or times of day. They tried to sound knowledgeable about art to impress her. But she actually didn't know much about the technical side of photography. So when Sergei asked, "How come you photograph so much purple? Is it symbolic in some way?" she was both surprised and pleased.

Huh? She turned and scanned the room. She was taller than the women and most of the men, even without the heels. Liesel and Griffon, both glowing, whispered near the military cemetery shots.

Harry was teasing Anna about her latest twitter post as they circled the room for the fifth time.

She could see in a kaleidoscope-sweep of the room her work. Present in almost every single shot was purple. Purple sunset, purple flowers, purple painted letters. Other colors, sure, but prominent in varying shades was purple. Even the dress Barney sent for her to wear was purple.

"I never noticed." She stared at Sergei's mouth, looked briefly at his shoulders, lingered over his crotch. She swallowed and led the way back into the flow of the crowd.

She could do things she had never done before. She could have a conversation and decipher the other person's opinions on his responses and not on what they were really thinking. She was in an art gallery, surrounded by people who wanted her photos. It tasted made up, smelled like a dream and sounded like a fantasy. It gave her courage, this new power. She could do anything.

Barney hugged her, careful not to disturb Sergei's hold of her. "Liesel told me I could hug you and I've always wanted to." He had touched her before, helped her to stand up from the hospital bed. She squeezed him close and projected all the love and gratitude she felt. They were both crying when she released him.

"Darling you're my friend. Not just my client." Barney was a good-hearted man who was in love with her art. Dianne had lucked out finding such a hardworking and patient agent. "Go. You are officially off duty. I'll call you tomorrow and tell you how it goes." They had done well, her and her photos. Barney shook Sergei's free hand, took a deep breath and headed back into negotiations with a movie director who wanted one of her photographs of a Search and Rescue Truck.

As Dianne and Sergei walked through the hotel, she tried to figure out the best way to ask Sergei for his help. It might be a huge favor or it could be a no-big-deal and she had no way of telling which.

Unless she asked.

It scared her not to know the answer beforehand. In high school she had gotten straight A's by reading the answers out of other people's heads, usually the teacher. She needed directions while traveling? The gas attendant or other drivers knew the way. To ask someone for something, not knowing their response, felt like a really big deal.

Sergei cupped the back of her neck, squeezed it. He broke the silence first. "How did you find Barney?"

"Internet." Distracted, she walked without worrying she would bump into another pedestrian.

He laughed.

"I'm serious." She looked at him, squinted to search for a clue to what he laughed about.

He shook his head and stroked down her arm to take her hand. All that bare skin, little echoes of warmth pulsing through her body.

"I'm sure it was hard before those type of things were available. Before you could get an internet connection." He kept their pace slow, guided them through foot traffic to get to the front of the Bellagio hotel.

"I stayed closer to small towns. Easier to limit my interactions that way. I'd befriend the local grocery store and they'd stay open late for me. They could order most things." She squeezed his hand. "But then I'd start getting...."

A large crowd was waiting for the fountain show out in front of the Bellagio. The city had a filthy feel to its streets, Nevada dust mixed with sweat and sin. The newer hotels were immaculate, but the older hotels felt threadbare. Then they tore them down and built new ones. Bigger, trendier concept hotels. The streets collected the grime that never washed away by rain. Everything else dissipated. The noise wore itself out in the early morning hours. The occasional wind filtered the air but the grime stayed.

"What?" He prompted her.

She realized she'd been scoping out the area for possible photo ops. Pleasant warmth pooled in her stomach, as Dianne tucked away her artistic thoughts. "People would think I was odd. Which I am. They would wonder if I was on the run or if I was worth enough money to live off of, enough to kidnap."

"Are you?"

She would have asked just as bluntly so didn't worry about manners when she answered him. "Yes, even before I inherited Grandma Maggie's estate. House, cars, empty safety deposit box, it's all mine now." She'd always had a small trust fund from her parents, which allowed her to live carefully. With the sales of her photos things got easier. It went from beef bouillon to steak. With Maggie's money she would be financially very comfortable.

"Empty?"

She nodded, closed her eyes a moment and brushed up against him as they walked. "That's what Dad said. He's going through her house now. I'll live there, for a while at least, so I can help Liesel."

"I'm starting my new job for NEWCo Labs next week," Sergei said. He looked at her, just stared for a second. "It's important. I'm excited to get started."

Dianne felt like he was trying to tell her something. She shrugged. "Tell me more about your sister Portia. Do you have other family?"

They stopped to wait for the water works, comfortable to linger without a new direction. "Two more sisters." She put her free hand on his chest, moved it side to side to feel the silk contour his muscles.

She waited for him to say more and when he didn't, she teased, "Bambi, Tiffany and Amber?"

"Yeah, how did you—? Oh, I see. You think they're stripper names."

Heat flashed across her face. "I am so sorry. I didn't mean...I just...."

He laughed, so weird not to know if he was laughing at her or not. "You've made other blunders and yet this is your first apology." Nice laugh though, it sounded real because it was half chuckle and all awkward. He was a really good looking, successful doctor and his weird laugh made him approachable. Pulled him down from some out of reach stratosphere to the mortal realm. She thought it was adorable. It made her feel proud that she could cause that reaction.

"Do you think I'm rude?"

"Sometimes intentionally. Mostly, I think you say things most people wouldn't be comfortable saying. You're very brave." His solid body fit against her palm as if her hand had been carved from his chest. Light bent to the surface, cupped the angle of his cheek. She felt deviant touching his chest in public.

She stepped in close to him. "So they're not called Bambi, Tiffany and Amber?"

He smiled. "No. I'm the oldest then Portia, Bailey and Zeeman." He nodded at her raised eyebrow over Zeeman's name. "Yes, really. With college and medical school I missed them growing up." He shrugged. "We're closer now." The fountains started. Pressurized jets of water choreographed to music and light. It was beautiful. Not something she could photograph. The beauty stemmed from the movement, the response of the crowd.

She wanted to whisper her request. *Be brave.* "I want to ask you something. I've never...."

His breath shortened and his eyes and body stilled. She stepped closer, more a shift or lean forward, already in his personal space, almost, almost touching.

"Will you go to the movies with me?"

"What?" His husky voice started a swirling vortex at the pit of her stomach. She realized it was attraction, passion. She wanted this man. She swallowed to moisten her dry mouth, licked her lips. "I've never gone to an R rated movie before. When I was younger, before my psychic problem became a problem, I was too young. I haven't sat in a theater since I was eleven."

"You want to see a movie?" He scrubbed a hand across his face—she leaned back to avoid it rubbing her own face—almost used his right hand before he remembered and left their hands clasped.

"I've seen movies on the internet, just not in a theater. A hundred plus people all watching the same thing yet having a huge variety of responses to it? It is the very definition of chaos." She watched, enthralled by the way his hair fell back into place like little metal springs compressed and released. Sergei rubbed the back of her neck and slid his hand down her bare spine, drawing her even closer. Pressing her into his body heat and her skin lapped it up like honey.

"I'll go with you but you have to go clubbing with me tomorrow night. Deal?"

"Clubbing? Doesn't that hurt?"

He kissed her. The slant of his moist mouth plied sweet pressure to her lips. He just pressed for a moment and Dianne was surprised that it tasted so good. A bit like dark chocolate, bitter yet so smooth. Her tongue slid along his lips. She tasted the laugh as his mouth switched playful to passionate. Holy shit, it was nice.

Kissed and kissed.

He sucked her bottom lip in between his teeth and nipped before licking the spot. She tilted her head and opened her mouth, trying to follow that delicious heat back into his mouth with her own tongue. He tried to pull back and she wouldn't let him.

"Dianne."

"What?"

His lips did this amazing thing, they flexed and held her own mouth, plump and receptive then firm and controlling. Rebellion. A potent drug that urged her to take, grab what she wanted and revel in the feel of freedom.

"Let's slow down, I'm not for having sex on the street." His major hard-on indicated otherwise.

"That's something else I've never done. Had sex."

He groaned, "Dianne."

"What?" His chin felt prickly with stubble. She grazed her lips over his jaw and felt little fires burn her mouth. Oh, and there was his ear. What did that taste like?

"We've attracted an audience."

She let go enough to read the man staring at them. "So? He isn't getting any either."

Sergei's cell phone rang as they walked back to the hotel after the movie. He was grateful for the interruption. Dianne was asking for the twelfth million time, "What did you think about—"

"Hello?"

Liesel said, "Sergei? I've been calling you for over an hour."

The kiss had hammered his nerves and had his hormones raging but the happy bouncing beauty walking next to him made him grin like a sap. Her enthusiasm was contagious and dangerous. And a huge turn on. Yeah—he adjusted mid turn, shifting his package to a safer location—huge turn on.

The art show had been a total rush. Dianne took amazing photos and she could work a room like a pro. He'd heard one fan whisper "endearingly unrefined." Two days ago she couldn't face leaving her hotel room, yesterday she retreated to sleep rather than deal with her problems but today she had touched Harry on purpose and used her ability even while touching him. He doubted she had even noticed.

He had told her about his job in D.C. as they waited for the movie to begin. Reminding himself that this—the building passion between them—stayed in Vegas when they resumed their lives.

"Sorry, just turned my phone back on. Dianne and I were in the movies." It was just after midnight and he wanted to track down the nearest all night eatery. Dianne's stomach growled in concurrence, despite the popcorn they had shared and the box of Swedish Fish.

"She's with you? She's with Sergei," she said to someone on her end. Liesel sighed, "Sergei can you bring Dianne here? Someone killed Maldecia."

Chapter 11

Griffon saw the two-man Harvest Team hover on the edge of the crime scene. The way they carried themselves, the clothes they wore, the knowledge and awareness in their eyes, acted like a beacon. It made them easy to spot even though it was a different pair of guys than the first night.

Jordan Mathews was personally sanctioning the Harvest Team and Dianne didn't read anything off them to indicate they were there to hurt Liesel. Yet, with the Ronin they were hunting, Griffon couldn't imagine they had gotten this far without video footage or a description of the guy. Hell, at the very least they should have his real name and fingerprints. They knew more than they were saying and until they got on board with being one hundred percent cooperative, Griffon would view them as a threat.

He tried to arrange for Max, his partner, to come help by acting as bodyguard, but Liesel wasn't having it. She was surrounded by all these super-powered people, so a normal would either get hurt in the cross fire or be unnecessary. Not her words, by any means, but the sentiment she conveyed.

Griffon did freelance work for the Army, acting as a target or combatant during training. The work kept his skill set strong and provided cash flow when business was lean. He could pick the veterans among the newbs from the burnt out innocence in their eyes. These two from the Harvest Team were world-worn, capable and confident, but possibly damaged.

Dianne? Griffon whispered in his head. Maybe she could read the team now that they were closer but he got no response from her. Either she was touching Sergei or was doing a search of her own.

One of the two lifted his head and looked at Griffon. And without any physical movement or talking, the other knew something was up and looked as well. They nodded to Griffon who nodded back. *That's right assholes, I see you.*

The first guy pulled out a cell phone and turned his back to make a call.

Griffon didn't need Dianne for this one. He faded back into the crowd and slowly circled around the crime scene. Vegas cops had shunted the four lanes of traffic into three and left a narrow strip of sidewalk for people to pass. The thick traffic was gutted with gawking bystanders. Huge spotlights had been placed to shine into the dark corners and illuminate the area.

As the guy pocketed the phone Griffon was there to withdraw it. Fluid. Fast is smooth.

He kept going through the tight crowd as he attached his own phone to the stolen one and used an app to clone the phone and all its information. He stopped on the other edge of the crime tape and chatted up a patrolman who kept the gawkers from entering the sectioned off area. He felt more than saw the Harvest Team head his way. He disconnected the phone and palmed the extra in a loose grip getting ready to slip it back.

"Keep it. Can't use it now." There was carefree respect in the other man's voice.

"Griffon," he introduced himself.

"Mathew."

"Sure it is," Griffon widened his stance, crossed his arms.

The guy smiled. He was older than his partner and definitely older than the previous two. Griffon wondered how long he'd been at it. Harvesting.

"Ultimately we are looking for the same answers here." For an I'm-on-your-side speech it had big gaping holes. He continued in his imparting-wisdom tone. Griffon's drill sergeant had sounded a bit like that when he wasn't yelling. Like he held the wisdom they all needed to survive the grueling torture of basic. "The casinos and businesses were quick to give video surveillance to the police. We'd like the chance to sit in on the viewing." Mathew's stern face stayed impassive.

"And you think I have that kind of access?" Griffon watched for the little physical movements that would convey unease or tension. A twitch in the jaw or flexed fingers. Nothing. The man kept emotion from showing better than Griffon.

With the slightest emphasis, "I think that the Amazon queen has access to anything." He pulled out a card which said Mathew above a ten digit phone number.

Griffon stared at the extended hand then took the card. "She prefers matriarch and it's not official until tomorrow."

"Matriarch. Hmm, fitting," this from the other man. He had the slightest down slip to his consonants which indicated an accent.

Griffon said Matriarch in Spanish to test the water, "*Matriarca? Si?*"

The man shook his head and said in what Griffon thought was Portuguese, "*País errado, meu.*"

He got the translation from Dianne—*wrong country, dude*—who sent a wave of warmth. The older man tightened and straightened his spine. Not old really, looked to be in his forties but with Mighty longevity that could be sixty.

Ft. Knox level steel doors on that one. I can't get anything and the other is a newb. Nothing new there.

"A Double with psychic abilities?" Mathew asked. Could he feel Dianne reading him?

Then in both of their heads, apparently, *Blue Hair to you, meu.*

The man's eyebrows went up. Then he pointed to the card and threaded back through the crowd. The professed newb moved confidently and easily behind his partner. Newb to the team but not new to fighting.

Griffon checked his pockets to make sure he had everything including the phone. He opened the cloning app and pulled up the call logs. Only one number listed in both incoming and outgoing and it was the same ten digits on the card. Perhaps some type of switchboard. Griffon dialed the number as he headed for Liesel's hotel room. A neutral voice answered, "Mathews?" Griffon closed the phone without speaking. Time to see what influence Liesel's new title would have.

-#-

Liesel finished answering the detective's questions. The cop was different than the pair that had questioned her after the airport attack. Probably a different division, precinct even, if they had that here in Vegas.

No, she didn't know why Maldecia was out on the foot bridge. Maybe smoking. She'd made sure the detective knew about the conference and disagreements over the bylaws and left it up to him to interpret how he felt most comfortable. If he wanted to think the Amazon thing was an exaggeration or untrue or possible and be okay with it, fine. Whatever. Her policy had always been complete disclosure and honesty. So far no one had scoffed and asked her to prove it, any doubt they had they at least kept it to themselves until out of earshot.

Harry entered the room and, after introductions, escorted the officer to one of the bedrooms so the cop could question her there. A sisterly check was sent and received: *Yes, I'm okay.* All nonverbal, no psychic needed. Liesel let out a sigh. She'd been overly harsh with Harry about the climbing wall. She'd asked her sister to come with her on this trip because she honestly thought she'd have more time to hang out, just the two of them. She missed doing sisterly things with Harry. So far they'd only had the few hours at the salon.

"A bit late to be working," Harry said to the officer. Six words, said with that tone, and Harry was bonding with the stranger. Her sister said it was a blue collar thing—the I-get-where-you're-coming-from connection—and had more to do with the handshake than the tone. Liesel had seen it at work, always impressed by how natural her sister made befriending people look.

"I work the night shift, even as a detective. We're open when the casinos are. Always." The officer smiled. "And with witnesses traveling in and out, we try to talk to them when they are willing. Even 3:30 in the morning."

Maldecia, despite being in her eighties, had not been frail or weak. Maldecia would have fought her attacker with spry grace and that left no doubt the killer had been a Mighty or an Amazon. The police were still working on identifying Liesel's airport attacker but he was not a Mighty or a Blue Hair.

Anna was on the phone with the Europe group to relay the bad news and see if there were possible connections with the missing documents and the Ronin the Harvest Team was harvesting. If the Europe group had missing documents or had received any threats that could help them figure out who was behind all of this. Griffon knew a guy in SWAT that vouched for him and he was down at the crime scene talking to the forensics crew.

A full search of the hotel and the attendees hadn't given Dianne any clues but she was determined to still work on it.

Which meant it was time to make a phone call and ask for reinforcements. Her people were covering all the angles they could, a Harvest Team was in place, and now the wife of an international dignitary had been killed. Time to ask for help.

She explained her idea to Sergei and then asked him, "What do you think?" Liesel sat on the couch with her feet tucked up under her, clutching her biceps to stay warm. The blue-haired doctor was lounging on the couch, keeping an eye on Dianne who was sitting in one of the wing-back chairs with her eyes closed, meditating.

"Maldecia's death might not be connected to any of us. It could be something from Maldecia's past. Her husband isn't known for his low profile. Or it could be one big fucked up mess." Sergei listened to Dianne's occasional outburst, like angry shouts at a television screen only she could see.

He looked relaxed. Vacation had a positive effect on him. "Not like you to cuss." Liesel closed her eyes, stared at the back of her eyelids, and took a moment to evaluate all the places her body was pinched tight with stress. Breathed a few times, relaxing her shoulder muscles, focusing on the positives of her life.

He snorted and Liesel opened her eyes in time to see him pull on his inner earring. "Yeah." He looked toward Dianne again.

Any other time she'd tease him about it—the bewildered look and awe of new love—but she had been in his place not that long ago. Scared and awed and giddy.

"The police will stay busy and Griffon will have something to growl at," Sergei finally said.

Liesel laughed, short, bitter, and closed her eyes. Yes, he would and man, was he good at it. He could corner a person and have them quaking in their Special Forces combat boots with very little effort. The bitter came from how she was missing seeing him work his magic. And that something as awful as Maldecia's death would necessitate him working his mojo.

"Only about 10 percent of murders are solved," Anna said. She came out from the second bedroom and looked a bit pale. They'd agreed that making those phone calls couldn't wait for Liesel to be done with the police but it was difficult news to convey. There were already pictures and video on social media so a phone call had been necessary and a kindness.

"Thanks, jolly ray of sunshine," Sergei said.

"Sorry." Anna sat next to Liesel. "They'll call us back. They needed the chance to process." Liesel would be able to take the phone call, provide a shoulder to grieve on, and a sounding board. She remembered making similar calls after Maggie's death. God willing, she would not need to make such calls for her mom for many, many years.

Liesel knew Mal's death had been a shock to her, she couldn't image how the Europe group would feel. Sergei took her hand and squeezed it. "Today we'll vote you in as Matriarch. All those plans you got swimming around in your head, you'll get them done. You're doing good things here. Always have."

Someone reassuring her felt way too familiar. She needed to believe in herself as much as these people did. Perhaps they just needed those reassurances in return.

Griffon entered the hotel room and a little spark lit his eyes as he looked at her. She smiled and watched him walk over. Anna popped up and took a seat in the other wing chair so Griffon could sit next to Liesel. He sat and kissed her hands. She let herself dwell in that electric moment. A thousand reconnections as each cell of her body warmed at his touch.

"Hey, I'm trying to concentrate here," Dianne yelled from her seat. "Stop with the sex thoughts. Crud. *I'm* not getting any." Anna and Sergei laughed.

Griffon ignored Dianne but got down to the business at hand. "If Maldecia had just fallen, she'd probably would have been fine, healed up quick. But she was thrown with enough force that when she hit the car it punctured a lung. They cleared the streets and got in as fast as they could but she was already gone. They continued to administer CPR until they got to the hospital. Then they called it."

"Called it what?" Dianne asked. "Oh.... I'm sorry," she whispered.

Liesel nodded her head, felt it brokenly bob and gritted her teeth to still it.

Maldecia had worked tirelessly through Europe beside her husband, both advocates for equality and education. Her gray hair and careful step made her look seventy when the truth could be a hundred. Maldecia and Maggie, two of her mentors. Women who had done more than just befriend a web designer with big ideas.

Gone.

She wiped tears off her face. "Anna contacted the family. I think we need to call Valdez, get her take on what are next step should be."

"She wants privacy for this one. Clear out."

"Dianne," Liesel tried to smile and shook her head.

"What?"

"I'll just duck into the hall," she pulled her cell out of her purse as she stood. Almost four a.m. in Vegas and the area code for the cell number was D.C. so, hopefully, seven wasn't too early to call.

"This is an unsecured line, Valdez, go ahead." With a greeting like that you didn't start with the how-are-yous.

"Agent Valdez, this is Liesel Grant. I need your help."

"Give me your number and I'll call you back." Agent Valdez sounded confident.

The hallway was empty. She stared at the carpet with its fancy pattern. Harry would know the type of carpet it was, the type of regulations the hotel had to adhere to with exits and weight thresholds, or whatever it was all called. She let her mind wander for the brief moment before her phone rang.

She slid it open and before she could say hello, "Liesel, sorry about that. I was in a meeting. What's going on?"

"Maldecia Farina was killed today in Las Vegas." She never

wanted this part of her life, passing on bad news, to get easy. She swallowed back the hitch of sadness. "Do you know of the conference?"

"I do."

Liesel could imagine the FBI agent in her power suit, all business hair and capable hands, standing just outside a major meeting to speak with her. "Then you must know Mal was here representing the European groups. Also, I was attacked at the airport two days ago. My attacker died but I'm worried these two might be connected."

She didn't include Maggie's death in her list of worries. Dianne was probably listening and she'd address that problem if she had to, but she still didn't think Maggie was killed or that her death was linked to Maldecia's. It felt different. Maldecia's murder had been violent and swift while Maggie had looked so peaceful, her brown hair in long braids, curled to her side against her white pillows.

Amazon FBI Agent Valdez had helped her and Griffon before. The secretive woman could probably command an army into battle or work covertly on her own to clear a compound of hostiles. She asked for a few details and Liesel told her about the Harvest Team and their hunt for a Ronin.

Valdez took a deep breath and said, "I can't go to Vegas, though I'd like to. I'll be in contact with the local office and we'll get someone there to check this out."

"It's probably not connected, or at least not something the FBI needs to get involved in—" Liesel paced the hall in short steps just in front of her door. No one had come into the hallway but she kept her voice down. Downplaying her concerns was habit, and the longer she spoke the more paranoid and stupid it all felt.

"Mrs. Farina was not an accident. There will be trouble because of her married connections, whether her death is attached to your attack or not." Valdez sighed. "And a Harvest Team? They aren't sent out over idle issues."

Liesel didn't know if she should feel reassured that Valdez knew about Harvest Teams or not.

"Senor Farina will travel to the U.S. Once Maldecia's identity is revealed to the public, media attention might be a problem." Valdez snorted. "Unless a Hollywood socialite breaks up with her boyfriend or some other worthy story surpasses it."

Liesel smiled at Valdez's derisive tone. They had met once and Liesel didn't know the Agent's first name or past. But there was mutual respect and trust between them.

"I just don't want to waste your time," Liesel said.

"You are not wasting my time." Valdez continued, "Vigilance is the price of liberty."

Liesel kept her sigh to herself. "All right."

"I'll be in contact. Please feel free to call me, anytime."

"Thank you."

"You're welcome, my queen." With a bit of a laugh, knowing Liesel hated that title, Valdez hung up.

The FBI agent got them hourly updates on the video feeds. Maldecia leaving the casino, walking with a large crowd through the foot tunnels between hotels, all of whom, if identified, would be questioned. They were emailed a few still-framed photos of possible suspects, but even before they'd received them Dianne had identified the people scanned and dismissed the possibility. The person could have entered a different way, all of which were slowly being checked. Liesel only forwarded pictures of the Mighty or male Blue Hair possibilities to the Mathews. Each picture was returned with a brief note: *Not person we seek.*

Liesel attended the voting then climbed into Griffon's arms to sleep the afternoon—between those hourly updates and the FBI visit—away. They'd hold her election this afternoon and then tomorrow people would vote for the board. The results would be announced in a general meeting and a closing banquet the day after. Two days of conference responsibilities.

Two days and Maldecia's body would be back home. Two days and Liesel could head back to Boise and set some of this chaos behind her.

Chapter 12

"Where are we going again?" Dianne watched the clutch of women from the couch. She had used some cream, the magnets—her fourth set—and Tylenol and was holding together without Sergei. She felt independent. In the last twenty-four hours she had gone to her first gallery art show, seen a movie in an actual movie theater, made out with a hot guy, and spent some time in deep meditation looking for the codex and the Ronin. People flexed in and out of her range but she was still able to sort of establish a book mark of where she left off. After a couple of hours, though, she started to loop through the same minds, like getting lost in the woods and going by the same boulder seven times before you realize you'd seen that before. She needed to eat each time, sleep. She planned on trying again in the morning but for now Liesel wanted to go out with the girls and Griffon couldn't tag along. Yes, Harry and Tammy would be there, but Dianne decided she need more protection than that.

Compared to that morning in Boise after the funeral, she wasn't jittery or high.

"Kee Ping set up a private viewing of Thunder from Down Under," Liesel said. Liesel Grant, now the official leader of the Amazons. Matriarch Grant. Her whole bearing now spoke of confidence and power. Like a mantle had settled over her shoulders as she was voted in. Dianne felt a deep loyalty to her new Matriarch.

Ping had booked the evening a week ago and decided not to cancel even with Maldecia's death hanging over them.

"Ping's a bit of a cougar, isn't she?" Griffon's sister-in-law Tammy said.

"So it isn't a lightning show?" Dianne questioned.

Tammy and Liesel laughed and Anna shook her head but smiled and said, "Thanks for not taking the easy route and..." She pointed to her head.

Jen, the Australian representative, was there too. Quite the gathering of single Amazons plus Tammy. "Any man off his face will drop his daks for a pretty Sheila," Jen said in her thick accent.

Dianne felt comfortable back in her old jeans and wrist bands, though the fitted button down was from yesterday's shopping spree. Last night's dress had exposed more than just her skin. Responding to Anna's words, "I'm working on it. The cream makes it easier. I can't hear past this sitting room and the four voices in here are easy to ignore. Easier, at least." Especially when she would much rather be thinking about Sergei and the kisses they'd shared in the theater.

Or worry about Maldecia's murder. If she'd had more control, sooner, maybe she could have prevented it. Scanned all the male minds and come up with something. Though there was no guarantee the mind she'd heard at the funeral was here. Or that the Ronin killed Maldecia. There was no guarantee that using her powers would do more than further tear down her resistance, shred her mental barriers. The Ronin and Maggie's killer might not be the same guy. Hell, a woman could have killed Maldecia. *Stop.* She took a breath and set aside her worry.

"Five voices," Harry said as she came in from the bedroom looking tan from some time at the pool.

"Thunder is a male review," Liesel checked her lips in a compact and tucked her lipstick in her purse.

"Review of what?"

Anna, annoyed by everyone else, mostly because she wasn't going, said, "They're strippers. Like Chippendale dancers." *Too young. Please. As if.*

Anna's mental annoyance was too loud not to hear. "Oh. What's a cougar?"

"An older woman after younger men," Tammy supplied, ready and waiting to head down. They were to meet Ping in the casino to have dinner before the show.

"I can tell everyone is excited," Dianne said. They were relaxed. Giddy almost. Triumphant over the vote and looking to relieve some tension after the chaos of Maldecia's death and the conference.

"Aren't you?" Tammy said.

No. In fact the more she thought about it the worse the idea seemed. "I don't think I should go. Picking up a bunch of people's sex fantasies?" She stuck out her tongue. Yuck.

Liesel laughed. She was determined to enjoy the night. "You can tell us what the men are thinking when they're stripping for us."

"Probably doing up their grocery list," Tammy quipped, tapped her foot and started flipping through a magazine.

Without giving herself a chance to think too much about the idea, Dianne said, "I need to make a call." Dianne stood and walked over to the phone and stared at it for a minute. She didn't like phones. She wasn't good with them. They made her nervous. The man from the audience with his fiancé, the one that had caught Sergei's belt, maybe they'd like to go. She called the front desk and told the operator the name she was looking for. As she said it, she got from Liesel's head that the non-belt winner was a Mighty. Something about an anniversary gift. Even better.

"Hello?"

"This is..." Her head went totally blank for a second. Crap. She took a deep breath. "I'm calling for James Carney Tanza. Is J.C. there?"

"Just sec," the Mighty handed the phone over.

"Hello?" J. C. said.

"Hi." She was supposed to say hi, wasn't she? "Uhm, is this J.C.?" Who else would it be, idiot? She felt her arms shaking. Sweat gathered in her palms. They were close enough that she could push to find them, tailor her words to their thoughts. Keep it together, Dianne. You can do this.

"This is J.C."

"Your voice doesn't sound girly at all."

"Excuse me?"

Anna threw a pillow at her and in desperation Dianne linked with Anna for guidance. "I'm sorry. Sometimes my mouth works before I tell it to. I was one of the performers at the hypnotism show two days ago? I hope you enjoyed the belt."

He laughed and Anna, across the sitting room gasped at being able to hear the conversation. "We...I mean I did." His voice sounded friendly.

"My name is Dianne Fender and there is a private viewing of Thunder from Down Under tonight. I guess it's a strip—" Anna cut her off and Dianne cleared her throat. "Would you and your boyfriend like to come as my guests? It starts at seven." There was silence on the other end and Dianne wanted to fill it with asinine things but Anna told her to wait.

"Hang on for a second," J. C. finally said. More silence. At least on that side of the phone.

"Dianne Fender, you get out of my head," Anna put her hands on her hips and glared.

"But you're so polite. It's like you're this book on how to act." Pulling the phrase from Anna's head. "Yes, a book on Etiquette and Manners."

"Still there?" J.C. asked.

"Yes."

"We'd love to come. If you are free for dinner before, we'd like to take you out. As a thank you."

"Say yes but that you're bringing a date," Anna crossed her arms over her chest.

"That sounds wonderful. I'm going to bring a few people but they'll pay for themselves. I can get us a table at Il Fornaio at the New York, New York. The host owes me a favor. I didn't rat to his wife that he's having an affair at the show."

"Dianne," Anna whisper-yelled.

"Oh, no. Don't Dianne me. This is going to be great. They have a really good chef."

From the distant side of the phone J.C. laughed. "Remind me to stay off your blackmail list. Shall we say in about a half hour?"

Dianne almost asked him 'say what in a half hour?'

Get off the phone before you make a mistake, Anna pleaded.

Good advice. "Great. Bye."

Now, besides having Tammy and Harry on hand, J.C., who was a cop in San Francisco, and his super powered boyfriend would be there. Yeah, they hadn't volunteered for guard duty, but she could convince them it was in everyone's best interest if they kept Liesel safe.

-#-

Dianne thought the semi-dressed men looked like golden, sculpted Adonis. Every single one of them. The show had more dancers but only four had agreed to do the private show for Kee Ping, which she had paid out the nose for. Dianne let the thoughts of the ladies and the two men surround her as the Performers—that's what they called themselves—came in to meet the audience. Guess when you paid that much you got the VIP treatment.

The room looked like a home theater with a small stage and only two rows of cushioned chairs.

Dressed in different costumes, the men handled the audience with experience. Each thought about the men's physique from the audience lingered or appreciated different things. Kee Ping loved the blonde's hands. Liesel thought the brunette's hair looked a bit like Griffon's but Griffon had the better butt. Tammy fixated on their eyes.

One of the dancers had his own moment of awe. He gazed at J.C. and his partner and wished he could be in such a committed and open relationship. J.C. held his partner's hand and they picked dancers to cheer for. Different from each other because that made it more fun, like some kind of sporting event.

J.C. and Orlando—call me Andy—figured that at least two of the performers were gay. The men had no mental reservations about dancing in front of gay men. Dianne checked.

The bald one—and boy howdy, he had a great set of shoulders—was the oldest. He didn't look all that much older than his companions but he thought forty was too old to do private shows for a bunch of oversexed women. Great shoulders didn't come with a great personality.

Dianne told him to mind his manners, totally channeling Anna when she did. Even though Anna wasn't there. His head jerked up and he smiled politely, totally fake, at Dianne.

"Did ye say something, my lovely Sheila?" He had an Australian accent. They all did. And every single spectator in the room melted at hearing his voice. Even Dianne melted a bit, despite knowing of his insincerity.

"You're a romantic. You'd think after doing—" she caught herself before she said just how long he'd been doing this. "After being a performer you'd be jaded. I see you're still hoping."

Hot body, the sweep and shallow dip of muscles, the ease and comfort of movement. As he moved toward her, heat infused her cheeks and her stomach flipped. Yeah, he was sexy.

"A Seer there? I've heard whispers amongst the staff that we have a psychic staying with us." He didn't believe it. He cocked a hip toward her, dropped his eyelids to turn up the charm. She read the intentional body language in his mind as he made the minute adjustments to indicate interest and to display himself.

"I've heard whispers that you believe in true love, that you're straight and single and..." She starred hard at him for a minute, deciding what to reveal, "And your new black puppy is named Shrimp. Then you can threaten to cook Shrimp on the barbie when he's barking at the neighbors."

The other three dancers laughed and one punched him in the shoulder. The violent one meant it as a sign of friendship. Go figure. Might be a Grant relative. "That's amazing." He reached out to take her hand and place a kiss on the back. Hope. His head was full of hope. Quick, hearing it coming, Dianne used Jen's sleeve and clenched her teeth in concentration.

Instead he got Jennifer's hand. Both Jennifer and the Aussie were surprised, not only that they were the ones touching, but at the electric current their connection caused.

Dianne felt their arousal like a flurry of heat that swirled through her. She froze, afraid to do anything but stand there. She throbbed with her pulse. The fiery ash settled in her nipples, singed her apex.

No more thoughts, time to block out the noise. Too much sex. She removed the tube of lotion from her pocket, she squeezed it and the puff of scent settled her.

"Jennifer is a veterinarian. Single. And older than you by two years. Older women always have a lot they can teach younger men. And you've always had a thing for them."

"Well, Jennifer, it is a right honor to meet you. And you don't look a day over twenty–five."

"Thanks," Jennifer stepped forward and met his charming gaze with a confident smile.

Dianne leaned toward Liesel and in a rather bad stage whisper said. "I'm getting out of here. All these horny people and I'm about to combust."

When she left, she put Harry in charge of Liesel. "Make sure she gets to Griffon safely." Tammy glared, outraged by Dianne's choice of guardian, but Dianne trusted Harry.

It was a full three floors and the opposite side of the hotel before Dianne stopped 'seeing' the dancers strip their clothes off. Holy cow, the brunette was very flexible.

She stopped at the bar and downed two shots of scotch. Then lingered a full ten minutes over a third. Then she switched to rum-and-Cokes.

Dianne unbuttoned another button on her shirt, desperate to cool her heated skin and yet unsure how. She knew about sex, had seen it. Had felt some of the horrible things about it when she touched people, like a rape victim. But because of the whole touching thing she'd not experienced it.

To say she hadn't considered sleeping with Sergei would be an outright lie. Even before they realized they could touch without him sharing his nightmares, she'd been deeply attracted, but she figured nothing could come of it. She'd thought the movie would be like a date and maybe lead to sex. Other people did that, had sex on a first date. However, she didn't have any delusions here. Just because her abilities were manageable now didn't mean they would stay that way. Next week she would be in Boise and he'd be back in DC.

Even now, she didn't know if he liked her, or if he wanted to hook up, or if he would think she was a bad lay and too innocent. How did women enter relationships, put their hearts and bodies at the mercy of men, based on trust?

Trust. A word to convey acceptance and submission. But not a real thing. Couples doubted each other all the time. She'd heard it. Even Liesel and Griffon. He hesitated to share his feelings because it made him vulnerable. Liesel didn't know how anyone could love or rely on her when she didn't trust herself. Yet, they said they trusted each other and loved one another.

She wiped the damp from her neck on her jeans and undid another button.

She pounded on the door in front of her. Then leaned her head against it. A gambler mentally counted funds and decided where he could pull more as he walked down the hall one floor below her. Why could she hear him and not Sergei?

She knocked on the door again, forgetting to raise her head. The vibrations made her head jar and shook some of the thoughts in there loose. Anna wasn't in their room. Now to just clamp down on the urge to go mentally looking for her. Dianne hadn't brought a key, assuming Anna would let her in or that Liesel would let her in if they returned together.

She turned and walked to the stairwell and headed up the two flights to Sergei's room. She knocked. She knocked again and when the door opened she swayed forward.

"Can I touch you?" She realized her blouse gaped open and tugged it closed.

"What?" Sergei rubbed his eyes, half asleep. "It's almost two in the morning."

"Really? I must have lost track of time once I got to the bar." She swayed again and braced herself on the door frame. "You don't have clothes on."

He looked down at himself, perhaps to double check. "I'm wearing shorts."

"Oh." She followed the contours of his sculpted abs, past a shallow bellybutton, to the waistband of his cut off scrubs. They hung along the curve of his hips and dipped low enough to show a patch of blue hair.

"Are you drunk?"

"Rums and Cokes," she said to that gorgeous bellybutton.

He sighed. "You're room is two floors down. Go back to the elevators."

"No."

"Give me a second and I'll get a shirt on. Walk you back to your room."

"No. No key." She ducked around him and took two steps into the room and then very gingerly, very carefully, fell flat on her face. "That hurt."

He lifted her easily and carried her to the bed. Just scooped her six foot plus frame up. Swoosh. It made the air in her lungs flip through her stomach. She floated. Not an altogether good combination.

"I'm not having sex with you."

"Good. Because I'm drunk." She toed off her shoes and pulled the pillow to her chest as he laid her on the bed.

"I'm glad were in agreement."

The third time he'd carried her to bed but the first time she was awake enough to say, "Thank you."

He didn't speak for a moment, then whispered, "You're welcome." He curved around her from behind and brushed a cool hand down her heated cheek.

"If I was sober?"

"Definitely." He pressed a soft kiss to the back of her head.

She'd avoided an awkward situation by soaking in alcohol, escaped not knowing what to do by hiding. Sure, it was for different reasons than the pain of her psychic abilities, but for the very first time she regretted taking the easy out, relying on a crutch.

Chapter 13

In the morning Dianne tried to kiss Sergei awake.

The hotel had planned the room with gamblers in mind. Heavy curtains to block out the sun and thick insulated walls to cut the noise from the family of six next door who were watching Sponge Bob in Spanish. But Sergei had left the drapes open and she could hear people walk past the thin door.

Dianne pressed the side of her face to Sergei's bare chest and stared at the blue stubble on his chin. The soul patch below his full bottom lip was a thick, rich, on-purpose addition of color but the fresh whiskers looked more like bruises or shadows. She pressed her lips to his chin then pulled back to watch his dark purple-black lashes flutter. She leaned in to kiss his mouth.

He turned his head away. "You want a kiss?" his words coated in sleep. "Stop drinking, no more drugs, one hundred percent there, and we'll see." He climbed out of bed.

Dianne checked to see if he had morning wood.

He tugged at his cut-off scrubs that had twisted on his waist. He had all these beautiful dips and twists and muscle and skin that showed each curve to best advantage.

She lifted him off the floor, cradle-style like he had her the night before, and dumped him in a chair. "I'm never 100% there."

His eyes narrowed and that space between his eyebrows shortened. "Sober." He blew out a breath and leaned back in the chair. "I'm not going to bother if you're going to destroy all my efforts."

She straddled his lap, her knees awkwardly pressed between his outer thighs and the arms of the wing-back chair. She wanted to be closer, to press back into this warm skin. "So the kisses are just another treatment?"

He rested his hands at her waist and stared into her eyes, pondering. Then he kissed her. He tasted stale, like day old microwave popcorn—morning breath—but his lips were full and warm and sent delicious tremors down her spine. Very nice.

Then an oily shadow laid over Dianne's thoughts like a soaked pair of jeans, heavy, dense. Someone was in danger.

Liesel would have liked to discover, in a totally different way, exactly how many green pairs of underwear she owned. As it was, walking into her hotel room and having them strewn across the debris was far less than ideal.

Her room was messy. Okay, that was an inadequate description. But she was having a hard time identifying this as *a* room let alone *her* room. The door to the sitting area hung off its hinges. The TV had been thrown out the window, probably onto the roof of the casino area, but she couldn't see for sure from the doorway. From where she stood to the window there was no visible carpet. The bed, destroyed. The mattress and drapes and bedding and bathroom towels, ripped into confetti.

Stay there. Do not enter the room. I'm sending Griffon. I'll be up as soon as I can, Dianne said, somehow knowing she stood in front of destruction.

A lipstick tube lay at her feet. In an alternate universe perspective—she felt the shock but was helpless to do anything about it—she saw the case, nudged it with her toe, and watched it roll.

She cocked her head to the side. Why was it on the floor?

The front of her shins felt hot and tight and refused to move. Her chest constricted as if pushing out all the air in her lungs, though she didn't breathe.

Griffon says he's coming, go open the door for him.

The lipstick was an asterisk mark on a red trail that ran over clothes, her laptop and luggage to the starting point on the dresser. Like a boat marooned on the beach, the dresser tilted to the right. A crack, jagged and rough, ran down its center. The laptop lay in two pieces.

Thump, Thump.

It's Griffon, let him in.

The hallway door stood solid among a mental fog just behind her.

Thump, THUMP. It crashed to the floor and Griffon came in, gun drawn. He took her arm and placed her behind him, one hand back on her hip, pressing to keep her close.

It's Frank.

Frank rushed through the door and if Dianne hadn't warn them Griffon would have fired.

"What's going on? You just suddenly...Oh, shit." Frank said.

"Call the police," Griffon said.

Minutes ago they'd been recharging with breakfast, eating these delicious puffy omelets with fresh mushrooms and spinach. She'd spent the night working out all her emotions by happily screwing her very own sexy boyfriend, who—bonus—loved her. Nights like that required serious carbs.

When Frank showed up, she had left the brothers to chat and headed to her own room to change before the first meeting. The conference goers didn't need to know she hadn't been in her room all night. Today, they would choose the board members and vote the bylaws in.

"I'm fine." She pushed Griffon's arm away. When the arm came back she said, "I promise to keep both hands on you, if you keep both hands on the gun."

He checked the other bedroom and bath before entering her room. He toed through the debris. "Nice thong."

"I didn't know I had so many green pairs." It was asinine but she couldn't think of anything else to say. Her mind didn't run through all the possible suspects or what this could mean. She counted her green undies. And the blue ones: four blue.

"It's clear." Griffon hollered back to Frank. He turned and gathered her into his arms. A warmth scented with security flowed through her body.

"You're shaking," She ached like after a run where she couldn't find her rhythm and had perhaps fallen down a mountain side.

"Dianne wasn't all that forthcoming on the details. 'Liesel needs help' and then the image of your room." He squeezed her and smelled her hair. "Took years off my life."

Dianne came in, giving a mental call as she led Anna and Sergei behind her. *I'm now entering the sitting room, don't shoot. I'm now entering the bedroom, don't shoot.*

"Dianne," Griffon asked, "When did this happen?"

"I didn't see it happen," Dianne said.

"I mean mentally."

"I didn't see it that way either."

"Window has been open long enough that the room is really hot," Sergei said.

The window was open? Oh, yeah the TV.

"The destructive nature denotes a female and a personal knowledge of the victim," Anna said. Thankfully, Anna wasn't lying broken among the wreckage. Frank gaped at Anna, his cell phone to his ear as he spoke with security, already done with the police. Anna had on a pair of leather pants that laced up one side and a dark red shirt. He eyes were heavily lined and she'd added red jewels to all her piercings. "I went to a club, got back as they opened up the restaurant downstairs for breakfast. Been there since."

"They didn't think it was you," Dianne said, "Just staring because you look hot in those pants. You know, like sexy," Dianne clarified.

"Did you touch anything?" Griffon asked Liesel. She shook her head. "We need to protect the crime scene. Liesel and I will wait for the police, but why don't you guys head back to my hotel room? We can meet there and figure out what to do next."

When Griffon said crime scene, a link snapped in place in Liesel's brain. Someone had done this. Her laptop wasn't just broken. Someone had snapped it in half. Someone had touched her stuff. Someone had destroyed the bed. Someone had pissed Liesel off and would pay.

"My room is closer," Sergei offered.

"Plus there are two new rooms with connecting doors, just a flight up. Robert at the front desk will bring us up a few keys." Dianne looked at the ceiling, showing the room mostly the white of her eyes. "You won't want to stay here. Plus, then no one but the six of us will know where the new rooms are. Seven with Robert. And then you and Griffon can be close but still private. Anna can have her own room across the hall—" she turned to look at Frank, her eyes suddenly hot. "It is not creepy."

"How'd you manage that?" Sergei asked.

She shrugged and said, "Todd is going to make an announcement in the next meeting this morning that you are—" She looked at Anna who sighed and crossed her arms, "delayed answering questions for the police concerning M's death but will be available later for questions?" She ended the sentence with an upward swing in tone as if verifying. Liesel nodded.

As the motley group filed out, Griffon gathered her close again. "It's going to be okay. I love you."

"I love you, too." They had messed with the wrong person. She was Liesel Grant. Amazon Matriarch and Griffon's woman. Bring it on.

At least the FBI were in place now to analyze everything. And timid, mentally shattered Blue Hair Dianne had pieced her powers together into an *uber* righteous communication center. Griffon bounced on his toes and scowled at the mess, a boxer waiting to come out swinging from his corner.

Woe unto the idiot that fucked with Liesel Grant.

Harry Grant had always been defined by her place in life. The youngest. Liesel's sister. Karma's sister. The athletic one, the construction worker. *Not* the Amazon. *Not* the leader. Not... well, not a lot of things. So, sometimes, when she felt petty and small and fucking starved for some ... identity of her own... Harry pretended she was an only child.

"Ty, you got any siblings?" Maybe he could relate. They'd walked through the New York, New York, done the gondola ride at the Venetian and now sat at the counter of a fifties style dinner eating ice cream sundaes with whipped cream and cherries. She had hoped to use whipped cream and cherries in a totally different way. Tydus McKinley was...courting her, it seemed, in an agonizingly slow way. Might have to do with being the Matriarch's sister.

She just wanted a diversion, perhaps a friend with benefits. He sparked her body but not her mind. He was guarded about his non-Vegas life and she wasn't drawn in enough to purchase admittance to his real life. That would make her responsible for his heart. The hell with that. She realized she wanted to get laid and Ty would do nicely.

The place had pulled original fixtures and parts from an actual 50's diner and restored them. They'd managed to smooth the transition from hotel to back-in-time seamlessly. Tydus had remarked earlier that he could still smell the linseed oil they'd used to varnish the floor. Too bad the food didn't have the same high-quality standards.

Tydus stuck out his tongue and licked down the side of the long teaspoon as he contemplated his answer. "Yeah, I have a sister." He licked chocolate syrup off his full bottom lip. "What's your sister doing today?"

"Probably working with Dianne." She bit the inside of her lip, thinking about ways to seduce him.

"Harriett," he said, lips pursed and eyebrows forward. He used her full name because she kept using his half name. "Dianne isn't some freak." Misreading her body language. "She didn't choose to be born different. This world isn't ready for people like her. They don't see the potential, the possibilities."

They didn't see? Did he mean Harry didn't see? "You feel very passionate about that." General non-aggressive, non-specific, multi-purpose answer. It slices, it dices, it gets the job done.

"My sister," he checked to make sure he had Harry's attention, then he plunged his spoon in his ice cream, tapped it to the bottom of the dish, dividing the creamy mounds, mixing the toppings. "Half-sister. She's a Blue Hair." He shrugged, looking at the counter. "She has superhuman hearing but as she likes to say, there isn't anything super about it. She hears every single sound. And the volume control is erratic so the ants on the sidewalk sound louder than your heartbeat standing next to her. She...." He sighed. "She suffers."

His mouth thinned and his bottom lip disappeared between his teeth.

"I'm sorry Ty." She brushed her cold hand up and down his bare arm. Trying to comfort but not asking questions, not delving deeper. Because he was still not relationship material.

"I try to take care of her."

"Half-sister from your mother's side?"

Distracted, he said, "Yeah."

That didn't sound right. If the mother had passed on one of the sister's two Amazon genes then mom was an Amazon and Tydus had a fifty percent chance at Blue Hair. The Mighty gene coming from his father. Yet everyone was entitled to their delusions.

She just nodded, counted quietly as she called herself a lust-crazy bitch, and then changed the subject. Yeah, she wasn't very good at the whole emotional support thing. "It's been nice spending the morning together. Want to go back to the hotel?"

"I need to meet with a client in a few hours." Not really a no. He chuckled and ate a bite of his ice cream. "Want my cherry?" No hint of sexual overture.

Maybe she could make the first move, just spell it out for the guy. She turned her body toward his and leaned on the counter, shoulder back to display her moderate chest to full potential. He glanced down and smiled as he handed over the maraschino. He followed it forward to kiss her cherry-full mouth. His eyes finally full of heat.

He had a very capable mouth, soft and warm. His lips as expressive in movement as they were in speech. He had a great mouth.

She smiled and he kissed her again. "Want to go dancing?"

"No," she didn't want to go dancing. She leaned back and laughed, not willing to be more blunt. Her cell chirped and she stood, one foot planted on the stool's bottom rung, to dig out her phone. Seeing it was Liesel, she tapped the phone to answer the call.

"Hey sis, what's going on?"

As sisters, you got pretty good at reading each other's voices, even with very little said. "Sorry I'm interrupting your fun." Liesel's voice sounded pissed, quieter than just plain angry. And though Harry could read the anger, it was totally different then the I'm-pissed-at-you tone.

"What's wrong?" Harry stuck a finger in the opposite ear to block the sound of gambling and diner behind her.

"My room's been ransacked."

"Oh, god. Are you okay?" Tydus stood and put money on the counter, steering her out of the diner, with a hand on her elbow, through the casino, toward the exit.

"Everyone is okay."

"Did they take anything?" Harry had been the one to discover the codex had been stolen. One broken window but nothing else out of place. The thief knew what they wanted and took it.

"I can't tell yet," and before Harry could ask another question, asked one of her own, "Where are you? Dianne couldn't find you."

Tydus held the door for her and she smiled her thanks as he steered her out toward the front door and the waiting taxis. "I'm in—hell, I don't know—north end of the strip. Almost across from the Stratosphere."

Tydus hailed a taxi and gave directions to the driver. She slid in and when he didn't follow, "Hang on Lies," she muted the microphone, "aren't you—?"

"Sounds like a family thing."

Oh yeah, family drama and antics were sure to follow. "I wouldn't come either." She smiled. "Thanks."

"Call me," Tydus said as he closed the door to the taxis.

Ten minutes after the police arrived, another knock sounded at the door. Griffon figured the Robert that Dianne had mentioned from the front desk had brought the new room keys.

Less than an hour ago, he'd had several years stripped off his life as he saw Liesel, probably the first time she'd been alone since the airport, step into the physical representation of hate that used to be her hotel room. So, yes, it was understandable that he was edgy. He just wished the anger wasn't accompanied by fear. He would be glad when they were all back in Boise. The threat wouldn't disappear but he knew almost every police officer, had an armory, and could hunker down and ride it out.

He checked the peephole. The older Mathew from the Harvest Team stood at attention in the hall. Shoulders back, chin up, like a drill Sergeant presenting his squad for formal inspection. Griffon opened the door.

"It came up on the police scanners that Ms. Grant's room was...?" The Sergeant's eye went wide as he saw the destruction behind Griffon; very telling since it was his first show of emotional reaction.

Griffon liked that the man got right to the point. "And that concerns you how?" Griffon sidestepped to fill more of the door way.

Junior sulked with his arms crossed and back to Griffon. Saying I don't consider you a possible threat. If the stance was more to guard their six his arms would be down by his side.

Sarge smacked the back of Junior's head. He stumbled forward then turned with a sigh. He didn't rub the spot or reprimand Sarge, which reminded Griffon these two weren't teammates. "The Modesitte don't play at diplomacy," the accent heavy but clear.

Sarge didn't censor the Modesitte—perhaps a Mighty family name—but continued as if uninterrupted. "Jordan expresses his gratitude for sending the photos and asked that we offer aid to a friend."

A very formal speech, slightly awkward despite his best efforts. Liesel ducked around Griffon and extended her hand "Mr. Mathew. Thanks for coming to offer me aid. It was very sweet of you. We are managing the situation." She smiled, head tilted and then offered her hand to the Modesitte. "Liesel Grant."

He shook her hand, tried to hide his awe and said nothing. Yep, boy, behold the awesome presence of Liesel Grant. Griffon didn't bother to stifle his proud grin.

"Do they know about Dianne?" Liesel asked him quietly.

He kept his eyes on the two men before him, using his body language and eyes to convey how absolutely deadly he could be if needed. "Yes."

"We have our Blue Hair scanning in intervals for Mr. Ole. And we have Jordan's email and the number you provided. We hope you find who you are looking for." Then with a regal air she turned slightly toward Griffon. Both a dismissal and a sign of support. "Griffon, the police have a few more questions and Harry's bribing some maids to help us clean the room up."

"Okay."

She nodded to the Harvest Team. "Gentlemen." She kissed Griffon's cheek and stepped back into the room.

"Mathew."

"Griffon," Sarge said. Neither addressed the Modesitte and the door closed.

Chapter 14

Sergei hunched over his cup of coffee, and let the fragrant steam sooth the tension in his face. A tall order. He still felt the intimate press of Dianne's body as it straddled his that morning, before they ran to check on Liesel. It would be a rebellious risk to take Dianne to bed, but he'd always been a risk taker.

They'd left Liesel's room with her strong insistence that they both eat. What good were they to her if they dropped from malnutrition? He'd put away a Monte Cristo sandwich and a full plate of fruit. Dianne was on her second plate of French toast.

"Have you ever been kissed? Before the fountain?" Sergei asked Dianne.

"Yeah." She moved her cup around the table. She tugged at her cloth bracelets, circled them.

"Did it hurt?" he whispered. His hand rested on her thigh, her hand covered it, pressed it down. Her touch linked them and allowed her the peace and quiet to eat her breakfast. She looked around the room and picked at her eggs.

"Very badly." Tears welled in her eyes. "I thought it had been left too long." Each word she spoke was carefully chosen. "I was turning twenty-one and didn't want...." Her voice stumbled and stopped as she blinked away tears.

Tears weren't along the path to getting laid, time to change the subject.

But she wasn't done. "Never having kissed? When you're a teenager that's okay. But I'd been on my own so long." She moved her hand, touched the top of his with just her fingertips then slid them down tracing his fingers. She lay her fingers over the top of his. "I met someone in a bar."

"Just a stranger?"

"Someone I knew from online."

"Really?" His dry throat clicked shut. The raw pain in her voice felt intimate, alluring. Pulled him to know. Someone that mattered? Where was he now? And what was wrong with him that he was glad that it had hurt. Sick bastard.

Dianne laughed and sighed, releasing the pain of that awkward moment with her breath. "I thought he... well, his life had been safe. He wasn't a doctor or cop or...anything horrible or tragic. Nothing that I knew about." She swallowed and looked from their pile of hands into his eyes. Before his question, she had been thinking about Liesel's room, grateful that their matriarch and Anna had both been out when the devil came knocking. Seeing that level of destruction...whoa. Her grandmother's body wasn't marred in any way. Maybe the killer was escalating. Poison or suffocation had ramped up to pure physical rage.

Sergei waited for her to continue. As she stared, his lashes lengthened, the color deepened, the little lines to the side became sexy, or at least seemed to. This new exciting twist of desire in her belly stirred an electric shiver inside her blood.

"What was in his past?"

His eyes were such a beautiful brown. "He was lonely. Had been since his wife died many years before. So much more intense because they'd had it so good."

Just below Sergei's nose was the swooping indent above his full lips, where the skin flexed as he spoke. He hadn't shaved, pale blue-white hairs forming along the curve. They rasped against her fingertip. She gasped at the thrill that ran through her body like a wave, a backward release of pressure. Her hand shook as she placed two finger tips to his bottom lip, barely there, barely touching.

"How does that feel?" she asked. Before he could speak, she tried to explain. "When Whitney Houston use to sing *I Will Always Love You*? Those unbelievable high notes of power that sizzle down your arms? That's how it feels for me. How does it feel?"

He cleared his throat and, instead of answering her, placed his same two fingers on her lip. He held his hand still and she played with the power of pressing in close, flattening her lip against his fingers. Pulled away, not really touching but hinting at it. She shifted her lip back and forth, felt her lip tingle, but it felt good, warm. She closed her eyes and lingered in the feeling.

Sergei, took a shuddering breath, "God, you're sexy."

She opened her eyes and stared at him. He had helped her so much, let her experience things. If they slept together, if she got to experience this, would it require her to trust him completely?

"Come back to my room," Sergei said.

There was an air of danger to his words that suggested crackling air and black clouds on the horizon. "Sergei, I want that. Sex. But I don't want...a relationship." Yeah, that was sure to save her from all of these emotions, by ignoring them.

He pushed her lip flat. "Stop thinking so god damned much and live. Just let go and live."

When he lifted his fingers, she said simply, "Yes."

They didn't make it to the hotel room.

Sergei touched people all the time. Patted a hand in comfort, inserted a tube past throat muscles, and held firmly to a limb as he set broken bones. He washed life off his hands, blood, bile, sweat.

And no matter how many naked bodies he saw or miracles he aided, he loved those first moments of sex. Always in awe of the build and fit and color of his partners skin, how it responded to his touch, sank as he pushed, gripped as he stroked.

Dianne. She added a whole different level to sex, a virgin not just to intimacy but to touch, to kissing, to afterglow.

He would be her first but he know he wouldn't be her last. Once she realized that she had control of her own powers she could sleep with anyone. Even if that trust only extended to the sheets.

"Dianne," he lifted her hand away from his nipple, her arm deep up inside his shirt, "Wait."

She groaned and the people on the elevator watching them turned their heads and scurried out of the elevator when the doors opened on the next floor.

"Did you do that?" Sergei asked, tried his damnedest to sound stern. It was no good. That kind of lust, the must-have-now response, was erotic. He laughed and pulled her to his chest. The elevator closed and continued up. He mouthed hotly at her ear and whispered, "Make sure the hallway is clear."

She arched into his touch. "It is."

He wondered if she realized she was using her powers while touching him. He let her pull his shirt off. She ran her warm hands over his bare chest, brushed against his skin, and kneaded his muscles. Like a standing message.

Erotic exploration.

The elevator door opened and he stepped forward to block it from closing as she bit his shoulder. A press of blunt teeth, then her tongue laved wet warmth over the mark to sooth the skin. He moaned and clenched his jaw. The cautious walk down the hall was going to be hard in these tight jeans. Already it added a tangy note of pain to his pleasure. "Come on."

She shook her head and mouthed against his nipple, "Now. Here."

It would be so simple to strip her, pin her against the elevator wall and take. Pleasure pushed him up to his toes, biting his lip and shivering. Then she sucked his nipple as she palmed his jean covered dick and he came. She laughed, this rich heat of sound rolling through her whole body. He shivered through an aftershock.

"That was hot." She kissed him and the elevator door tried to close on them again. When he urged her forward once more she finally left the elevator. He marched her along one-handed, trying but failing to not notice the way his jeans stuck to his pubic hair and thighs. He needed out of these jeans.

"Are we done? How long before we can try again?" Her tone curious, not bothered that he had come first and so quickly. He smiled, and thumbed her hand in his. He shifted uncomfortably as he took out his key and prayed the green light would register the first slide of the card.

She went in first and dropped his shirt on the floor, then just waited and he slowed enough in his mute frenzy to stare. To look. Clear, open face, with the beautiful eyelashes around the hazel eyes and that full mouth. Her pert little breasts and that tight ass curving into long stellar legs.

He placed her hand on his elbow, pressed to let her know to keep her hand on him, then undid his jeans, pulled them down his legs as he toed off his shoes.

"You're not wearing underwear." She tilted her head, cheeks flushed as she watched his body appear. She was letting him have something, though she didn't fully understand how much, and because he was enough of a bastard to want it anyway, he took her trust and tried to give her something in return. His thoughts.

"You have this amazing mouth." Free of clothing, he reached up and pressed his thumb over her bottom lip, watched it spring back. It thinned as she smiled. "You're so sexy and kind and..." and he sucked at this whole talking thing. His dick stirred with interest again.

"Let me touch you." He undressed her slowly, stripped each lawyer away with a gentle hand, touched or kissed or licked the flesh as it was revealed. "It makes me so horny to see your bare skin. All these long sleeves and covered skin but then you reach for something," his palm skated along the waistline of her jeans. "And I'd see your stomach or back or wrist and, oh," he gritted his teeth and moaned.

She breathed in quick bursts, eyes half-lidded, pulse thumping through her body. Her panties were wet. "Oh, god that is so fucking hot Dianne." He stroked her through the material and she arched forward to push into his hand.

"I guess we're not done?"

He looked her in the eyes and smiled, winked. "No."

"Good."

He led her to the bed and had her sit. She kept a hand on his shoulder as he kissed from her knee to her lacy edged underwear. He slid his tongue inside and she shuddered, "Sergei."

He was glad they hadn't made the bed yet, the white sheets a perfect back drop to her bare skin. "That's right *Svyet*. My sun, so hot," She laid back on the bed, keeping her fingers in the bristles of his hair. He pulled her panties to the side and licked and sucked and kissed. She twitched and squirmed. It was such a power rush to watch her, at first uncertain then needy and finally embracing her pleasure, pressing in rhythm, urging him to the right place.

She tasted so good.

She let go of his head and came as she gripped the sheets. He kissed up her body, lingered over her breasts as she shook through aftershocks. He propped himself on an elbow and watched her glassy eyes.

"You're smirking," she said.

The sound of her breathy, husky voice made him smile harder. "That was awesome, feeling you come against my mouth," she blushed. "Knowing I was doing that to you. Helping you feel so good. So yeah, I guess I'm a bit—"

"Smug?"

"Pleased."

She touched his check. "I think I'm lying in a puddle."

He laughed, feeling so light and happy and that finally sobered him. The vulnerability was black coffee strong. Sergei rolled them away from the wet spot. "Come touch me."

She looked at him for a while and he just waited. She would say what she thought he should hear. Finally she started to explore his body. Detached, analyzing, seeing were all the scars or freckles or hairs were. Touching but without heat. He gritted his teeth and did his best to hold still.

He had a great body, cut with muscle, skin soft, and blue. Blue from the pale hairs on his arms to his almost hairless chest. The thin patch of hair on his torso gathered over his sternum and pointed down his body, darkening to a royal blue and thickening as it trailed to his bellybutton. It went further, nested around the base of his balls but his dick distracted her. She touched it with just her finger tips. "It's silky." Then curved her hand around, "and hard."

"And sensitive." He took her hand and helped her relax her grip.

She giggled at his strangled tone and felt his dick jump in her hand. The muscles in his stomach tightened. Another stroke and squeeze and his hips lifted slightly. "Wow, that's so cool."

He shook his head and closed his eyes. She wanted them open so she kissed his hip, right next to the royal blue hair. It felt like hair, smelled muskier than the hair on his head, was softer than the bristles of his chin. His eyes were still closed. What would it take to get him to open his eyes? She licked the spongy tip of his dick and jumped when he moaned. "Cool."

"You said that." He had his eyes open and reached out a hand to stroke her arm, shoulder, hair. She leaned forward and kissed his mouth as she stroked his hard length, feeling her hand dampen. He tasted weird, tangy, and it was a minute before she realized she was tasting herself. A bolt of pure desire thumped through her and her toes curled and she shuddered.

She kissed and kissed and kissed.

Playing with his tongue and nibbling at his lips, quickly he was lifting his hips and thrusting his tongue into her mouth a counterpoint rhythm. He was going to come and the thought startled her out of sync.

"Dianne," he moaned.

"Aren't we supposed to...?" She couldn't think of the right words, she just knew she wanted him in her. Now. She toyed with the idea of letting him go, breaking contact, and seeking the answer in someone else's head. Sex Etiquette. But she didn't want to share this.

"Will you...?" She hesitated, knowing that some people found it offensive. But he had used it. "Fuck me?"

He kissed her, pressed hard at her lips for a minute then reached down and slid a finger into her hot folds. "You're so tight and I don't want it to hurt."

"I can take—"

"This isn't a bravery or strength contest Dianne, I want it to be good." He said with quick defensive anger.

Geez. "It's already been good." He groaned as she pushed into his hand, trusting that she was safe, that he would do this right. He added another finger then rolled her to her back. She felt the heat of desire building again. She really liked that feeling. Like kinetic power storing heat in her limbs and core, ready to zap her with a surge of pleasure. He settled himself between her legs and thrust in hard.

"That hurts," she yelled at him and smacked him on the shoulder. Really she was just surprised and felt stretched and awkward. He held tightly to her body, prepared for a fight, then relaxed as she didn't pull away. He covered her face with kisses, pressed his teeth to her chin, drifted lower. As he sucked her nipple she let go of the last of her tension, felt the pain slip beneath delight.

"Here it goes again." Like riding a roller coaster, perhaps, since she had never done that either.

He laughed and stroked harder, once then little ins and outs. In, and out. Her mind melted and she felt only the rolling pleasure of his body. "Sergei. Sergei, Sergeisergei." Saying his name faster and faster, panting and then she came hard, feeling him tense and shutter a couple of thrusts after her.

As she regained her breath she tried to speak. "Now there are two wet spots."

He laughed so hard that tears gathered at the edge of his eyes. He rolled her to the center, used the sheet to wipe them down. His hand stilled and he looked up at her. His skin paled. "We didn't use protection."

"I'm clean. I don't have AIDS or anything."

"Pregnancy?" His voice edgy with sarcasm.

"Mood killer." She pushed his chin out of the way and settled her head on his chest. "They have those morning after things, right?"

"Yeah," his voice was tight, hesitant. He rubbed her shoulder.

"And next time we'll be more careful."

He shook his head, but she felt him smile even though she couldn't see it. More a carnal knowledge of just how he straightened, stilled as he grinned. And they both drifted to sleep.

Chapter 15

Sergei laid for a moment adjusting to the weight of his empty arms, listening for Dianne. He heard several clicks and lifted an eyelid to stare across the room. Dianne, naked, took his picture. She smiled over the top of her phone at him and then turned the phone a quarter turn before taking another shot. She walked around the bed. He tried to follow her with his eyes.

"Hold still."

The sheet barely covered his hips and with a naughty laugh he pushed it lower to show his pubic hair, made sure his hipbones were on display. She laughed too then knelt at mattress level to take another angle. As he laid there listening to her laugh, he thought about how infrequently she laughed. Even when she made others laugh or gasp in shock, she stayed level. Only the gleam in her eyes gave her away.

It was early afternoon. Hopefully post any cleanup effort in Liesel's room but before the vote.

"How do you feel?" he asked.

"Good."

"I'm sorry about the condom."

"You're clean—"

"I am but you'll need to remember for your next lover that—"

She turned quickly and went into the bathroom slamming the door behind her. He groaned and closed his eyes. Handled that well, bastard. He'd call a local pharmacy and make sure they had Plan B available and go pick it up for her. Get a box of condoms. He used his phone to pull up a list of pharmacies that carried what they'd need. Turns out they delivered.

She poked her head out of the bathroom a few minutes later, eyes huge, looking like a lost child. Adorable. "Want to take a shower with me?"

Adorable? Man, he walked an *uber* thin line. He'd sure as hell better watch his angle or he'd fall and land on his own scalpel. "Just going to avoid—?"

"Yes, I am," she said quick and loud. She bit her lower lip. "Lots of people...well, relationships take time and this may or may not work. And, well...." She sighed and looked at him again. A direct stare. "I'm hoping it does."

"Because I can touch you."

"Asshole," she yelled and went back in the bathroom leaving the door open.

"Dianne? Come on, you're great, but just because we can have sex—" The rest of his words were drowned out as she turned on the shower.

She yelled out through the open door. "If it was just sex I would have slept with you the night of the hypnotist."

"The night we were busy with the Harvest Team? The night you chickened out and left me to deal?" he swung his legs over the side of the bed. He didn't hear what she said next. "What?"

"Get your blue ass in here."

He leaned in the bathroom door and she peeked out from behind the shower curtain.

"It's not just sex, or gratitude. I like you." She reached out and grabbed him and pulled him in the shower.

Shit, she was strong. His shins hit the tub. The water was hot as hell and he hissed. She took up the soap and started to scrub at him, talking the whole time. "You're not fake around me."

He snagged the soap out of her hands and glared. No, he hadn't charmed her like everyone else. But he had still lied. He turned down the water. "We're not scrubbing for surgery here."

He handed the soap back and watched as she washed her own body, sliding the soap in a casual way over her pert, brown nipples. Oh man. The best thing in the world was wet skin. He felt loose and rested and hungry. Classic symptoms of extra oxytocin from great sex.

Hey. Serious conversation here. His overheated body needed to chill.

She had to see him. He needed her to see him. To really see the darker side of him. But confessing those things was scarier than multiple gunshots with an unknown street drug in play. For the first time in his life he wished someone could read his mind.

She needed the truth. He had never removed a bandage slowly and he wouldn't start with Dianne. "How did you take my picture?" The soap smelled gender neutral and the bathroom matched the theme of the room, Vegas hotel. He slid the soap between his fingers absently. "Wasn't it hard to focus when you weren't touching me?"

"You mean the mental noise?" she asked. "I used some of that lotion."

His laugh sounded cruel even to his own ears. "That witch doctor's sludge?"

She washed the last of her shampoo out of her hair and stared at him for a minute. "What do you mean?"

"It's fake, a placebo. It doesn't actually work," he scoffed.

"The magnets?" Her eyes wide and guileless.

"Fake," he made sure his voice sounded flat, uncaring. He scrubbed extra hard with the shampoo, ran the suds down his body.

"You've used them before," part accusation, part dawning awareness.

"My father. And my baby brother Peyton." Even knowing he was about to say his brother's name, in the middle of trying to flatline his emotions, still his voice quivered as he spoke. He could hide the hurt from everyone but himself. "He killed himself and eventually my father stopped believing. Or just wanted the real drugs more."

"What about the wide angle lens and the hypnotist?" her tone sounded metallic.

"Now that's just you being impressionable." He tilted his head back to rinse the soap off, waited for the boom.

She didn't slap him. Not his Amazon.

Her fist connected at a sharp angle to his chin and he cracked a tile as his skull hit the wall. He shook his head, sending water and multi-colored stars everywhere as she climbed out. Her hand shook as she closed the shower curtain, the metal links clanging against the shower rod. He rinsed the rest of the way off, felt his chin carefully and listened as she dried off, cussing and muttering to herself.

Bandages. Yep, just rip them the fuck off.

He waited for her to leave the room.

He picked the broken tile off the tub floor and chucked it into the trash. She knew now. Good. Right. She would pull back and he wouldn't have to work so hard to protect his heart. He wished she'd hit him again so the ache in his head matched the one in his chest.

Sergei had been asked to hold Dianne's hand during the vote to make it truly secret. The vital information about her being able to use her powers while touching him? He left that out of the briefing. Nothing like a little self-torture to erode the soul. And being close, touching her, wanting when he couldn't and might never again? Torture. Maybe he needed to think long and hard about constantly putting himself in difficult situations.

His internship in D.C. started in a week. D.C. was the exact opposite of Hermitville, Nowhere State, USA, taking photos of heroes from a distance. He'd done the right thing not only telling her the truth, but breaking things off now so they could gain some closure.

Frank, Griffon's brother, had rigged four computers on a secure network to act as ballots. Each person signed in as if logging into HOAX and were routed to an anonymous database to vote. Votes were also taken from absent members the same way and monitored by Freddy Rayne back in Boise to verify no cheating. The results were instant and confirmed within five minutes.

Just a matter of getting those present to line up, vote, and move on. He clicked his choices and lingered over the submit button because Dianne tapped her shoe. She worked hard to get the sneaker to make a noise. He directed them to the back of the room and took up wall space. He could let go, head back to his room. But he couldn't let her go until she understood. He'd required her trust, manipulated her feelings and betrayed her. Didn't she want better than that? She sure as hell deserved way better than him.

Though they were holding hands, Dianne avoided him. She stood childishly as far away as their clasped hands would allow. Their arms pulled at the shoulder sockets. Even now, that made him smile.

"I'm not sorry." He wouldn't stand here at opposite ends of a taunt arm, ignoring each other. "This is who I am. You must see that. I give people what they want and smile. But the whole time? I'm thinking about what's in it for me."

Sergei yanked her to him, wrapped a steel arm around her and continued in his hushed tone, "Stop it. We are totally wrong for each other. Finishing my residency? Easier to get what I want when a person likes me. Helping Veranda? She feeds me, watches my place when I'm gone. I'm manipulative and dark and you have to see that."

She knew the truth now. If she could look past that maybe they could enjoy the sex as something temporary and fun. "You have to. You can't be with me and not see that side. You can't choose me when you don't know me." Fuck, he hadn't meant to go that far.

She stopped struggling and stared at him, eyebrows pinched together as she frowned. "What are you talking about? Who the hell is Veranda?"

He continued to speak quietly, hoping she'd do the same. Yeah, it didn't sound like Dianne did quiet. "I tricked you. Made you believe."

"But it helped me. It made me stronger. I believe in myself now and...." She shook her head. "Dark side that wants to help Blue Hairs and your sister Portia? Dark side that's determined to protect me from you?" She rolled her eyes. "You're such an idiot. Do you know that? An idiot." Not keeping her voice down, not his Amazon.

He let go of her and tried to march away, but she grabbed at him again.

"Sergei. Sergei, stop." She dug in her heels. "I see you," she whispered, finally dropping her voice. Even though nearly every eye was already trained on them. "And you're wrong." She pulled him around. "What? You think you're so special? That you are the only one on this planet that thinks things that they don't say? That have ulterior motives for helping people? You're so normal it's boring."

He jerked back from the slapping words and she got really close, pushed him against a wall and kissed his swollen jaw. What kind of argument was this? Perhaps two Blue Hairs couldn't do anything the regular way.

Tammy Griffon cleared her throat and announced the winners. "Philip Ralphe." Philip's supporters applauded.

Dianne ignored it, kissed his chin again and waited for the noise to subside after, "Emilio Corby," was announced for the second slot.

"Most people have a mix of reasons." She wrapped her arms around his neck, let herself hang a bit from his stiff frame like a baggy sweater. "Some are noble reasons, a few good reasons, and the rest are selfish. All in one person." She pulled his body close for a real kiss. "And? So? That's normal. I'm the expert here. Listen to me."

"Jennifer Hadley," Tammy said and waited for the applause to subside, not a long wait since far fewer had voted for the Aussie.

"Now that you're done being stupid, can we go back to your room and have sex?"

Dianne didn't see the truth. She didn't realize that he acted without regret.

He moaned into her neck, shook his head and tried to listen, process what she had just said. But how did you ask for reassurance on something that big? Ask for her to say it again? "Really?"

"Yep, sex would be great."

He laughed and so did she. She squeezed him and said, "Oh, the thought? Inner side that isn't perfect? Yes, really."

"Sergei?" She said names so rarely, just spoke and expected people to know she was talking to them. "I've seen black hearts. Their actions speak as loud as their thoughts. You do good." She looked down at his shoulder, pursed her lips. "That's why I'm with you. So, yes really. You're normal."

"Boring?"

"Average even."

He tilted her mouth and pressed his lips against hers, licked his way in, pressed his teeth against her bottom lip as he drew back.

"Fourth and final board position will be held by.... Oh, me,

Tammy Griffon." Tammy blushed and nodded to the audience's vocal support.

Sergei vaguely heard Tammy give congratulations and reminded people about the closing banquet. It all meant that he could take Dianne back to his room so he could have all kinds of selfish sex while making her come twice as much.

Dianne had honestly thought she would be safe. That the only one in any real jeopardy of getting his heart broken was Sergei. She had even warned him off, that she wasn't looking for a relationship. Way to think ahead, Dianne.

He peeled her sock off, the last article of clothing between them, and placed his warm mouth against her calf, kissed slowly up to her knee, licked a slow path along her inner thigh. Thank god she was already sitting on the edge of the bed or that tongue would have made her fall. She stroked his head, shoulders, back, trying to keep him close, unsure if she wanted him to take her now or linger. Yes. Both.

Instead of giving her oral, he fluttered kisses up her stomach and pressed her back to lay on the mattress and then he drew her nipple into his hot moist mouth. His lips rolled her tip as it tightened in a desperate effort to stay in his mouth, reaching up toward him. He braced himself above her, so only his mouth touched her. But it felt like he'd attached a silky cord from her left nipple to her clit and with each tug, lick, suck it was as if he tugged, licked, and sucked her clit. Which felt amazing. Hot damn.

He pulled back and blew on her wet skin. The breathy tickle caused bumps to breakout across her chest. Cold torture compared to the immense heat of his mouth. She groaned.

She pulled at his shoulders. *Come back, touch me. Right there.*

He switched breasts. The clever man had attached that imaginary cord to that breast as well. He bit her, pressed blunt teeth into her tender flesh and she hollered. He licked the sore flesh, grinning the whole time and then, with her clinging on for dear life, sucked with a rolling tongue as he massaged the other breast.

The unexpected, blasting orgasm tilted reality and grayed out her vision. So caught up in the sensation, just feeling, she hadn't realized how close she'd been.

"I wanted to do that really bad," he said. His shoulders shuddered and he pressed his sweaty forehead against her neck, nuzzling in, breathing sexy pheromones into her skin. Getting her ramped up all over again.

"Suck my breasts?" she smirked.

"Make you come from just touching your breasts."

She pushed and rolled him onto his back and straddled his hips. He smiled and stroked her hip, his erection pressing up between her legs. She squirmed just to see him bite his lip and moan.

She started to pull the bands off her hands. "My favorites burned off in the fire." Okay, slightly out of left field, but the good Doctor could keep up. The first one was doubled on her right middle finger, a cloth ring. It rolled off and she snapped it like a rubber band at the alarm clock. "I bought these in the hospital gift shop." She dropped the two on her right wrist to the floor. Her finger and wrist had tan lines where the hair-ties had been, the skin pale and waxy like fingertips fresh from a long soak in the tub.

He took her bare wrist and kissed her pulse point, rubbed his thumb over the paler skin.

She didn't want her hand back. With a single hand twist she pulled off the three from her left wrist, tossed them over the bed. "It was a way to pretend."

"That you still had hair?"

Okay, so she didn't know why the sudden urge to share. People took advantage of other people's soft-spots impulsively. Show any weakness, reveal a hidden truth and people revealed *your* secret, broke your trust, and tore you open. It seemed to be a survival instinct. Destroy before being destroyed. She'd worked her whole life staying guarded. Pretending not to have a single insecurity.

But with Sergei, well she wanted him to know her. All of her. Wanted to give him all that she had. Her body. Her thoughts. Her crazy-ass adventures as a photographer. Her soft spots. And yeah, it was a way to say 'thank you' to the man who'd made living possible but it was also....well, maybe she loved him and wanted to see if he really could be trusted. The placebo mojo aside he was a good man. For now she'd keep that weakness to herself.

"A way to pretend that my home hadn't melted with the fire; that I was in time to save   Grandma Maggie." He pulled her into a hug and she realized he wasn't hard beneath her any longer.

"You did the right thing, Dianne. You helped those people."

Yeah, and she knew she would make the same choice again. Regret only made her the victim instead of fully capable of steering her own fate.

The last band was another one doubled on her left index finger, between knuckles, half way down her finger. She took his right hand and rolled the band down his pinky finger to the base. "You can keep this one."

Ridiculous, right? To give a naked guy waiting to get laid a hair tie when he didn't even have long hair? But she felt vulnerable and exposed, completely, for the first time since she was eleven. Not only was she out, but she felt free. She liked this, felt safe that Sergei would protect her, wouldn't take advantage of her vulnerability. Because heaven knew she didn't have a chance in hell to know what he thought about her soft underbelly.

This was why people bared their souls to doctors, on reality shows, and to strangers in shopping malls. It felt damn good.

He turned his hand this way and that to look at the cloth ring. Then he lifted her up and seated her on his hips, pushed deep inside of her.

"We've got to talk about your delivery," she moaned as she arched her back, straining down to get him even deeper as he finished hardening. Neither of them were fully ready but the heat built with a hip-bucking intensity that had her thrashing back into each of his thrusts.

"So good," he moaned.

He looked so good with his muscles straining, his complete focus on her face as he guided her up and up and up and up. How could they call it a crash or fall when you flew so high. It was more like reaching the sun and being engulfed in flames, but in the good way.

She laughed at the thought, at the pure happy energy flowing between them and he came, shouting her name, holding tight to her hips and her own orgasm just behind him. How could she not when he was so sexy?

Safe? Nope, she was far from the land of safe and had no interest even looking up the embassy. Safety was for sex-deprived cowards. And she was on the sex-full, coward who'd sucked-up-the-courage-and-taken-what-she-wanted side. She found her band around his finger and traced it. *Mine.*

Griffon sat at a round table facing the lit podium where Liesel stood. He had a couple of hotel security people covering the area, he'd checked the place over—every inch—himself and as the final official scheduled conference event, Liesel was as safe as he could make her outside a full secret service lock down.

"Let me tell you a story," Liesel said. The way the audience settled, stilled, at her simple words was a type of magic. Dianne might be psychic but Liesel had power in her voice. Lights dimmed so people could eat and still see Liesel. Griffon was tired of conference food and couldn't wait to get home and eat a bowl of cereal in his own kitchen.

"Lindsey Delphi joined the Marines right out of high school. She wanted to feed the crave she felt to help others and knew that serving her country and then later using the GI bill to pay for a college degree in nursing would open many opportunities to help."

He'd had his eyes open wide when he leaped into this relationship with Liesel. He knew about her controlling family, about her hectic work and volunteer schedule. He had even known that, given the chance, she could kill a man with her bare hands. He didn't know a thrashed bedroom would hurt worse than an hour spent interviewing emotional, crying, teenage girls. So he had come to a very important decision.

"She has described the need as 'an ache, a listless sorrow.' She took to military life like bee to pollen. She met and married another soldier and with six months left of active duty, they decided to start a family. She got pregnant immediately, often the case when you think things will take longer, but no worries because the timing would be fine.

"Twins, a joy and definitely a purpose to life. Then, when they were a year old, her reserved unit was called to go to Iraq. Like any mother and soldier she struggled with leaving but found relief in knowing her husband would be home with the kids. Until his unit was called as well."

Griffon hadn't known that he'd willingly step into protector mode and sacrifice himself and, if needed, others to save her. His love for her had made him worry. Was he vulnerable for feeling so deeply? He could no longer have these loose what-ifs, hanging over his head.

"Grandparents stepped in and filled the gap but Lindsey, not realizing how her Amazon body would be torn with the need to protect her kids, started to deteriorate. She held out, six months and she'd go home. One month left and her son was diagnosed with leukemia. One week, home on leave before her term of enlistment was up, enjoying the healing freedom to nurture her family and she was stop-lossed."

"What's that?" Dianne asked those around her. She could have asked for the information mentally or just pulled it from one of their heads. He saw it as progress that she wasn't resulting to those tactics.

Anna answered in a hushed tone. "The military has the right to extend your term of service without notice, indefinitely, during a time of war."

Liesel had continued undisturbed with her story. "—Lindsey's lawyers have contacted me. They want to show that she was driven to AWOL because of her genetic makeup."

Dianne again, "They made her choose between her family and her country? That was stupid of them."

Dianne was such a trip. Determined to help, confident that people would just believe whatever she told them. Had she ever considered working as a private investigator? "Every soldier, Amazon, Mighty or not, has to make that decision. If not us, who? Someone must defend this country," Griffon told Dianne.

"Yeah, but she should have just been medically discharged. Her body was destroying itself. Or the Red Cross could step in—" Dianne said.

There was hushing from the rest of the table. Griffon scanned the room, making note of all the familiar faces, looking for agitation. He heard another part of Liesel's speech. "—medical research we have done to understand if our quick healing can help cancer patients. If we can donate blood or organs that quickly replace themselves—"

"Can we re-grow a whole organ?" Dianne. Who else? Griffon didn't bother hiding his grin. She'd read it from his mind anyway. He suspected that half of the outlandish things she said was on purpose. If she asked more questions while respecting their mental privacy, he was all on board for that. Plus, seeing Anna Marie loose her temper made him laugh.

"Depends on the organ," Sergei said. The man liked to give Dianne plenty of opportunities to create chaos. He must think it just as funny as Griffon. After the social with the donors and the families, Griffon had decided that Sergei was a pretty decent guy. He could work a room with his proper doctor bedside manner but he was always politely respectful with Griffon.

"Ssshhh." Dianne just quirked an eyebrow at the person trying to shush her. The lady promptly turned back around to look at Liesel.

"That is the future for Hoax. To offer information and support for our members. To create a place in this world where we are welcomed and we can feed that need to protect, to help. Before we wrap up this conference I want to thank a few people."

Which she did and people clapped appropriately but she didn't talk about her attack at the airport, or the death of Maldecia or even her thrashed hotel room. Which in Griffon's opinion was what the conference had entailed.

People stood and were passing goodbyes around. He picked up conversational snippets as he canvassed the room, keeping an eye out for concealed weapons and any signs of anger.

"I'd thought she'd say more about her historical research."

"All of that is on the website for people to read and access, this stuff was new."

"Do you know if the speech will be up on the site?"

"I saw someone recording it, it'll be up one way or another."

Dianne turned to Sergei, cocked her head to the side considering him and then smiled nice and slow.

"Griffon's on duty." Right? Not needing to wait for an answer. "Let's go back to your room."

Sergei didn't say anything, just took her hand and pulled her along behind him.

Once they were back in Boise, Griffon would implement his plans to protect his queen bee. One of which was to move her into his home and office. Way easier to keep an eye on her if she was underfoot 24/7. Now to convince the headstrong leader that she could rely on him to watch her back. Because he decided to propose. That way the whole world knew he loved Liesel Grant, Matriarch of the Amazons, and would sacrifice everything to keep her.

She does know you'll watch her back, Dianne whispered. *You are the only person she feels safe around.*

Not only person, Griffon sent back.

Sure, she feels safe with others, but on guard to protect them too. You can protect yourself.

He smiled and several conference attendees scattered away from him like fleeing birds. Well that was something.

Chapter 16

After the closing dinner Dianne led the way to her new room that connected to Liesel's. Anna, if she wasn't off talking to the boy she'd met at the club, would be across the hall. Dianne had needed access to her clothes and wanted to take his picture again but this time with her actual equipment. The pharmacy had delivered their order and Sergei strategically placed condoms all over the room and bathroom. Exhaustion had folded over them like a warm blanket and they slept for a couple of hours before he kissed her awake. Now they lay under the dim light of the lamp in each other's arms, each caught up in their own drowsy thoughts.

Afterglow made Dianne feel as vulnerable as hanging from a high-rise to get a shot, the camera stuck with Velcro to her climbing harness. And not just because she was naked. She felt open. Safe. Which always heralded danger. Not that she'd photographed a high-rise, let alone done so without clothes on.

Maybe she was as bad as Sergei believed himself to be. Picking at other's mental walls to her own purpose. Shielding her soft spots by stealing or tearing down his armor.

"Sergei, tell me about your dad and brother," Dianne said.

He absently stroked her back. During sex Sergei was speechless but after he got talkative. "My earliest memory of my brother Peyton is feeding him. He'd cry if anyone else touched him..." He gasped and looked at her, stroked her face, "Do you—" He swallowed. "Do you think I turned it off for him?"

Dianne shrugged.

"Oh god, and I left. I went to college when he was only six and," he placed his head in his hands, gasped a tight breath in, "it got so bad for him, Dianne. He was so distant and remote from everyone and so caught up in being perfect and—" He took a deep shuddering breath that raised his chest. He sat up and pressed back against the head board, raised his knees. She sat next to him, leaned her head on his shoulder.

"I thought things had gotten better. He was on medication and it seemed to help. I came home for Christmas and he was sooo thin...." He shifted to place an arm around her and pull her into his warmth, maybe remembering.

"Could he hear your thoughts?" she pressed a quick kiss to his flat brown nipple and turned her head. She felt bad but clueless how to make him feel better.

"No." He laughed, bitter. She didn't push for more but felt privileged when he continued. "That next summer I was home for two whole weeks. He planned it so I'd be the one to find him. Tried to save the girls from that." He picked at the hotel sheets covering their legs.

She watched him swallow. She felt broken, as if his words just tore open her soft spots more instead of building up her armor. When he told her in the shower, she'd barely registered the words, too angry, too shocked to understand what he was telling her.

"When I had three days left, before I had to go back to school, he killed himself. That way there'd be enough time for the funeral." His voice was quieter and more matter of fact, less emotional. Yet, she knew how painful the memories were for him.

"He must have felt it was his only choice. He could have done it anytime, whether you were there or not," Dianne said.

He coughed. "Would you choose that?"

She wished she could draw the memory out of him, banish it to a bright land. Or share the burden of it. She placed her fingertips over his heart in a semicircle, pushed down and imagined drawing it out.

Would she choose death? "No. I had other ways of getting out. Money. Freedom. My family didn't have to see me suffer because I wasn't there." Now, all she had to help Sergei were awkward words that she hoped would ease his pain. "How old was he?"

"Eight."

"Good grief. He was born with this? I was strong, right off. But the mental journey through blades and fire didn't hit until I was eleven. Eleven years to be semi-normal and I was out of society at sixteen. Absent all but physically by fourteen."

So young and to know nothing but chaos and pain. She remembered taking her truck and parking it in Yellowstone. Living in the cab until she bought her Airstream trailer. She had loved the peace and the freedom, had started to heal. Not to have that? That would have killed her eventually. "He couldn't help being sick."

He didn't say anything. She lifted her head to look at him. He stared at the window and didn't look at her as she waited. "What about your father?" Dianne said.

"He didn't know how to help Peyton. It scared him and he just hid further." He spoke but the words clattered, laid flat in the air. His body settled into stone.

It wasn't what she'd meant. "When did he start hearing other's thoughts?"

Sergei shrugged. "He's never said. He was that way when my parents met though. He controlled it and could work and function fairly normally with drugs. By the time I left for college he was on full disability." He threaded his fingers in her short hair, rubbed the back of her neck.

Dianne shook her head. If Sergei's dad was so incapable then why have five children? "Asshole. Way to look out for his family."

Sergei's head jerked up then he sagged as she finished speaking. "My father? Yeah."

"I didn't mean you." Surprised that he'd even think that, she sat up to watch his reaction.

"Good," back to stone.

"Were you an asshole too, though? Or did you help?"

He smiled, shook his head. "I like how unfiltered you are. I helped." His body softened as he pulled her back to his chest. He kissed the top of her head. "Sent money. Still do. Play handyman when I'm home." He explained about Kathleen and Thomas, the children he had helped create to pay for school and life.

"In a cup? What did you use to get excited?" She smiled and wiggled closer as she closed her eyes, laid her head on his chest again.

Laughter rumbled through his chest and into her. "I am actually shocked you asked me that. Shouldn't be surprised but am."

"So what did you use?"

He laughed some more. "Dianne."

It made her glow with pride to make him laugh. She kept her tone matter of fact, worked the innocent angle. "Girl on girl? That's supposed to be a guy's ultimate fantasy."

He pulled her up slightly so he could whisper in her ear. Why would he whisper? It wasn't like anyone was around to hear. She grinned and did her best to stifle a laugh.

She pulled back, eyes huge and cheeks hot. "No. Way."

He nodded.

"Sex Pistols and Seven of Nine? The band doing her?"

"No! Listening to the music and thinking of her." His checks purple with embarrassment.

She shrugged, pursed her lips in consideration. "I could see the appeal."

He groaned and pulled her in for another kiss, both of them laughing.

The new room didn't have a mini bar like the last one so Sergei ordered a pizza at two in the morning. They ate and slept in-between very one sided wrestling matches. Hard to wrestle with someone who is determined to let you win. The hours stretched out before him, aware of time like he hadn't been in years. In a couple of hours he'd meet Portia and John for a late breakfast and by this tomorrow he'd be back in DC.

The drapes caged the morning light. Rays, like little fingers, reached across the carpet at the bottom of the curtain. Sergei laced his fingers behind his head and leaned back in bed to watch Dianne, her eyes glassy with afterglow. He needed more time. He would tell NEWCo that he had a family emergency, dip into his savings and follow Dianne to Boise. They could spend a few more days together. Hell, the job didn't start for a few more days. Maybe he could just change his flight to Boise. She needed the help cleaning out her Grandmother's house and he needed more time.

A little voice reminded him about his policy on bandages—rip them off quick—but this was different. There weren't any open wounds here. Plenty of sharp objects to puncture his heart but no wounds just yet.

"What would happen if you touched yourself?" Sergei asked.

"That sounds," she searched for the word, "kinky. I have satellite, I've seen porn. Had satellite." Dianne climbed out of bed and started digging in the blankets for her underwear.

Sergei rolled his eyes and tried again. "When you touch people you see their worst memories, relive their fears. Is it the same each time you touch them?" He scooted to the edge of the bed, kept the sheet over his lap.

"Each time I touch? Who needs a second time?" She tugged her underwear up and wrestled her bra on.

He stood, let the sheet drop. "You didn't try? You didn't go back and—"

"No." She threw the blankets out of the way, looking for the rest of her clothes. "You don't know," her voice louder with each word. "You don't—"

"Stop it." He grabbed her arms to sooth her agitation. Just held her still. But she continued to yell so he pressed her against the nearest wall. "Shut up and listen. If you touched someone with the same ability as you, what would they see?"

"What the hell? I don't know. Let go," she yelled, her throat wide with the effort.

"What's your biggest fear, Dianne?" he whispered.

"Why can't you ever just ask plain the first time?"

"Dianne?"

"You are. Okay?"

"What?" He must not have heard her correctly. The very idea that she would fear him jumbled his thoughts like an EKG reading. Shocked. With the way she fought, he had figured her fear was being out of control. Had even suspected, over the last few days, there would be a tragedy in her past. It would explain why she didn't like it when she thought Harry and him were fighting.

"What?" he said again.

"I don't know what to do with you. I don't know what you want from me. Of me." She tried to pry herself loose but he just tightened further. "I can't read you."

"And why is that such a bad thing?" Seriously, her fear was of being normal? That didn't make sense. She'd worked so hard this week to learn control of her abilities. He'd watched her use her powers to look for Maldecia's killer, the Harvest Team. When they had first talked on the phone, no way would she have been able to do any of those things. She hadn't taken so much as a Tylenol in almost forty-eight hours. Could she really be afraid of that?

Oh god, Dianne wanted it back. The pain and confusion and escape of mental chaos. Like a caged wolverine, she clawed up his chest and pushed, the connection to reality gone. A desperate need to flee or to submit to the pain again, to hide in the mess. Anything was better than this. Exposed before? What a fucking joke. She was such a naive twit.

He slammed her against the wall, her head denting the sheetrock. White dust like dandruff rained on her shoulders. She'd been at it for a while and he shouted her name again. And again. The red marks on his chest from her nails started to bleed. She tried to push past his mental block, see the people in the next room. Anything.

Bang, bang.

Two gunshots into their connecting door and Griffon stepped into their room. The hotel was so not going to host the Amazon convention ever again. "Put her down," Griffon yelled and Dianne realized he'd been pounding at the door. She hadn't heard even the physical noise until the gunshots.

"Hell no. Stay the fuck out of this," Sergei yelled back at him.

Griffon aimed at Sergei. "I said. Put. Her. Down."

Dianne brought her hands up to her ears as if the noise was there. As if she could trap it in her head and escape. "Don't fight. Don't fight. I'll be good. I'll be good."

Sergei swept a gentle thumb over her bare bicep. "Good for who, Dianne? *Svyet*, good for who?" So gentle. The soft compared to her own brutality laid her heart stark.

"Sergei!" Griffon warned.

"Let go so I can hear!" Her throat hurt but she continued to yell. "I have to know." She clawed at Sergei's arms, the white furrows popped to the surface then turned red like his chest.

She yelled at Griffon, "What are you thinking?"

Griffon flinched, a hand to his ears. He moaned.

"Griffon," Sergei said, "please."

Finally Griffon, hand still pressed to his ear, stepped back into his own room. As the P.I. was leaving Sergei had her against the wall with another shaking thunk. The connecting door swung shut. "*Svyet*, be good for who?"

Dizziness swamped her and she felt herself stagger though she didn't move. Vertigo. Mental swirl.

Sergei knew she'd been able to use her powers before while touching him. Why not now? Did he push back at her powers or was she just so worked up that she couldn't focus enough to hear?

"God damn it. Dianne. Try. Try!" So much adrenaline pumped through his system that his head floated. As Griffon entered with his gun, Sergei's heart rate had kerthunked faster than a Sex Pistols' song.

He couldn't let this amazing woman believe she was somehow weak. He couldn't watch her dwindle away like his father or run toward the point of suicide like his brother. She needed to know. He'd be left behind, unable to provide touch, peace, and she would suffer. He wouldn't be able to help her from D.C. This would be his gift back. A repayment for the things he'd done.

She would embrace her true self and he could live knowing he'd done that. That he'd healed her.

"My parents."

"You won't understand unless—" he hadn't heard her and Dianne couldn't bring herself to say it again so she leaned in to kiss him, distract him. He pulled back, "No."

That stung worse than any manhandling had.

"Tell me who—"

"My parents," she yelled it this time. "They—" she quieted her voice, afraid others would hear, afraid that she'd sound childish to the man that she had begun to love. Begun? Shit, she did love him. "Why couldn't they love each other?"

"Lots of people go through divorces."

"But they didn't. They didn't just stop, move apart. They seem...to thrive on it. The pain they can inflict on each other. And then," she hiccupped and realized she was crying. "Then she would come into my room...after he had stormed out of the house...and she'd yell at me. That it was my fault. But it wasn't. It wasn't." She knew that, of course, had known even all those years ago but that debilitating doubt had invaded her days until she couldn't function without seeing the truth. Even later as they fought she would look, dig through memories looking for the root of the hatred. They didn't know, no longer cared why.

"Was she the first mind you read?" He loosed his grip but his body sagged into her, covered her.

Cold, she shivered and tried to absorb his heat, tuck in, a new hidey hole. He pulled back. "Yes. Her and my father's. I needed to see if they hated me, if they really wished that I hadn't been born."

He swallowed and let her slide down the wall. He shuddered as he brushed debris off her shoulders. "Did they?"

"I embarrass my mom." She blushed at the raw pain she heard in her own voice but couldn't stop the flow of words. "She feels so awkward when I'm around and she's always glad to see me go," she whispered, her cheeks heated with shame. She kept her eyes open so she could see his reaction.

He searched her face, placing his hand on her chin to tilt her eyes up. "She's only human. None of us are perfect." He said the last with a deep aching sigh of relief, letting go of a weight on his own shoulders, his arms gathered her close.

"She should have been more. She's my mother," Dianne wiped her tears away.

"You've seen what mothers do, what people are capable of. Yet, you believe in them."

She shook her head to deny his words.

"Sergeant Sparks. Barney. People who you couldn't read, yet you knew they were good." Sergei kissed her cheek, her shoulder, tender with no particular heat behind it.

Someone knocked on the broken door. Dianne yelled at the top of her lungs, "We're fucking. Leave us the hell alone."

Sergei just lifted an eyebrow, his chuckle soft.

Liesel yelled from the other side, "I'm stronger than both of you. If you don't come out later whole and healthy I'm busting heads."

They breathed and listened to her stomp away. "Should we tell her it would have been better to threaten us with Griffon?" Dianne threaded her fingers between his, palm to palm.

"That man is bad-ass scary," Sergei murmured, shivered.

Dianne giggled and then sobbed, her emotions still too close to the surface. He pulled her in close and stroked her hair, giving her silence and time.

"And your father?" Sergei eventually asked.

"I pretend for him. Pretend I'm okay because he feels so responsible. He loves me." Her father did love her. And the rest wasn't her responsibility. "I'm sorry and thanks and I just don't want to talk about it yet."

"Time to process?" Sergei asked.

"Yes, please."

"What is Liesel doing?" His voice smiled but his face didn't. There weren't the straightened shoulders or stillness that denoted a smile.

Dianne could tell that Liesel was bargaining with the hotel and Griffon was talking to the police—he had fired a weapon after all—and it freaked her out. She could control this. Even when Sergei touched her. Once she was calm, no longer panicking, and her ability was this easy pliable force that bent to her will. She gathered herself together and sent a wave of total trust to the people questioning Griffon so things would go whichever way he wanted to spin it.

Sergei kissed her, heavy on the passion, and she realized she was only in her underwear and Sergei was naked. Sergei smiled. Maybe knowing what she had just figured out.

"Griffon now knows you're blue everywhere." She kissed the red claw marks on his arms, glad to see the marks on his chest start to scab over. "Does that constitute as a fight? Can we have make up sex?"

He stroked her scalp and it felt sore when he touched the back, but didn't really hurt. "Fight or not, we'll have to pay for the door and the wall. We might as well get our money's worth from the room."

"You're such a charmer."

Instead of climbing back in bed Sergei led her to the shower, a companionable silence between them. Maybe they both needed time dwell in their own thoughts.

Chapter 17

Sergei kept looking at his watch until Portia's hand covered his wrist. "Are we keeping you?" she raised an eyebrow.

"Sorry." Sergei drank the rest of his coffee and took the lid off. He wished he had more concrete answers for them. Something kept him from making another false promise to reassure his sister. They'd gone down the list of family, gathering intel from each other. Their sister Bailey had a new job for better pay but hours she hated. His mom was on a gardening kick. He had given his update for Portia to pass to their sisters, mostly rehashing news about his new job and how glad he was to be done with his residency.

"It's about a girl," John said, referring to Sergei's distracted behavior. His brother-in-law John crossed his arms and leaned back in his chair. Smug bastard. Sergei considered pushing until the chair fell over.

Portia looked like a brunette version of Sergei. Same eyes and build, clear that they were siblings even with her breasts and pregnant belly. John had deep brown skin, a wide nose and a goofy sense of humor. They were going to make beautiful children.

When he had first met John, he did the cool, older brother thing to test John. He wanted to see if Prince Charming was the devil incarnate. Not really creating a friendship but checking him out, getting the guy to trust him so he could trick him into showing his true self, before Portia got hurt.

Yet, it was Sergei who had been acting like a wolf in sheep's clothing.

Dianne might think he wasn't evil, but he regretted that. Their friendship had survived, thankfully. Even now he strategically steered away from his fears and doubts and stayed in control of the situation.

He gripped his knee as a wave of lust smacked him. A random but frequent thought of Dianne's smooth inner thigh, the red carpet to paradise. A quick look at his sister and his body behaved.

"Really?" Portia wanted to know. "A girl here? But you've got a life in D.C."

"Doesn't have to be a permanent thing," John said.

The tight roll of paper that created the lip of his cup peeled off like a croissant, in layers. He focused his attention on dismantling the cup rather than look at his sister and have her read him so easily.

Portia broke bits of her scone off and ate them. All delicate femininity, even though she could bench press her husband. She laughed. "Looks serious."

"Sitting right here," Sergei said crossing his arms.

"Okay, so dish."

"No. Not serious." Though he wanted it to be. Wanted it to mean as much to her as it had started to mean to him. "Can't be because of that life in D.C.," he said with a nod to John.

"Where does she live?" Portia's eyes shined in glee at his discomfort. "Oh, wait. The hermit artist right?"

"Don't," Sergei warned, pointing a finger at her and giving her his stern doctor routine. "Don't be like that. She's good."

"Sure." Analytical, detailed-oriented, practically a walking resume, Portia didn't "get" art. She thought the Sex Pistols were talentless noise makers. "She could live in D.C. Not really any roots to yank up."

"Don't think she's equipped with roots to plant." Sergei groaned. "And what the hell we talking roots for?"

John snorted.

Sergei pushed on his chair and John dropped all four chair legs to keep from falling back on his ass.

"So what's the problem?" Portia finished her scone and John pushed his unfinished bagel in front of her. "You want the time to develop this thing between you? You can do that long distance."

He wanted more than a long-distance relationship. The thought sounded so petulant in his head. Fuck, maybe he was deteriorating to a hormonal teenager tripping out over whether Dianne would go to the prom with him.

"Hell, NEWCo has sites all over the US. Do you have to work the D.C. location?" John rubbed his wife's lower back in slow circles, neither commenting on her appetite despite the fact Portia had protested even the scone. John texted Sergei after each doctor appointment, sending information like blood pressure and blood levels. He'd even seen video of the ultra sound. Everything looked really healthy.

The NEWCo Lab hire had come at the heels of his grant acceptance. The grant would cover his salary and lease anywhere. NEWCo would put forth matching funds and maintain the business end so he could get lost in his research. The additional capital would cover an assistant, maybe even two.

"Figure out where she'll be and work there or you know, compromise."

Portia wiped her mouth with a napkin. "That would require talking about their feelings," She laughed, "and—"

"Portia," Sergei looked at her under his eyebrows, all gruff menace. "I'm falling for her." Saying I-can-talk-about-my-feelings, though he'd chickened out and hadn't used the L word.

"Like this?" John kicked at Sergei's chair and he gripped the table to keep from falling.

"Asshole."

John shrugged. "Made you smile." In the same tone a kid would say monkey's always look.

Portia took his hand. Her small hand such a contrast to his big hand. "You deserve happiness, Sergei. You don't have to keep that distance anymore. You'll be there for us, no matter what. Let us be there for you." She teared up, sniffed, and reached frantically for a napkin to dab at her mascara. John handed her a soft Kleenex from her purse.

"Waterworks," John said and gripped his chair in anticipation for Portia's retaliation.

With a laugh she kissed his temple and switched topics. "Zeeman is dating a teacher's aide."

Sergei rubbed a thumb across his sister's hand and thought about Dianne. And the fact that NEWCo Labs had a site in Eagle, Idaho.

He'd checked when he'd consider job options to move closer to Liesel and the world she was creating. How far was that again from Boise? Commuting distance surely.

Eagle, Idaho, might be a great place to convince her that they made sense.

The camera equipment was all brand new and didn't need cleaning but Dianne pulled it out, taking a mental inventory of the different pieces. Her head was plenty full with old memories of her parents that only a few of the thoughts around her surfaced.

It was weird not having several packs of batteries in her case but Barney had gotten her top of the line rechargeable gear so there was cables instead. She checked on her phone for a portable battery pack and ordered one that would fit her needs. Four lenses for different shots and distances, two sets of filters, and a quarter tripod, were also in the bag. As she checked each piece for function and made sure everything was cleaned and organized the way she liked it, she reached out to check on Liesel.

The matriarch was next door answering email and catching up on calls. A local FBI agent, Griffon, and a few guys from hotel security would go downstairs that afternoon with Liesel to see people off. They would make sure everyone got checked out, nothing was left behind, and that Liesel presented a strong front for any remaining dissension.

Anna had just gone to sleep. The guy from the club—she hadn't gotten his name—had thankfully left after they hooked up, no strings, no drama. Dianne would check with her later and make sure she had plenty of condoms.

Harry and Griffon had taken his nieces swimming with the Corbys. Dianne took a moment to look in both Amy Griffon's and Jesus Corby's minds. They'd both been kidnapped a couple of months ago, and though several years different in age, were fast friends. The kids had named themselves The Conquerors and talked through skype weekly. Dianne thought that was healthy, even admirable. To unite under a common struggle instead of hiding from it.

She remembered the nights curled under the blankets, unable to get warm, little trembles cycling her body as she tried to sleep, tried not to cry. Tried to convince herself that she wasn't bad or evil but just a kid. She wasn't the only person damaged by their parents, not by a long shot. As she focused she could push all the other thoughts to arm distance.

Sergei was right. She really could control her abilities. Sure, random thoughts still pulsed behind her own but it was like working in a noisy office. She could ignore them for the most part, turn them out when they got particularly loud, tell them to hush. She even got the mom, two rooms down and across the hall to stop reading and take her kids to see the free tigers at the MGM. It was just a matter of finding something for them to do and letting the mom know. She probably thought it was something she had heard about and forgotten.

Dianne pulled the camera out, set it on the edge of the dresser, and took her own picture. There was an app so her cellphone could work as a remote control and she spent several minutes figuring out how to set it up and not accidently take a picture of the pores on nose. Her hair was a mess. He eyes were still blotchy from her earlier tears. She used the heel of her hand to wipe her eyes and let her messy hair be. She had on a tank top that barely came to the waist band of her loose jean shorts, a pair she'd bought in the shop days ago. She thought about shaving her legs or painting her toes or doing any little thing.

All these oddly normal thoughts that had nothing to do with pain or looking for the bad guys or well, anything. She folded down her equipment and looked at the digital viewing screen. The camera did both digital and film. Her age showed around her eyes yet she looked more confident. Her mouth wasn't pinched with pain. Sergei and done some of that but mostly it was her. Grandma Maggie would be so proud of her.

Liesel asked if she was okay from the other room. Perhaps her grief was loud as she remembered Maggie's deep warmth, kindness. *I miss her but I'm supposed to. I need to feel that. Let it process instead of trying to make it go away.*

Liesel put her phone down and drew her legs up on the couch, getting comfortable for their mental chat. *When my father died it was so weird sitting in the living room and realizing I was waiting for him to come home.* She turned and looked out the window but mental saw a green lawn and an irrigation ditch. *I'd find myself by the large window looking out. Or outside by the huge tree we had and just looking up and down the street for him.* They both sat in silence for several minutes until Liesel continued. *I still miss him. Still see him in other people. But it gets easier.*

Dianne wiped her cheeks and eyes again. *Thank you.*

Anytime and always.

I'm going to test the light settings in the casino. Are you going to be okay?

No one knew they'd even moved rooms and Liesel was determined to stay where it was safe so no one else got hurt trying to help her. *I'll wait here for Griffon, promise.*

Chapter 18

Kee Ping planned to stay young and unattached as long as possible. Her Amazon grandmother had lived until she was 120. When she did die, it was in a car accident—drag racing.

Ping looked fifty-five and happily led an independent life with men in and out. Relationships that provided companionship. Until Dr. Itou Jun, a total nerd. He was a neurosurgeon and, in his mid-thirties, half her age. He had none of the romantic skills her normal lovers had, nor the good looks. Ping, damn it, had fallen in love for the first time. Fallen hard.

Ping finished her blog post about the conference and that Liesel Grant was now the Matriarch of the American Amazons. She provided a link to Liesel's site and the bylaws and went to check her email. Someone knocked on her hotel room door.

"Flower delivery," the young man said as she opened the door. A dozen red roses? She appreciated it, she did. But Jun should have sent two dozen or an exotic arrangement. She buried her face among the silky petals, scented the full perfume and tipped the bell hop.

The card was sweet. More than sweet. Agitated, she tossed the card at her laptop and sat at the end of her bed. The petals felt incredible between her fingers. She should at least call and thank him for the flowers. Ping kept the vase in one hand as she dug her cell phone out of her purse. What time was it in Tokyo? She pushed and held down the fifth button.

The first blow struck the back of her skull. It snapped her head forward, her tongue catching between her teeth and blood spurted across her shirt.

In that split second between impact and realization her body retreated from the pain. Dropping to her knees, she raised her hands to cover her head. The cartilage in her knees crinkled and popped. The moisture in her mouth disappeared with her gasp of air.

But she wasn't going out like this. Cowering, flighting. She would stand and fight. With a Shishi roar, she rolled to the side and felt a heavy object connect with her arm. The damaged arm dropped like lead weight to her side, limp, in shock at just what had happened too it.

She was surprised to see her attacker. It made since. All nicely puzzled together now that the larger picture was revealed but the true surprise was how she had missed it.

She reached up to grab the bat as it swung toward her for the third time but her left arm still wasn't cooperating and her single hand wasn't enough to stop the bat reaching her forehead. Her last thought was a yell. DIANNE.

Dianne felt the air clutch to the sides of her lungs. Kee Ping no longer sent horrid thoughts. She was no longer able to think at all. Her skull split open. Dianne was three floors and half a hotel away and yet she could see a piece of the bat embedded in Ping's skin. Could see it clearly because the attacker stared at it and tried to decide if she should remove the bat before she left the room.

Dianne hit the door to the stairwell, running before she realized what it was that made her run. She called for Griffon and Todd and the head of Security and the chief of police. The chief was outside of her three mile range but several of his officers thought they were getting emergency calls over their police scanners. The Amazon convention. Again. Anna and Liesel were both safe in their rooms and she kept them there. Not broadcasting her fears to disturb their peace.

Griffon was the only one yelling back. *Wait, don't go in alone. Wait.*

"She'll get away," Dianne yelled out loud and through the mental link, vaguely aware she was shoving people out of her way, too focused to let any thoughts in but the ones she was gathering like an army.

But we know who it is now. We know. Griffon said again.

I won't let her hurt anyone else. She's leaving the room.

Her body was built for speed and she was in good shape yet she pushed her limit, stretched her legs a bit farther, and reached a bit further.

Which direction? Good. Check Ping.

She's dead. What's the point?

Check her! Griffon yelled back. *And keep sending us her position.*

Just outside the room she battered against a thin cloud of thought, like the hazy trail she felt when people were asleep. Like she'd felt just before entering the forest fire to help the couple, that almost child calling to her. Kee Ping was alive. Dianne caught on the shock and she stumbled mentally.

She lost the fleeing attacker for a moment as she focused on the cloud. Kee Ping was alive.

Sergei. Would he hear her? She'd never heard his thoughts but did he hear hers? Now, when she desperately needed his help, would he come? *She's alive.*

The door stood open. Wet rose petals covered the floor. Their color mixed with Kee Ping's blood. The penny smell and the blare of sun through the window beat on her senses. Ping must have knocked over the vase as she struggled with the attacker.

Crap, Dianne had lost her mental connection. *Griffon?*

I'm on the stairwell. She isn't here. Griffon seemed okay with this mental assistance, but others it was freaking them out, even with the calm reassurance she emoted with each thought.

Sergei. Kee Ping is alive. She needs Sergei. Dianne knelt and took Ping's hand. Skin to skin and she felt the smooth glide of rose petals between her fingers then the squish of her brain as the painful blow from the bat shoved her head forward. *Shishi, lion warriors fight. They do not flee.* She stopped the slideshow of the attack, refocused.

Security flipped through video feeds trying to track the killer's path. Todd organized a group of Mightys and Amazons to search the casino and restaurants in pairs. Frank was curbside waving the police in.

The police are here. I'm going to call for an ambulance. She couldn't sense any within her range.

"How about you use the phone like a normal person?"

Dianne opened her eyes to watch Sergei run into the room with a large first-aid kit. Two hotel maids came in behind him with towels and sheeting. One maid had been a nurse in Argentina before coming to the states. Odd that would surface among all the other wavelengths of knowledge.

Thank god. You can hear me.

Dianne didn't feel any pain. Not even the smashed brain Ping felt. Thousands of thoughts, but no pain. She picked the minds she needed easily out of the maelstrom around her. No hesitation.

"Call 911." On the floor, Sergei opened packages of gauze, shredded sheets and took Ping's vitals.

Dianne? Griffon asked for direction. No one knew where Ping's attacker had gone.

They'd lost her. And so had Dianne. Shit.

One of the maids used a cell phone to call 911.

Dianne, ignoring everyone and everything, sat cross-legged on the floor, surrounded by blood and petals. Sergei, feet away, tried to stabilize Kee Ping. She turned it all off. Severed all connections and started clean. Empty, void. Then thought one thing.

I'm going to get you, Valasca Perch.

Chapter 19

Ten minutes later Dianne kept looking. The problem was Valasca wasn't Valasca. She saw herself as something else. Defined herself as mother or by a career choice or some life accomplishment. Like the Times reporter at the gallery or Todd's accountant Amanda or even the Argentinean nurse. She couldn't focus on Valasca because there wasn't a Valasca.

Dianne focused on the hate within three miles, narrowed it down to one mile, relatively speaking. She'd never been very good with measurements. Just like her searches after Maldecia and the Harvest Team but this time infinitely easier. It was like when she struggled to set up a photoshoot and it wouldn't come together, the light and composition would be off. Frustrating until she had an epiphany and it suddenly freed her, made her powerful. Everything aligned for the perfect picture.

This time motions felt familiar and automatic, like she'd developed an efficient process. She knew this equipment and used it well. She listened for intense heartbeats. No lazy gamblers, no comatose TV watchers. She filtered it further, focused, shifted out the happy, agonizingly slowly to only those with intense hate.

The paramedics took Kee Ping out of the room on a stretcher and headed for the roof where she would be Life–Flighted to the hospital.

It took a simple mental look over her shoulder to see the different teams doing on foot what she was trying mentally. Still looking. Valasca wasn't in her room. She hadn't come up on any of the security feeds.

Sergei finished washing his hands in the bathroom sink. As he walked toward her, keeping her range focused became easier. He dampened her powers.

Not too close.

"Say when." He stepped another two feet closer.

When.

He sat on the floor, a foot from her. Sat and waited.

I've got three. Griffon, I'm not sure which one. Should you split up?

Instead of answering he said, *You're freaking the police out.*

Chill, coppers. This is Jean Grey from the X–Men.

Sergei laughed. It sounded broken, a damaged record that skipped and scratched. Not the laugh she loved. She sent him a mental hug, stroked a hand down his bare chest without touching him.

Split us up. Which way.

There is one in the buffet room. Sitting in a booth. Not eating. The mind is so dense with...darkness. I can't read it.

She tried to connect to someone sitting near this person yet no one would look that way. Perhaps recognizing and responding instinctively to danger. She didn't want to force it and alert Perch to her presence.

After sending hotel security after the first one, Dianne switched to the next one.

There is one on the fourth floor. They're washing their hands. I can smell the soap.

It made her head hurt to get deep with that one. Wash, soap. Dig a bit around the cuticles. Increase the water's heat. She didn't know if it was her own pain or the person's pain that she felt.

And the third? Griffon urged, as she sent the police after the fourth floor hand washer.

The third is...It's a Mighty. So not her. But....

The Mighty was looking at a leather parchment. Hieroglyphics in techno hologram scattered like pigeons on cobblestone away from his eyes, keeping only inches out of sight, never letting him see. The very vivid smell of leather, the tinge of sweat from his brow as he concentrated.

"Sergei. I found the codex of the Amazons, the McKinnon leathers." Dianne spoke out loud for the first time in what felt like hours. She opened her eyes to look at him.

He sat there, inches away, impervious to her ability to read minds and yet the struggle was obvious. Sergei clenched his fists and the muscles in his arms jumped at his skin like caged animals. His eyes saw what she saw. Her mind opened wide. Saw Tydus Vaughn McKinley, also known as Ole, smooth a hand over the leather of the codex. They both felt Tydus realize his mind had been invaded. And they both knew, just as Tydus knew, that he would run.

Sergei crossed his arms, an extra restraint.

The Harvest Team? She didn't feel them. Maybe if Sergei stepped back, if she focused only on contacting the Team.

How had she missed that? Except he'd made sure they never met. She was at the hotel when the airport attack happened. She hadn't attended the workshops and when she'd gone to the vote she'd held Sergei's hand. He wasn't registered for the conference so she hadn't scanned him. He kept moving each night to a different hotel.

"It doesn't matter. Find Valasca before she hurts anyone else." Sergei swallowed, clenched his fists on his thighs.

She reached out and touched his hand to offer comfort, to let him know that she cared deeply. As all the thoughts and mental connections left her head she realized that one mind was missing: Liesel's.

Harry took a fortifying breath and squared her shoulders before she knocked on Tydus's door.

"Harry, am I late?" He checked his watch. Chest bare, his perfectly defined pecs flexed as he stuffed his hands, stiff armed, into the pockets of his tailored slacks. "Not that I'm not flattered by your eagerness but I need more time to get ready. Why don't you meet me down in the casino?"

She leaned to his side and looked into the hotel room at the open suitcase on the bed. But she didn't say anything. He'd been avoiding her and Todd had mentioned seeing him at the front desk, settling his bill. She thought it was weird, especially since he had been staying in the Paris Hotel initially. Yet, he didn't owe her anything. Except it got her adding things up and it was quite apparent the man had been lying to her. She couldn't let him leave until she had a chance to tell him off.

"I'm totally anal. I know. Who packs the day before they leave? Me, I guess."

"Tydus. Let's try something." Harry kept her voice even. Her jaw jumped as she pushed her teeth shut.

"Experimenting," he wiggled his eyebrows "I'm up for that." He leaned, hands still in his pockets, against the door jam. Further blocking her view of the room. Giving overt sexual offerings for the first time. Busted and he somehow knew it.

"You try not to lie to me for five minutes and I won't kick your ass for all the old lies," she kept her tone playful. After all, she could be wrong about the lies and he might be able to talk his way out of this.

Even before she finished speaking his demeanor changed. He straightened his shoulders and his face relaxed into blank, no–emotion gambler.

She didn't want it to be true. What she thought he had done. That anyone was capable of that and could flirt with her...Her stomach flinched away at the thought. She'd liked him and trusted him, allowed him access to Liesel.

"No one likes being called a liar," even his voice was flat, unemotional. Not even the heat of outrage.

"That's a very good beginning. Seeing how it's true." She walked around him and he reached for her arm to stop her but expecting it she was able to avoid his touch and go to the other side of the room. Turned to face him. She didn't need to share with the whole hotel her embarrassment.

"You're not a business consultant," Harry said, almost hoping that he would deny it. All this time she'd convinced herself that this was a convenient fuck. She didn't get any action anyway.

He laughed. "Is that what this is about?" He shook his head and tried his charming slow smile, head cocked endearingly to the side. So easy to buy into the innocent side of the look despite the dark warning. "So I lied to impress a beautiful woman that I've got the hots for. So what? I'm sorry. Harry—"

Harry had to tell him how she'd figured it out. *See the holes. See how smart I am.* "You never checked the stock market. You didn't know who Sheldon Adelson was. And when I talked about Linux you thought I was referring to some construction equipment."

"I told you, I'm sorry." He reached for her again and she avoided his hand. She stepped to put the sitting area table between them. An apology but not an explanation.

She continued her spiel, urging him to do the same. "So I had Griffon to do a background check."

"Now that's bad of you." All innocent charm gone, scary man came out to terrorize. His eyes darkened and his shoulders and chest tightened. Fear chased down her spine then he smiled and she swallowed the gasp. "You should have come to me for an explanation. Don't you trust me?" All smooth talking sexy boyish honesty. The liar.

"You were in Boise. Why were you in Boise?"

"Boise? I've been to Boise a lot. I've told you I travel for work," Tydus motioned with his hands, pointing to her.

"As a business consultant."

"No—"

"You've only been to Boise once."

He got an oh-shit look. *Yeah, I pegged you, you bastard.*

"The end of August. Why were you in Boise?"

The codex had been stolen in August and if he was the one who had swiped it his questions about Liesel and Dianne made sense, since he wouldn't be able to read it.

He crossed his arms and leaned away from the table. "I was there to see my sister."

"You have no sister." All the records for a Tydus McKinley were fakes.

When Liesel had told her about the Ronin the Harvest Team was looking for she'd thought of him but Ty wasn't out of control. He wasn't the raging bull in a china shop they had described. Not a bad guy. He wasn't even a Mighty. But he was a thief and a liar. "You lied. So, I get to kick your ass."

He threw back his head and laughed. Until she slammed the table into his nuts, pushing against the wall behind her to get the biggest impact. He stumbled down to a knee but rolled out of the way as she tried to connect the same way with his head. She put one foot on a chair and the next on the table as she leaped over the top, clearing the furniture and his prone figure.

A black leather book, frayed around its leather edges, lay on top of his suitcase. She grabbed for it as she ran past to the door—reflex, not really thinking what it was.

The hotel door was on a spring-loaded hinge and had shut behind them as she came in. If it had been open, she would have made it.

Four floors above Dianne, Liesel sat in her new room in the first tower. Dianne had sent Griffon with the police to the fourth floor hand washer in the second tower across the hotel before she realized Liesel was out of the action. If anything, she'd wanted to keep Liesel safe, exclude the matriarch to keep her from racing off to stop the killer. Not realizing that she didn't even know of the threat. The hotel security was in the restaurant questioning the woman in the booth. And Valasca Perch, heart rate normal, a chilling peace and contentment filling her mind, rode in the elevator up the first tower. Heading for Liesel. Heading to kill her. She heard about the gunshots and knew which room Liesel was in.

Valasca had killed Maldecia and Ping because the women had sided with Liesel. She trashed Liesel's room when she found the place empty after her election as Matriarch. Now the board was in place. A board that supported the morally degenerate and wrong bylaws. Valasca had to do something.

Dianne filled her head with Liesel's danger. She felt Griffon's heart kick up even before her own did. She ran for the stairwell. Her hands, covered in Kee Ping's blood, slipped off the door handle to the stairwell without opening it. But with another jerk, she and Sergei spilled into the stairwell, jostling a maid on her cellphone. Their steps echoed hollow off the cement and steel stairs.

Liesel. Liesel. Valasca's coming for you. Hide.

She's already here. Dianne, she has a gun.

The image of Valasca pointing the gun at Liesel spurred Dianne's body forward like nitrous oxide in a drag race. She felt Griffon stumble, his chest ripping open with adrenaline and pain. She heard his audible shout across the hotel. *NO.*

Liesel, Sergei and I are almost there. Keep her talking.

Harry was slammed into the door like a wrecking ball. The door handle caught her below the ribcage and she could almost hear her ribs cracking.

Tydus pushed into her. If he hadn't she'd have slithered to the floor, unable to stand on her own.

What the hell was going on? You slapped the guy or kneed him in the nuts and—even-steven—he let you storm off in a bitchy snit.

"You think you're so smart, cunt? Then you know I have to kill you," he whispered the words in her ear.

"Not going to happen, asshole." What the hell? She knew he had lied, might even be a thief, but kill her? Did he think such a threat was funny? No way was this over. "Back the fuck off. Or better yet—" Dianne stretched to her fullest height, clasped her hands together above her head, her side ignited with fire, and slammed her elbow with all her strength into his face.

He staggered back and she wrenched the door open. A blow to her kidney from behind pulverized her body like a granite shockwave. He'd used every ounce of strength and her jaw sagged on its hinges. Flaming acid ripped its way through her body.

She leaned heavily on the wood door. Blood splattered the front of her clothes in pulses with each heartbeat. She must have coughed that blood up. She detached from the pain, groaning yet separate. Her head bobbed and before she blacked out she heard him say. "Not so smart now, are you?"

It jarred her back from the faint. Still in the hotel room, he reached around to get her before she could close the door. She caught the door handle and slammed the door closed on his hand, using her weight to propel it forward. He howled and a door across the hall opened.

"What the shit is going on?" It was Jennifer. The Aussie from the skin fest with Ping and new board member.

His hand got a hold of Harry's shirt and tore. She banged the door on his hand again. Or tried. His superior strength caught it and wrenched it open. He no longer looked distinguished. His nose was bloody and his eyes blazed with totally-pissed-off-deranged-killer. His hand bleeding, his eyes red.

Harry stumbled away from him, falling backward into Jennifer's room. On hands and feet she crab scuttled out of the way as Jennifer banged the door shut in Tydus's face. He pounded his fists against it and one of the hinge screws fell to the floor.

"Better—" Harry swallowed the blood and bile in her mouth, "call the police. That door isn't going to hold." She wasn't safe yet but her body sagged, drained. She clenched tight to the only thing keeping her conscious, sheer will.

Jennifer stepped toward her bed, pulled a two foot machete from underneath and her cell phone from the night stand. "No worries." She cocked her hip, full Aussie Sheila. "This here isn't for looking pretty."

Though Sergei called for her to wait, Dianne got to the room before he did. The carpet blurred under his feet yet he felt each movement stretched out. Too slow. Dianne was running without thought of protecting herself. Into danger. And he felt inert.

He didn't hear Dianne's thoughts.

The connection ceased. Gunshots ratcheted through the air. His steps faltered.

Dianne had grabbed Valasca from behind and wrenched her arms and the gun upwards, the bullet fired into the ceiling light. Sergei entered the room as broken glass rained on Liesel, cutting her hands and arms as she raised them to shield herself.

Dianne's palms were connected, flesh to flesh with Valasca's arms. They both screamed in pain and Valasca dropped the gun. It bounced once on the carpet and laid still.

God damn, why hadn't he gotten here first?

The two women crumpled like a card tower, slumping together like unused marionettes as they screamed, pain expelled vocally.

Sergei pulled Dianne away from the prone woman and gathered Dianne into his arms. He touched her skin wherever possible, lifted her shirt to press his hand and whole arm around her bare stomach. His lips pressed against her temple. His other hand clutched above her heart.

She stopped screaming.

"Come on Dianne. Are you okay? *Svyet*. Look at me." Her heart rate was normal, her body temperature normal—or so some clinical bastard told his head. But she wasn't okay. She wasn't.

"Liesel?" Griffon yelled.

"Here. I'm in here," Liesel called while she picked a large glass shard out of her hand. For once the medical doctor that operated under Sergei's skill refused to leave one patient to help another. Doctor and shady punk and caring brother all wanted the same thing, Dianne to be okay. No one was going to separate them until she was.

Griffon sprinted up the stairwell of the first tower, his sight a double vision of the steps before him and the end of the gun as Liesel stared at Valasca. He knew the type of ammunition the gun held, how best to disarm and restrain the shooter, how to snap her neck. All useless information from this far away. Third floor and, as if closing one eye, he could no longer see through Dianne. "Liesel!" The police were still several floors behind him. He reached her floor and ran full-out, down the hall, yelling as he did. "LIESEL."

Please. Please.

"Here. I'm here. I'm okay." He was in the room and holding her, oblivious to the scene around him. He didn't feel the last dozen steps, as if he'd teleported on her voice into her arms. "I'm okay. Are you—" she gasped, her breath ragged like she had just finished her morning run, "okay?"

He turned to look for the danger, to keep himself between her and the gun. But the gun rested against the far wall. Valasca lay on the floor like a fleshy mannequin, un-posed and lifeless but eyes open. He searched for a gunshot wound. On Valasca with his eyes, on Liesel with his hands.

Relief, all the more intense for fear that had ridden his spine seconds before, swept through his body like oxygen in a drown victim. *Thank you, God.* He took a rattling breath and pressed Liesel closer to his heart.

Then he saw Sergei. He was holding Dianne and weeping. Tears ran down his scruffy cheeks as he cradled Dianne in his arms.

"Help. Please help."

Sergei lost time. It floated out of his grasp as he stroked Dianne's bare skin. Instead he saw his brother, strung from the garage rafters, his feet twisting with the rush of air as Sergei opened the door. He'd pulled him down, did CPR, knowing that as a Mighty he hadn't died from the initial drop, had allowed himself to suffocate.

Sergei hadn't been able to save him. Didn't know enough like the use of a tracheotomy to open the collapsed throat, electric paddles to restart the heart. But now he was a doctor, thousands of emergencies under his belt, and yet he couldn't help Dianne. She didn't have a gunshot wound, hadn't stopped breathing. But she was empty. Gone.

Sergei, Dianne whispered, and at first he thought it was out loud. But her mouth and eyes were closed and her throat had not moved to produce sound.

"Dianne?"

Sergei, she's in here with me. I can't get her out. Help. Please help.

How? How could he possibly help? "Help. Please help."

Liesel pulled firmly out of Griffon's grasp and knelt next to Sergei. She pressed a hand to Dianne's head, one of the few uncovered places of skin Sergei wasn't touching, and told Sergei to let go. Liesel took shallow breaths and swallowed back saliva to keep from puking. She hid her other hand from Griffon. She needed to help Dianne, one of hers, and knew Griffon would worry over the blood. Leading her people, healing them, that mattered, drove her to be their leader.

"Let go, Serg," Liesel said again.

"She needs me. I'm keeping her safe." He no longer cried but made a pain-filled keening noise as he rocked back and forth. "If I wasn't touching her she'd end up like my father."

"You mean she'll end up like Valasca." Griffon knelt to check the woman's pulse. "She's alive." He waved a hand in front of her face then he rolled her over and cuffed her. *Trust no one.*

"Let go Serg. You're blocking her ability. Let it take its course." Liesel helped him lay Dianne out on the floor. *Please let this be right.* Sergei brushed Dianne's hair away from her face and let go. *I believe in you Dianne. You were given these abilities to help me and you have. Now let go. Come back.* She repeated the words in her head and focused them and her warmth on Dianne.

Chapter 20

The hospital lights above Sergei's head were like a sick hopscotch pattern. Some blacked out, some turned off, and some pounded your retinas into seeing dots of color.

It felt great to be back home. And though this wasn't his hospital, it was the same. Nurses and doctors looking respectable and haggard. Announcements, in code, over the PA system. The antiseptic, filthy-death smell of the hallways. And he knew his way in this world. He'd journeyed back and felt strengthened by his surroundings.

You're grinning like the Cheshire cat.

"I like to think of it as a hero's victory grin," Sergei said.

"Watcha, Tall Poppy coming through," Jennifer chirped from her seat next to her Thunder man. It might have been polite to ask Jennifer and her boyfriend-the-stripper how they were getting on but Sergei couldn't be bothered.

Tell me about Harry, Dianne whispered in his head.

"This would be easier if we cut out the middle man. Or woman," he said instead of answering her.

Jennifer doesn't mind.

"I don't mind."

"I thinking it's creepy." Za, the dancer, said. The dancer was dressed modestly in slacks and a polo shirt. He held Jennifer's hand and had one heavy booted foot up on his knee. He looked like he sold cell phones at the mall instead of stripping down to his skimpy jock strap at the screaming of strangers. Guy reminded Sergei of a couple of high-end and not so cultured prostitutes he'd helped in the ER. It could be dangerous work. Stripping, especially in nice venues, was at least safer.

Since Dianne couldn't hear Sergei's thoughts, she listened to him talk out loud to Jennifer. Sergei in turn listened as she talked in his head. She'd taken vigil up at Liesel's side and wouldn't leave.

"Harry is up in the O.R.," Sergei said. "The doctor, good guy, is repairing her spleen and kidney. She has three broken ribs and a dislocated shoulder. But she should be fine. Thanks to Jennifer."

"Wish the guy hadn't run off. Sure like a pound of his flesh." Whatever mental image Jennifer was broadcasting with her words had Dianne agreeing wholeheartedly.

Liesel and Griffon were answering questions for the FBI in a conference room two floors down. Liesel refused to leave the hospital while Harry was in surgery and Dianne refused to leave Liesel's side until she knew that Griffon had finished his own questions and could be with Liesel.

Her thoughts hesitated, *I'm sorry Sergei. Tydus is gone. Took all of his stuff with him.*

"Not that little black book Harry thought was the Amazon book," Jennifer said. "I've got that."

What little black book?

Sergei felt Dianne travel through Jennifer's memories—working in remote-control mode—and focused her senses. Almost as if Diane had held the book herself.

"You're right Za, this is creepy." Jennifer shivered as Dianne left her mind.

It's Grandma Maggie's. It was her father's diary. My great grandfather's diary. He must have killed her to get it.

Grandfathers keeping diaries. His grandfather, Dianne's grandfather. Tydus had spoken of his Great Uncle keeping a journal as well. He'd have to take up the tradition for his nieces and nephews.

"Didn't Griffon's brother Frank investigate a robbery that involved safety deposit boxes?" Sergei said.

"I don't know. Did he?" Jennifer asked.

He's talking to me, Dianne reminded her. To Sergei, *I think so, but I can ask Griffon.*

"What if they were Maggie's bank boxes? You said there was one in her will that turned out to be empty."

He wished he could offer comfort as she realized what this meant.

Sergei pulled at his blood-marred shirt and jeans, trying to get comfortable in the stiff and thinly padded chair. Would it be too weird to mail them to Veranda back in D.C.? No one got blood out better than Veranda.

Dad figured she'd just forgotten to put whatever it was back.

"So Tydus, steals the book and goes after Maggie so she can't tell anyone what is in it?" Jennifer said.

Harry must know. He killed Liesel's old assistant Penelope and attacked Anna. Harry must have figured it out. That's why she confronted him.

Sergei knew the thought of Maggie's killer escaping had to weigh heavily on Dianne. She was quiet for several minutes. Jennifer and Za spoke in low tones and Sergei shifted his body away and stared at the opposite wall to give them privacy. Though Jennifer was the conduit, it felt more like he had an ear piece in and heard Dianne's voice through it. Separate.

If a whole Harvest Team couldn't bring Tydus down....He refused to offer false platitudes about catching Tydus. Going forward he needed to be honest with people instead of telling them what he thought they wanted to hear. If things worked in his favor, he could relocate to Eagle, Idaho in a couple of weeks and start his job for NEWCo with Dianne at his side.

How's Ping doing?

He avoided the dark fear that still clutched at his heart. It had settled in his chest as he entered that hotel room.

He sighed. "Don't know yet. It'll be touch and go for a while. I spoke with her boyfriend on the phone. A doctor at a major hospital in Tokyo." Sergei rubbed a hand across his blue stubble. "I think he'll come and stay with her. If she wasn't an Amazon she would have died by now. We just don't know."

Why are you smiling now?

"I was thinking about your question on whether or not Amazons can grow new organs." A shower and a shave and ten minutes where he wasn't in jeopardy would go a long way to making him feel normal. That sounded good. Not realistic while his heart was owned by another, but good.

When she didn't say anything more he asked, "How's Griffon

doing?"

His nerves are pretty badly frayed.

He sure as hell wasn't the only one. "Well, it's not every day a Gynophobe proposes."

Sergei scrubbed at his face, checked his watch. "I want to see you." *Need to see you.* Both Ping and Harry had been in surgery for hours.

They're almost done. Griffon just proposed and they're kissing and I'm doing my best to let them have their mental privacy.

"It's easier now," he spoke only to Dianne because Jennifer had realized she didn't need to listen for Dianne to hear him.

Thanks to you.

"You worked hard for it. You deserve it."

Your father deserves peace to. I don't know why I'm different.

"He destroyed his body—" realizing that he was still talking through Jennifer, he stopped. "I wish you were here." A throbbing pain spiraled through his chest and he took a couple of breaths to let the pain abate, blinked moisture out of his eyes. His father was too weak to fight for control as Dianne had, did. Chandler Sky had cooked his brain in drugs until he lacked the ability to control it. Or maybe he just didn't give a fuck.

I'm coming.

He laughed, tilted his head back and stared at the ceiling, seeing her below him urging him on with moans. Her words spurring him to his own orgasm. He blinked the tears away. "I've heard that one before."

There was so much he wanted to tell her, so much that needed to be said. He shook just at the memory. He bit his top lip to stave off the tears. Rubbed his hand over his spiked blue hair.

Valasca had seen, felt and heard each of Dianne's most painful moments. Her constant mental noise, her flesh burning off her bones, her mother calling her a freak. It went on and on and Valasca couldn't handle it. Her soul had retreated, and now was in deep hiding from her mind.

Sergei had waited. Had painfully watched Dianne fight to expel all the mental shit that was Valasca. Twenty minutes, doubting himself. Twenty slow minutes, doing nothing but waiting. A single paramedic worked around them to help Liesel and get Valasca ready for transport. Another full team across the hotel saving Harry's life. Then his sunshine, his *Svyet*, had reached out her hand and touched his thigh and Sergei had gasped a breath so hard into his body that he had shook with the effort. "Please say you're okay. Please." He had knuckled away a tear and grasped her hand, pressed it firmly down on his thigh.

I'm okay, Dianne had said. *I'm going to sleep. Will you hold—?*

Before she'd finished the thought he had swept her up in his arms and tucked her into his neck. "I've got you."

Now in the hospital, his body still quaked with adrenaline. Ready and needing to fight for Dianne.

Dianne walked down the hall from the elevators and sat next to Sergei in the hospital chairs, took his hand. With that touch the pain in his chest doused, the coals steamed.

What Dianne had seen in Valasca's head she wasn't saying. She stroked his blue cheek. "You need to shave." Then she brushed her bottom lip over his stubble. Felt it prickle. And slipped into a kiss. She tipped her head and her tongue stroked his. When they pulled apart she tucked her head under his chin and threaded her fingers through his.

"I love you Sergei," she whispered.

Whoa. That felt incredible. He squeezed her hand, felt the coals go out. Only Dianne would follow up an admonishment to shave with a declaration of love. He formed the words in his mouth but couldn't let go of his jaw enough to say them.

He kissed her head on his shoulder and squeezed her hand again.

"I do," Liesel said.

"And do you Jim Griffon take this lovely babe," the Elvis impersonator indicated Liesel, "to be your hunk of burning love, until you join the big rock concert in the sky?"

Griffon didn't care that this was ridiculous. He didn't care that he was wearing jeans or that Liesel didn't have flowers, or a ring, or a proper preacher. And neither did Liesel. He'd had Dianne check.

She's in love. And the rest doesn't even occur to her. Dianne reassured him again.

Harry was slightly propped up in bed fighting to stay conscious. He and Liesel stood in the doorway of Harry's room so the rest of the crowd could watch from the hallway. The hospital staff had balked but there was absolutely no way they could make Amazons, Mightys or Liesel's family leave.

Liesel wore a simple white blouse and the same skirt he'd almost swallowed his tongue over when he'd first seen her in it. She looked happy and that inner light made her shine. He tucked a strand behind her ear and cupped the corner of her jaw, used his thumb to stroke away a tear as it slid down her cheek.

Griffon would do the ring, flowers, and photo thing with her family back in Boise. That alone spoke volumes of his love. "I love you Liesel Grant."

"Hound dog, your line is 'I do,'" The impersonator hadn't charged extra to come to the hospital and conduct the service in Harry's room. Which was pretty decent of him so Griffon would try not to glare at the man. But no promises.

"I believe in your good nature." Griffon placed her hand over his heart and covered her hand with his.

"You could've paid extra and written your vows ahead of time." The Elvis voice was turning into a Texas drawl.

"I trust you. Completely. And will give my life to protect you." He took his eyes off Liesel long enough to stare at Elvis. "I do. Continue," daring the man to say anything else.

Elvis swallowed then said, "By the authority I obtained from this here State of Nevada. I pronounce you married. Hurry up and kiss the girl so she'll quit with the crying."

Frank was his best man and Dianne was Liesel's maid of honor, honorary positions as official witnesses to sign the license. Though Dianne was quick to assure anyone and everyone within visual distance that she was no longer a maid. *I've been thoroughly de—*

maidened by Sergei. Just ask him.

Liesel laughed through her tears and held tight to Griffon, her hand still pressed against his heart.

Medicated oblivion didn't really count as rest. Harry had had little sleep and the hospital staff had given up trying to restrict her visitors. They barely lifted an eyebrow when the whole Harvest Team came to her room. Sixteen Mightys. Eight Mathews and eight Modesitte men. They walked through the room in precession, shaking her hand or placing flowers on an available surface before quietly heading out the door.

The Harvest Team's differential treatment of Harry felt odd. They had conferenced with the medical staff. They had covered her expenses and they wanted all the extras done, specialists brought in. Full and high end physical therapy. The deluxe treatment.

When only two remained, the oldest stepped forward. Harry recognized him from Griffon's description of Sarge. "My name is Mathew. Ms. Grant, I'd like to ask you a few questions if you feel up to it."

Harry scanned the two Mightys standing at the end of her hospital bed. She hurt and she wanted Tydus caught but these guys were the Harvest Team. Would they kill him if they caught him?

They were more diverse than she would have initially thought, their height and skin tone varying across the full spectrum. All stiff military posture, short hair, serious expressions. The way Liesel talked, this polite treatment was against the grain for these guys. What was up?

She pulled her eyes back open when they slid shut. "What's he done? Why," she swallowed a few times and felt a cool hand settle on hers. She swallowed again to moisten her throat. "Why harvest?"

"The man you knew as Tydus McKinley, which we think may actually be his real name, was Ole to us." The younger man, his tone carefully polite and gentle. "Ole worked his way up in the Modesitte before suddenly leaving for America."

Mathew said, "We believe he stole the...your sister's research next."

"Yeah," she nodded. He'd pretty much confessed as much when she'd cornered him.

"Then he approached the Mathews to work with them," Modesitte said. "We have clear indications that he went after those kidnappers in California."

Harry pulled her eyes open again, they were so heavy. But her head was clear. Her sore throat from the tube during surgery made it hard for her to speak. She settled for, "Why the medical?'

They were surprised, perhaps thinking she wouldn't know about that yet. "He's Ronin. We should have had him by now." The Modesitte said, "You're the first person to survive a fight with a Mighty gone Ronin."

Mathew added, "Usually the destruction is complete."

Harry sighed and took a moment to think. "No record under McKinley, try Kinley or Vaughn." Harry coughed to clear her throat. "He's a Blue Hair."

"What?" Mathew said.

Harry tried to lift her hand and tap her nose. "Can smell. Everything." That was how she had known he wasn't just a Mighty but a Blue Hair.

The guys exchanged a look. "That might explain why he is able to somewhat control the rage. Funnel it." Sarge squeezed her hand to reassure her. The gesture reminded her of her father. She remembered her dad's hands the clearest. Her tiny hands wrapped around his fingers as he helped her walk.

"We've prepared for this, setting aside funds to help those who are injured, but they never injure." Modesitte's shoulders slumped, even his fists bunched inward. "They take a person down and then shoot. A single to the head."

Harry's breath caught in her throat. Liesel's secretary Penelope had died that way and so had the men who captured Liesel in California. Tydus had done that?

She'd thought him a lying thief. She would dump his ass and they'd go their own ways. Maybe, if she could find proof, tell the police about her suspicions. But a killer? And she'd blithely walked in. So stupid. So. Stupid.

"The attacker at the airport?" Modesitte said. "His family received a hundred thousand euros. It was Ole, or McKinley." Modesitte straightened his shoulders and released with a sigh. Paced his breathing for a moment like a swimmer doing laps. Back in control. She knew what that was like. She'd wake up from a nightmare where water pressed her down until her lungs could no longer pull in air. She'd work hard to regain her balance, even out her breathing.

"The family says he was paid to deliver an antique knife. A collector's item. Perhaps he ran because his visa had expired," Mathew said.

She had blindly walked into death's cave. It felt distant probably due to the medication. The danger was a vague concept, she made it out, no matter how damaged her body was, so it all felt unreal.

"You're very lucky," Mathew squeezed her hand again.

And they thought what? That she'd tried to stop him? Discovered the truth and fought to capture him? If only.

"He has a sister, a Blue Hair. He has limited," she coughed, "computer knowledge." They passed her some ice chips and she sucked on one just long enough to moisten her throat. If they could take this guy out before he hurt anyone else and especially before he could come after her or her family, she would help them. Please God, let them catch the bastard. "What else do you need?"

Chapter 21

One month since Vegas and Sergei had been conned into turkey dinner with the family. Instead of having sex and overindulging in each other, Dianne followed Sergei to New Mexico for Thanksgiving. After spending weeks apart—him packing up his apartment, saying goodbye to Veranda, getting NEWCo to agree to the move—he was about to drag her to the floor and....

Yeah, not an activity for family time. He couldn't even bring himself to cuss in his head in front of Portia and the baby. Dianne had spent the same time in her grandmother's house in Boise, getting it ready for them to live together. It was 2.78 miles from Liesel's house and office. Close enough she would be able to keep an eye on their matriarch.

"She doesn't like the coffee you keep drinking in the afternoon," Dianne told Portia as she touched his sister's bulging belly. "It's hard for her to sleep."

John laughed, "Told you." He sat on the armrest of Portia's chair and stroked his wife's hair, obviously trying to ease her tension. Their to-be daughter was a Blue Hair and Portia had asked Dianne if she could tell what the mutation would be.

Sergei sat on the couch and wrapped his arm around Dianne. He felt his niece like a bright bliss on the edge of Dianne's thoughts. The blurry patterns seemed to make sense to Dianne. He liked that she would share this special connection with him.

"She's healthy and doesn't have any abilities yet," Dianne said. Nonchalantly.

Portia shivered, began to cry.

Dianne turned to Sergei and asked, as if they had left the conversation and were picking it up after a brief pause. "Do you know what the codex really says?"

Sergei passed his sister some Kleenex. "And how would you know?"

"I don't but I'm a good guesser." She ignored his derisive snort. "It says that the child is given...love. A family that loves her and she'll manage whatever comes her way." Dianne stood to hug Portia then John. She touched and hugged all the time now. Only when she was touched without warning was it a problem.

She sat back on the couch and leaned into Sergei. "Look at Phillip and Wendy's son. He's fine because he has the love and support he needs."

Who? Oh yeah, the new board member with the mixed family. Their son was blind.

"And though not quite the same thing, Ping as she learns to walk again, has the love of her new husband." She kissed Sergei's cheek and then told John and Portia, "My vote for a baby name is Janis Lynn Hambly. Just saying."

Portia snorted and John asked if Portia paid her to say that.

Dianne talked over them, "You love her already. And with me as an aunt she'll be extra blessed."

"Aunt?" Sergei said.

"Don't worry, I'll get around to asking you to marry me soon enough." Dianne waved her hand at the room. "I want candlelight and romantic music and nudity. This won't work."

Candlelight? Sergei quirked an eyebrow and laughed with Portia and John. Their laughter had a hysterical note to it. The sound his patients had when they expected the worse and were given a clean bill of health.

"Dianne Fender will you marry me?" Sergei left the eyebrow up.

"Only if you really, really love me."

"I love you." He didn't remember the first time he said it. Perhaps he had finally whispered it back to her in the hospital. Or over the phone every day for the past month. It was true and always would be.

She smiled and kissed him, pulled back just enough to say, "I'll have to take your word for it."

The End

About the Author

Amberly lives in the Northwest with her husband, two children, and their cats, Cat and KitTon. Their home has become a PC graveyard where games and gadgets are discarded for the latest shiny. She likes to read in bed, write in coffee shops, knit, and cuddle while watching Netflix or Hulu. Amberly acknowledges that she has issues with being too succinct. Feel free to ask her questions about herself. She's not shy. Follow her strange life on her website at www.amberlysmith.com or look for her on Facebook.

Thank you for reading Some Assembly Required. We hope you enjoyed it. If you did, please consider putting a review on Amazon. It's easy and reviews are what writers live and die by.

www.ingramcontent.com/pod-product-compliance
Lightning Source LLC
Chambersburg PA
CBHW050044180626

46810CB00002B/881